MW01487011

WHAT ABOUT THE BODIES

WHAT ABOUT THE BODIES

A NOVEL

KEN JAWOROWSKI

Atlantic Crime

New York

FIRST EDITION

Printed in the United States of America

First Grove Atlantic hardcover edition: September 2025

Library of Congress Cataloging-in-Publication data is available for this title.

ISBN 978-0-8021-6547-3
eISBN 978-0-8021-6548-0

Atlantic Crime
an imprint of Grove Atlantic
154 West 14th Street
New York, NY 10011

Distributed by Publishers Group West

groveatlantic.com

25 26 27 28   10 9 8 7 6 5 4 3 2 1

To Michele DiPietro Jaworowski
You and me babe, how about it?

WHAT ABOUT THE BODIES

CARLA

ONCE, WHEN I WAS a girl, my father took me to the racetrack. My mother was in the hospital yet again with the ovarian cysts that plagued her, and my dad—a drunk who enriched our lives only by skipping town a couple years later—wasn't about to stay home babysitting or waste his precious, unemployed time visiting his ailing wife. Not when the horses were running and the beer was cheap.

After scoping out the first three races, he bet the fourth, on the far-right long shot that looked not a lick different from any other nag in the lineup.

"Why that one?" I asked.

My father hissed a stream of smoke, stifled a belch, then glanced down at me.

"You can always tell a winner at the starting gate," he said. His warm, wet breath smelled of menthol Kools and Miller High Life.

The bell rang and the gates crashed open. The horse shot out like its tail was on fire and never once lost the lead. As it sped farther ahead of the pack, my father roared, oblivious that the beer in his hand was sloshing over the top of his cup and onto my head. Ten minutes later he pocketed $556 and drove us home seat belt–free and halfway hammered. He repeated the remark and chuckled a few times on the way back, wholly convinced of his mantra.

He was wrong, of course. At least with the word "always." I'm forty-five now and have had several people surprise me over the years: a few longtime losers who turned their lives around, a handful of early superstars who went on to spoil whatever they touched. Still, there's a good amount of truth in his saying. For most of us, so much of who we are is little different from who we first were.

For me, only once was I absolutely certain that I'd seen a winner at the start.

My son, Billy, was born underweight and jaundiced. But when they placed his scraggly body in my arms, I blurted out a laugh, joyful, because I saw, and I knew. No matter that behind him were generations of busted homes, broken noses, and unplanned pregnancies. No matter to any of those things, and no matter to so many more.

I tell you, when I first set eyes on him, I *knew*.

And nothing since has shaken that belief. Not his stutter, which tangles him in words and too often leaves him misunderstood. Not this unfeeling small town, which tried its hardest to poison his dreams. And not its bankrupt school system, with its mocking bullies who leaned against his locker. No. My only child, sensitive but inwardly strong, sucked up each adversity. Then he put his head down and soldiered through them all, and later waltzed out of Locksburg, Pennsylvania, something so many try to do but never can. Myself included.

Billy came home last night from M.I.T., where he's studying software engineering. He'd finished his freshman year and hung around campus for another month to fill a staff vacancy in the computer labs. He's on full scholarship—my god, I practically quiver when repeating those two exquisite words, along with the school's three magnificent initials—yet he rarely misses a chance to earn extra money on top of the savings he's banked from the odd jobs he's taken since he was twelve.

I was happy to see him—always am, this time a little selfishly: free labor. My restaurant is slated to serve its first meal in four months in an old barn that I'm converting, and I'd be behind schedule even if the grand opening were scheduled for a year from now. By the time Billy heads back to M.I.T. in the fall, we'll have done everything from sanding the wooden floors at the entrance to installing the exhaust fans in the kitchen. He's already completed the computerized ordering and billing systems. Took him an afternoon to write the software. Would have taken a paid pro two weeks.

The restaurant is my hope that I can end up differently than how I must have appeared at the starting gate, and at pretty much any time before I hit forty. When my dad abandoned us, my mom and I kicked around central Pennsylvania, wherever she could find a job that fit her skill set of mopping floors and making beds, and her penchant for usually showing up on time. I began waitressing in high school, nursed her through her sickest years, then ended up living with a guy, Eric, who I was about to leave and ditch this Podunk too. Then, two days before implementing an escape plan, my pregnancy test showed a plus sign. Three months later, Eric made his own getaway. Last I heard, he was somewhere in Ohio. And I've never left Locksburg.

With Eric gone, I sleepwalked through endless days waitressing and spent the evenings driving Billy an hour and a half each way to Harrisburg for speech therapy when his problems arose. Most important, I tried to be his friend, since he had so few otherwise. As forty limped past, and with Billy gearing up to go away to college, it was clear that my chance for a last chance was passing me by. If I kept doing what I've always been doing, I'd stay where I've always been.

So I signed for a loan and bought the stone-walled barn and the two acres it sits on and began remodeling. Along the way I quit smoking, cut my hair severely short, and took up jogging. And the more changes I made to myself, the more I felt myself changing.

I was determined to be someone different than who I was at the starting gate.

This morning I knocked and walked into Billy's bedroom to find him in front of his laptop. No surprise there. He was logged on to the *Locksburg Leader*, reading a story about the one-year anniversary of Doreen Shippen's disappearance. I read the same piece in the newspaper that was tossed onto my driveway yesterday. Most everyone in a fifty-mile radius is obsessed with the case, and the *Leader* finds any excuse to recycle the tale and to print letters from homegrown amateur detectives who offer up their theories, which usually involve Doreen's former beau, who was the last known person to have seen her. I wouldn't be surprised if Billy was conducting his own investigation. He's naturally curious about mysteries. He's naturally curious about everything. I love that about him.

Doreen went to our local school with Billy and the rest, and in every old picture of her that they print, she appears to be half a moment away from comically rolling her eyes or saying something outrageous to shock the photographer. Born to a single and frequently absent mother, the girl vanished a week after their high school graduation. At first it was assumed that she had decided to leave town, though evidence soon pointed otherwise: Her meager bank account sat untouched, and everything she owned remained in her bedroom. According to cell phone records from the night she disappeared, her last call was to her old boyfriend turned drug dealer. Yet the cops couldn't find enough evidence to charge him with anything other than a parole violation that they were holding him on.

"So sad," I said when I peered over Billy's shoulder at the screen.

"Any w-word on the cuh-case?" he asked.

"Read the story," I said.

"I have," he said. "I mean, any ruh-rumors?"

"Not that I've heard," I said. "Don't get caught up in it; you've got other things to worry about, with school. And with me. Come on. Let's get over to the barn."

We got there earlier than usual and Nestor was already on-site, coffee cup steaming with the undrinkable dollar-store sludge he brews on a stained secondhand pot. I'd hired Nestor for more than I could afford, which means a buck above minimum wage, in cash and under the table. He puts in almost double the hours he's paid for, saying he's happy to keep busy since he retired five years ago. I think he's eager to get away from his wife, whom he never misses a chance to grumble about.

The day's undertaking was to complete the countertops in the open kitchen, where diners will be able to see flames flaring around stainless steel cookware and salivate when hearing the sizzles. Or so's the hope.

"'Sup, Carla. Hey, Billy," Nestor called out. Billy held up five fingers, hi, never speaking when a motion will serve him just as well. We began work and fell into a rhythm, communicating in the Morse code of gestures and grunts that the three of us use to minimize talk and increase our labor time. Two hours into it, Billy stopped, as if an unexpected idea had shouted his name from across the room. He took a moment, scrutinizing the place.

"Mom? Where did yuh-you get the money for all this?"

"I guess you should know. Besides the loan and the savings, I mortgaged the house."

"Why?"

"Well, to get the money for all this."

"And what if this doesn't . . . you know? What heh-happens to our house?"

"Billy," I said, "I think it's going to work out."

I thought that's all I'd say, but then the truth popped from my mouth. I'd been bottling it up, and before I could hold back the words, I said: "I'm forty-five. If I don't do this now, I'm going to end up as another townie loser."

"You're not a townie luh-loser."

"I know you think that way. And I love you for it. Only . . ."

Right then I longed for him, for anybody, to understand my life. To know how sad I sometimes get when thinking of all I've never done—and that's nearly everything, since I've accomplished so little. No travel. No money. No education. I thought about telling him how, when I was a girl, I was dumb enough to believe that I was special, someone who would go out and conquer the world, or at least fight it to a mean draw. To recall the plans and the ideas and the energy I once had makes me cringe in embarrassment when I see how things have turned out. It also steeps me in melancholy and sinks me into a funk that can last for days.

But who can really, deeply understand another's life? All the nuances and the memories and the secrets and the dreams, accumulated second by minute by hour over days and months and years?

So instead I said: "Billy, I just don't want to die as a waitress who never took a chance at anything."

He paused to consider that, then gave me a pressed-lip smile and nodded. We returned to work in silence.

Ten hours later we'd finished the day's jobs, except for that part over there that we'll take care of when we find the one tool, and the piece behind the thing that I'll replace when we get the other shipment in. Nestor wrote down what needed to be done, expanding our to-do list rather than trimming it. Then the three of us ended the day much the way it began, with raised hands, bidding good night instead of good morning. Nestor said he'd stay behind to finish some other job he'd found, then lock up. One more excuse to stay away from his wife.

Back at the house, I cooked homemade linguini with pesto, tomatoes, and cheese, a dish that's planned for the restaurant. From the clicking of the burner to the placement on the table: fourteen minutes. Granted, I prepped the pasta and mixed the pesto yesterday and had them ready in the fridge. But still. You can't say that's not fast, especially since the presentation was photo-worthy. Billy hardly looked at the food. He finished the dish, mumbled a thank-you—What? No compliment, not even an *Mmmm*, you little jerk?—then went upstairs.

I was in the kitchen a half hour later when he came back down. He hadn't changed his shirt or pants, even though I'd heard the shower running and his hair was wet.

"Gross. You put those sweaty things back on after you showered?"

Billy glanced at his clothes as if he were just noticing. He *was* just noticing. He stared at me, perplexed. Confused. Some other emotions too, ones I couldn't immediately decipher. But there were many, and they were upsetting him. I could see that much.

"Billy, sit down," I said.

"I don't wuh-wuh-wanna sit down."

"What's wrong?"

"Duh-duh . . ." The word lodged in his throat. I stopped myself from helping him. I guessed he was going for "dishes"—did he feel guilty about not helping me clean up?—but I waited, as I always did, for him to push it out on his own.

Finally he said, "Doreen."

"Doreen Shippen?"

He nodded.

"I wonder about Doreen too. But who knows what happened. Why are you thinking about her?"

"She's buh-buried in our yard," Billy said.

REED

I WAS STARING out of the window when Greg came in and sat on my bed and sighed like he often sighs. He waited for half a minute before he said: "You were up here the whole time."

I did not say anything because the way he said it, it was a statement.

"You couldn't come downstairs?" Greg said.

That one was a question. Still, I did not say anything. Technically I could have come downstairs. But I did not want to come downstairs.

"It was our mother's funeral," he said.

I said: "It was not her funeral. I was at her funeral. This was the reception. So you are wrong."

Greg sighed again.

"Even Little Jimmy was down there, sitting nice and shaking hands. And he's only five."

I did not say anything.

"Were you embarrassed?" Greg asked.

I did not say anything. Outside, a bird flew off the tree that Mom planted when my dad died in an explosion at Locksburg Chemical Industries when I was a baby twenty years ago. "I watered that tree with my own tears," Mom used to say, and for a long time

9

I believed her until one day I said: "I do not think that is true. There is not enough moisture in tears to water a tree." And Mom said: "Oh, honey. I never realized you'd take that literally. It's only a saying. But sometimes it feels like I did. Do you understand what I mean by that?" I did not understand what she meant by that, so I was honest and said no and she smiled a bit and she said, "That's OK. I hope you never do."

"We need to talk," Greg said, which meant that he wanted to speak and he wanted me to stay quiet.

He stood up from the bed. I was still staring out of the window. My room overlooks the backyard and there were cigarette butts on the grass, four of them, from guests who had gone outside to smoke. They were not Mom's cigarette butts. She always used the coffee can to put those in, after she smoked the cigarette down until there was no tobacco left and the filter started to burn. Then she would look at the butt with no more tobacco and say, "Good to the last drop!" and cackle. Some people would call it a laugh but it was a cackle. I like that word, "cackle." I suppose I will never hear her cackle again.

Greg said, "Do you remember the conversation we had, about two years ago? When you, me, and Mom sat down and we talked about what would happen when she died?"

I remembered the conversation. It was when Mom had recovered from pneumonia and she said that we should settle some things in case she ever got sick again and passed away. So I sat at the kitchen table while Mom and Greg talked. Mom said Greg should sell the house and keep the money but that he must use some of the money for me. "Talk to Mrs. Salter about her rooming house," Mom said to Greg then. "She loves Reed and would rent him a room." Greg nodded and told Mom that that would be a good plan. Greg said he would stop by every day to check on me. Mom said that would be fine. She said, "Well, that settles that."

But it seemed like Greg was about to unsettle that, now that Mom was gone.

"I promised Mom that I would look after you, and I meant it. But that was when things were different. Things aren't the same now, are they?"

I did not say anything, though I wanted to tell him that things are never the same, whether two years go by or two milliseconds. That has been proven by science.

"At the time, I thought, you know, we could get you a room at Mrs. Salter's rooming house and she could help you out some, and I could stop by once a day."

"That is what you promised Mom that you would do."

"I know. But Mrs. Salter is moving and selling her place. She's going to live with her son in Shamokin. Plus, when we talked about all this, I was married to Maggie."

"You are still married to Maggie."

"Well, I haven't seen her since she left last year."

"Why did she leave last year?"

"That's not polite to ask."

"You once said that we could ask each other anything."

"Almost anything."

"Then you should have said: 'Reed, we can ask each other almost anything.'"

"I don't need you to tell me how to speak."

Apparently you do, I was ready to say, but I knew that would make him angry so I did not say it.

"Anyway, Maggie isn't here anymore, so I've got my hands full with Little Jimmy and with my job. And now Mom's gone. So . . . I don't know what to do, Reed. I'm thinking that . . ."

The things that he was saying made me very nervous and I began to put my fingers in my ears and rock back and forth. But I stopped and moved my hands down to my lap when I remembered what Miss Barbara, my counselor, said two years ago when I was a senior in high school. She said that if I was really nervous I should try to act like I was not nervous and maybe try to explore different options to make things better. So I said to Greg: "I can live here. When Mom would go out, I was alone a lot of times."

"You can't live here. This house is falling apart. It costs more than—"

"I make money at my job."

"You're a bagger at the supermarket, Reed."

"I could get a second job."

"No you can't. The state program that pays for your employment covers only twenty hours a week."

I did not say anything.

"There's . . ." He started to speak and stopped and I could tell it was something that I would not like to hear, so I put my fingers in my ears. I could hear Greg talking, so I rocked back and forth and hummed to keep the sound out.

Greg never teased me when we were growing up. Instead he ignored me and many times acted as if he did not know who I was. It was almost as if we were not real brothers. One time I was walking on Carlyle Street and came to the corner. Greg was in his car with a girl and they stopped at the traffic light, right there. I said, "Hi, Greg," and held my hand up. Greg kept staring straight ahead,

12

waiting for the light to change. When it did, he drove off very fast. The girl looked at him, then at me, and appeared to wonder why Greg did not say hi back.

When I heard that the room had gone silent, I took my fingers out of my ears.

"You have to listen," Greg said after a little while. "There's a place in Pittsburgh. It's for non-neurotypical people. I researched it online. I'll show you. It seems like a great—"

I put my fingers back in my ears. The word "Pittsburgh" hurt me to hear. Mom took me there once and I hated it, with all the cars and the horns and . . .

Greg took hold of one of my arms and pulled. My finger came out of my ear.

"Listen to me!" he yelled.

"Aaaahhhhh!" I yelled back. Then I screamed again: "Aaaahhhhh!"

Greg stood up and I stopped yelling. When I calmed down I said, "Sorry," because I *was* sorry. I do not like to scream. But I was still upset. So instead of screaming I pressed the deep cut on my forearm that I had gotten a few days ago. That pain helped me to take my mind off Pittsburgh.

Then I thought of something.

"I could stay with you," I said to Greg. Then I added, "Please."

"I can't even talk to you, Reed. You scream and you—"

"I will not scream. I can stay with you."

He went silent for a little while.

"I dunno," he said, and when he says that, he usually does not know. He is honest like that. He likes to think about things before he makes a decision. Sometimes he thinks a lot.

I said to him, "I could clean out your basement and sleep there and I would not bother anyone. Unless you wanted me to babysit Little Jimmy. I could do that. It would save you money."

"You want to live with me in my house," Greg said. It was not a question. But still I answered.

"Yes."

"And you want to take care of my five-year-old son."

"Yes."

"Reed. You do realize that, a few days ago, you killed our mother?"

I did not say anything.

LIZ

SURE, I KNEW where I was: sitting on a high stool in a dim corner of Maxie's, where I'd pushed aside a beer-sticky table to make space to perform for the eleven people there, bartender included. But the song I'd just played was a new one I'd worked on for months, and it came together so gloriously that if I were headlining a sold-out show at the Hollywood Bowl, it couldn't have been any more magical. My guitar faded on the final note and I got that breathtaking feeling you get when you know you couldn't have done a single thing any better.

The small crowd clapped.

"Thank you. I appreciate it," I said, and meant it. I paused to savor the sense of pure satisfaction. Oh gosh, how rare such moments are. All my cynicism seemed to melt away. Then I smiled warmly at the audience. "I wrote that one when—"

"Hey! Heya!" someone shouted from the bar. It was a stringy-haired woman who'd thrown open the door and lurched inside at the end of my previous song. I'd ignored her then. But her screech was now eighty decibels too loud for the tiny place—no one in Maxie's is more than twenty-five feet from anyone else—and she was waving a hand high. I sighed. Raised my chin to acknowledge her.

She slurred, "I got a request!"

I gave her the flat stare I reserve for drunks and hecklers.

"Maybe later," I said. "Right now I'm playing my own music and—"

"Bon fuckin' Jovi!" she said, and looked around for a laugh, as if she were the life of this poorly attended party. Her grin exposed two missing teeth.

"Sorry," I said. "No can do. But I think you'll like this next song."

"Wait, wait, wait!" she yelled. "Sing . . . what's that one called?"

"Anyway . . ."

"'Baby, We Won!'—that's the name of the song! Yeah, sing it!"

My eyes almost rolled into the back of my head. That cheap pop-country ballad was fouling the airwaves nonstop lately. The tune was as cheesy as a brick of Velveeta, rhyming "love" with "dove" and overvibrating the guitar to milk the mawkishness. I loathed its clichés and its dishonesty, and the unearned exclamation point in its title offended me.

"Anyway," I repeated with some grit. I wrestled back the urge to sneer at her, then sought out the friendlier faces. "This is also new. It's called 'Two Travels.' I hope you like it."

Miss Stringy mumbled, and just as I was about to play, she opened her mouth. But instead of an insult, out blasted a quart of whatever she'd been recently drinking, mixed with what appeared to have once been a TV dinner. She retched again and a second helping of chunky puke splashed to the floor. The entire room instantly reeked.

"Christ!" Craig the bartender barked. "That's it! Closing time!"

My meager audience rose and fled, followed by Miss Stringy, who was wiping her lips with a used bar napkin that someone had sneezed into earlier. When the door shut, only Craig and I remained. The silence hung in the stinking air.

"Well. Otherwise, I think it was a good set," I finally said.

Craig didn't answer. Only looked down as if wondering whether to leave the vomit there and clean it up tomorrow. The way the place usually smelled, he'd no doubt done it before.

"You sounded nice, Liz," he said, and reached into his pocket. He handed me two twenties. "But, you know, you're not exactly packing them in."

"Tomorrow night will be better," I said.

"Yeah, I wanted to talk to you about that. Let's hold off on any more shows, OK?"

On the ride home, I opened the windows and cursed the world. I tried to blame jackasses like Miss Stringy for my contempt, which seemed ever present these days. But I knew this was no overnight transformation. It took twelve years to make me this way.

When I was eighteen, I had a choice: go to college, or try to make it in the music business. "Believe in yourself!" every treacly tune told me. So I moved to Philadelphia and played to surly drunks in cheerless bars, then came home to a dank basement apartment to watch the silverfish skitter across the cracked, water-stained ceiling.

When I was twenty-two, I had a drink with a friend who offered me a job at her start-up tech company. If I took it, I'd have hardly any time for my music. "Don't ever sell out!" the Hollywood movies said. So I declined the job and went on a two-month-long, self-funded tour of the South and Midwest in the hopes of getting noticed.

Instead, I performed for minuscule audiences in third-rate dives, then returned to Philly exhausted. A year later I read a story in the *Inquirer* about how the tech company had given stock options to all its employees, who were now millionaires, even the janitor.

At twenty-seven, I limped back to my hometown of Locksburg, Pennsylvania, practically penniless, after learning that the old crow who'd been cozying up to my widowed father had rushed him into marriage then hurried him into Hillview Living Center once he began showing signs of Parkinson's disease. Soon she controlled everything that was once his and mine. "Never give up!" the sappy novelists wrote, so I refused to stay sad for long. I kept striving and played on nearly every stage within twenty-five miles, often for free, which, when you count the gas and my time, means I sometimes paid to sing to haw-hawing boneheads who'd spill a pitcher of beer and yelp in the middle of a song I'd spent a year writing, practicing, and putting my heart into. When I wasn't performing or working, I was sending out demo tapes and emailing producers, who, in the rare times when one deemed me worthy of a reply, said thanks but no thanks, and best of luck.

I was remembering all that as I drove to the clapboard house I've rented since returning to Locksburg: a two-bedroom dump on the ass end of town. There I sat in the driveway that ran in front of the place. If my disappointments weren't bad enough, with the loss of my gig at Maxie's, I had no money coming in and was hip-deep in debt. My secondhand, fifteen-year-old Chevy broke down last year, leaving me with the choice of paying $1,900 for a rebuilt transmission or untold thousands for a new car. I used the bulk of my savings for the repair, only to have the cylinder head crack in the winter. Since I'd sunk all that cash into the transmission,

I figured it would be foolish to junk the car, and spent another grand on it.

As I parked, the Chevy shuddered, warning me that another regularly scheduled breakdown was soon to come.

I didn't have to wait long.

I woke in the morning with a plan to visit my dad. I locked the front door, put the key in the car ignition, and heard the whirring of the ignition with no turnover.

"Fuel pump's shot," Luke, the guy who calls me his girlfriend, said when he stopped by my place later that afternoon. "Didn't you notice any problems, Liz? Didn't you even—"

"Do not come over here and chastise me, Luke."

"That's nine hundred bucks at least." He sounded dejected, if only for himself. Luke had no car of his own, and my breakdown would rob him of the last-minute, *Please, Liz, please* rides to work that he often begged me for, to save him from being fired for yet another lateness.

I groaned. "I don't have the money."

"Neither do I," he said. "But I know someone who might cut you a break." An hour later Luke borrowed a pickup truck and hooked a chain to the undercarriage to tow mine to a house five miles outside of Locksburg. The place was a hundred yards down a dirt road and forty years past its last paint job. A mountain of a man with a long beard and two fingers missing on one hand stepped outside and stood there, unspeaking. The word KAP was tattooed on his neck in four-inch-high capital letters, as if he were afraid that someone might not see it.

"Hey, Kap!" Luke said. "Here it is."

Those five words jiggled with nervousness, the first time I've ever heard that in Luke's voice. It was enough to make me uneasy of this Kap guy too. He wore jeans and leather work boots in the heat of June, and a dark T-shirt that I could tell smelled of sour sweat, even though he was twenty yards away. I hoped we wouldn't get any closer.

Luke unchained the car then opened the hood of my Chevy. Kap didn't bother to look inside. After a while he said, "Come back tomorrow."

"You got it, man!" Luke replied too eagerly, and we took off in the borrowed pickup. I noticed that Luke drove away faster than he had on the trip there.

The next day Luke borrowed the pickup again and we returned to Kap's place. The guy came out of the house wearing the same clothes and a similar pissed-off expression. Luke quivered as he had the last time, with a false friendliness in his voice that all three of us could recognize, and at least one of us—me—was uncomfortable with.

"Hey, hey! All fixed up, Kap?" Luke said.

After a long pause: "I said it would be, didn't I?"

"Yeah, that's great! You always say you're a man of your word!"

"Seven-fifty."

"Uh, I thought you said six hundred?"

"Your fuel line was rotted too. Gas leaked all over my garage. I oughta make you pay for cleanup."

"Aw, sorry about that, Kap."

"So I replaced the fuel line. Even cut you a deal, since I had a line laying around here I could use, rather than buy a new one. So seven-fifty."

"Yeah. Right. But you said we could pay some now and the rest later, right?"

"How much you got?"

My checking account was already overdrawn, and my single credit card maxed. I had $40 from my Maxie's gig, and when I searched around my house for something to sell, the only thing outside of my guitar was a 1913 buffalo nickel, the first rare coin I'd bought with my own money, when I was a girl and collected coins with my dad. His new wife had everything else, but I'd kept this one with me for luck. Although it delivered little of that, it never failed to remind me of the sweet times I'd had with my father in his tiny home office, examining the coins he loved to collect. It hurt so much to sell. Ed, the owner of Berwick Numismatic, traded a lot of coins with my dad over the years and had mercy on me. He bought the buffalo nickel for $150, exactly what it was worth, and was nice enough to say that he'd hold it for a month in case I wanted to buy it back. Fat chance of that happening.

"We got $190," Luke said to Kap.

Silence.

"Well, you gonna make me ask for it?" Kap said.

Luke walked forward and offered him the bills. I half expected the guy to grab Luke's hand. Luke must have imagined the same, because he quick-stepped back. Then Luke nodded toward my car and said: "The keys in there?"

21

The guy slowly counted the money, leaving Luke to stand there with his unanswered question in the air, embarrassing Luke with the silence, but not enough to have Luke ask again.

After a full minute, the guy said: "When am I getting the rest?"

"Like, two weeks. That good?"

"You said a week."

"Did I? I swear we were, like, 'Two weeks,' right? When we talked about it?"

"A week," he said. "Don't make me come looking for you."

Then Kap's eyes crawled over me. "Or you either."

I drove away from Kap's and felt the car hesitate a few times. I hoped it was temporary: The last thing I wanted was to go back and complain about the repairs to that ill-tempered creep. I stopped at Fast Eddie's Sunoco to put in $4.27 of gas with the change that I had emptied from a jar in my kitchen. Luke saw me there and pulled the pickup into the lot.

"Where are you going to get $540?" he asked.

"What do you mean?"

"What you owe Kap. Seven-fifty minus one-ninety."

I was too tired to correct his math.

"Honestly, I don't know."

"Liz, you better find the money. And you better find the money soon. Do you know how I know Kap?"

"How?"

"From Carroll Valley prison. He practically ran the place. He's done some bad shit."

"How bad?"

"Trust me, this is not something you care to know."

"And what kind of name is Kap?"

"No one's ever had the guts to ask him. I sure ain't. Anyway, don't worry about his name. Worry about the money. He wants it when he wants it, and he does not fuck around."

"OK," I said, and pulled out of the lot to get away from Luke, who was using the *Are you stupid?* expression he'd been giving me a lot lately. Even though Mr. Einstein—whose own schooling ended in the eighth grade—hadn't even used his two-year prison stint to get the G.E.D. they offered.

So I drove toward home and tried to keep it together—and almost succeeded until "Baby, We Won!" infected my radio. When the singer crooned, "Follow your dreams!" I exploded.

"I followed them!" I said and smacked the meat of my palm against the steering wheel. "And where did it get me? Tell me that, ya fuckwad!"

I had a lot more to say but muttered it mostly inside my head, as I usually do when hearing phrases like "Seize the day!" and "Try new things!" and "Take some chances!" Those clichés are so easy to regurgitate, but they never take into account the failures and the missteps and the madhouses that await the vast, vast majority of those who set out to succeed. No one wants to talk about all of life's losers, do they? "Baby, We Won!"? Only the rare few do.

My rant ended, though, when I realized that there was only one way for me to get the car repair money, as well as the funds for next month's rent. And that realization sent a tear down my cheek.

The buffalo nickel I'd sold was the second most important thing I owned. My guitar is the first. I've talked to it, written songs with it, and taken care of it like I would a beloved child. For years people have been telling me that the tenor guitar is out of style. "Give up that sound" is the most frequent comment I get from other musicians, though not far behind is: "Real country singers don't come out of Pennsylvania," no matter that I'm alt-country, and heavier on the alt than on the country. "You sound too much like Neko Case" rounds out the third spot for the most dispiriting remark that's offered as advice. But my guitar and I stood against all those opinionated jerks—fiercely.

And now I would have to pawn it.

There was no other choice. I'd already gotten and spent an advance on three weeks of pay from my school year job as a receptionist at Locksburg High and had nothing else to sell.

When that understanding slammed into me, I sat in my driveway as that lousy song petered out and tried to convince myself that the pawn would be only temporary. But why lie: It would be months before I could save back the money for the guitar, and by then the pawnshop would likely have sold it, and my dream would finally die. Not that it had ever really lived.

I tried to stir some self-righteous rage and get incensed at the music world. Fuck them all anyway. Fuck the shitty bars and their ass-grabbing managers and their low pay and their high prices for their watered-down drinks. Fuck the record companies with their Ivy League assholes who don't care about anything other than the next hot chick with maximal cleavage and minimal talent. Fuck the other musicians, so many of whom got where they are through corporate connections and bullshit backstories and expensive lessons paid for with Daddy's cash. (One of them was a guy I met in Philly, where he was playing folk rock under his real name, Liam

Pennsky, after graduating from Yale. Now he is Robby Rangle, with a Texas accent replacing his New England preppy drawl, and two hit singles under his fake name, one of them about an old brown horse that he surely never rode outside his New Haven dorm room or his Philadelphia condo.) Fuck them all, along with the loud-talking, too-lazy-to-clap audiences, the four a.m. bedtimes, the bone-weary exhaustion following the shows, and the heart and the soul that you put up on display on the postage-stamp-size stage, only to have some cheap-looking chick raise her hand and call out, "Overrr here! Cindy! Overrr here!" to flag a sozzled friend who staggered into the bar in the middle of the set that you had to beg to get.

I swung the car door shut and went inside for the guitar, then picked up the case without looking at it, humiliated at myself for what I was doing. I went out to the car, put it in the back seat, then returned to the house to wash the tears off my face. Maybe appearing less desperate would get me a better price for the guitar.

And while thinking that thought, the realization hit me again: *Oh Christ, I really am going to pawn my beautiful guitar. I can now sink no lower.* That pushed another tear out of my eye.

My phone rang. An unknown number, probably some telemarketer, which is the only thing I get these days except for Luke, who's usually calling to apologize for something crude he said while drunk or asking to come over with laundry he needs washed, because it would cost him nothing to do it at my place. I wiped my eyes.

"Hello."

"Hi. Is this Liz?"

"Yes."

"Hi, Liz. This is Belle Chapman."

25

There was no way I'd heard that right, of course. I was tired, miserable, and stuffed up from the crying and nose blowing. I sniffed and brushed my hair away from my ear to hear better.

"I'm sorry. What did you say your name was?"

"Belle Chapman. How are you?"

I pulled the phone away, quick, to see the area code: 615. Nashville. Then I slapped the phone back onto my ear.

"I'm, uh, you know . . . you know . . . good. You know. Good."

"Good," she said.

"Yeah, it's, you know . . . good."

"That's good," she said.

"Yeah, it's great. Yeah. No. Actually, I'm great."

I smiled automatically, because I once read a psychology article that said a listener could hear the positive vibes in your voice. I glanced in the mirror. I looked like a grinning roadkill raccoon.

Belle Chapman said: "You sent me some tracks. Ten of them. Maybe six or seven months ago? Sorry it's taken me so long to get back to you."

"That's . . . no problem. No problem at all."

"I was working with a couple tours in Europe, then had to spend some time in L.A., so it's been hectic. But when I got home, I listened to your stuff and . . . wow."

"Wow," I repeated, because I had no words of my own and because I was talking to Belle Chapman, who produced three No. 1 albums in the past two years, and when she says, "Wow," you say, "Wow," too.

Belle Chapman said, "They were excellent. I must have listened to them a half dozen times this past weekend."

Forget the roadkill raccoon: My mouth dropped open like a gasping, beached carp.

And the phone went silent, because one of us should be talking, and that one of us was me. But I couldn't find anything in my maw other than air I could barely breathe. And the music producer Belle Chapman was on the other end of the line. And the music producer Belle Chapman was waiting for me to say something. And the music producer Belle Chapman finally had mercy on my soul and spoke first. And the music producer Belle Chapman said:

"Do you have a minute to talk?"

And I realized two things above all the things I've ever known in my thirty years on earth: (1) that the music producer Belle Chapman just asked me to talk, ostensibly about my music that she listened to a half dozen times this past weekend and said, and I quote, "Wow"; and (2) that this could be the start of something huge. So I announced to myself: *When you answer her, Liz, you make sure it's memorable because—not to get too far ahead of yourself—this could be the response that both of you remember and talk about at Grammy Awards ceremonies and record label lunches and Hall of Fame inductions. And not to pressure you, Liz, but the next thing that comes out of your mouth absolutely must be original and savvy and a teeny bit clever.*

"So, Liz?" the music producer Belle Chapman said. "Do you have a minute?"

Seize the day! I yelled inside my head. *Take your chance! Go for it!*

Then into the phone I said, quite brilliantly:

"Uh . . . yeah."

27

CARLA

BILLY WAS A SERIOUS KID, but he had a sly comedic side that he occasionally employed. During his interview for M.I.T., he told the professor that he was captain of the high school d-d-debating team. The professor shifted in his chair and himself started to stammer, scrambling for a response, before Billy grinned to signal that he was joking.

I could see this was no joke, though. Yet every bit of me had to hope that it was.

"C'mon, Billy. Don't play around like that."

His silence was crushing my heart, my spirit, whatever I had inside me that was now confounded and agonized. A heavy kind of panic grew in my mind and rolled down to my shoulders; I felt them slump. I kept waiting for some break in Billy's expression. None arrived. When the quiet became too much to bear, I said:

"You say she's in our yard. Is that metaphorical or ironic or whatever that's called?"

"Doreen's body is buh-buh-buried in our yard," Billy said. "I p-put it there."

"Why? What—"

"She did it to herself! She made a mistake and . . ."

"I don't understand. Anything. Help me here, Billy. Please."

"The party . . ."

"The graduation party, at Leo's? Where she was last seen?"

"Yes. I wuh-was there. I told you that."

At the time Billy had been surprised to be invited. But everyone from his graduating class had been invited, and most had shown up, crowding into their classmate Leo's house and yard. The police narrative, gleaned from interviews, put Doreen there, swilling beer and playing drinking games, until she called an ex-boyfriend who now served as her dealer and asked him to deliver some drugs to her. She told some friends she'd be back in fifteen minutes, went outside, and never returned. Her dealer swore to the police that he'd met her on the corner, a hundred yards from the party. He said he drove with her around the block, gave her what she asked for, and dropped her off at the same spot. It didn't help the dealer's case that they found her cell phone in his glove compartment.

Billy said to me: "I had a beer and hung out at the puh-party. Then I went in the kitchen and some of the guys were asking me lots of questions. I realized that, you know, they didn't care about my answers. They only wanted to hear me st-stutter. They kept going on and laughing at muh-me."

"You didn't tell me this."

"It's always the same. It never ends with those guys. So I luh-left."

"Then what?"

"I had parked on Smick Street, in front of the vacant lot. Doreen w-was in the lot."

"What was she doing?"

"Sitting on a tree s-stump. I didn't see her at first. Then she flicked her lighter in the dark and that caught my eye. She said:

'Why are you leaving?' I said, the party s-sucked. She said that's what she always admired about me: I could l-leave someplace whenever I w-wanted. Not like the others, who hung around when they didn't want to, afraid that people would talk about them when they left. That's why she was sitting outside. She wanted to be away from everyone. I said, 'I'm heading home.' She said, 'C'mon, let's take a ride.'"

It was easy to imagine how Billy must have felt: A June night. A cute girl asking him to be alone together. Even if she was only being friendly, her suggestion must have overfilled his stomach with butterflies.

"What about her cell phone?" I asked. "The cops say her dealer had it."

"She told me the dealer kept her phone, since she didn't have enough money to pay him. Cuh-collateral, until she sold some of the drugs at the party and paid him back in a couple hours."

"Then what happened?"

"We cruised around for a while, listening to the radio. She wanted to luh-light up something. I said no. I can't get caught with anything like that in the car. She said, 'Well, let's go somewhere where I can smoke.' So we came back here."

"I was in Philly, wasn't I?" I asked, though we both already knew that I was. Temple University had a weekend workshop for those interested in opening a restaurant. I'd recently started toying with the idea and took the two-day class to learn about the financial end of the business. I'd stayed overnight in a dorm there as part of the package.

"Doreen . . . she took out t-tinfoil and stuff and . . . Mom . . . I never took drugs in my life. I tried puh-pot twice and hated it. That was in my junior year . . ."

"Billy. Don't worry about any of that. Tell me the story."

"Doreen said, 'Try this. It'll stop your stutter.' I know she was joking about that part. But . . . when I breathed it in . . . everything felt so intense. And so calm at the same time."

"Heroin?"

"Yeah. Then she said if I really wanted to feel good, I should inject it. I didn't want to do that. So we smoked some more. Then I inhaled real deep . . . and I p-passed out."

"Did you get sick?"

"No. I woke up in the morning. Doreen was there with a n-needle in her arm. She'd decided to inject it. I ruh-read that overdose victims die within minutes of the injection. I saw the clock. I'd been passed out or asleep or whatever for four or five hours, so she was duh-dead for about that long. She was cuh-cold as ice."

I could guess some of the rest. I'd been asking Billy for months to fill in the ancient koi pond in our yard. He loved the pond, but the last fish had died a half year earlier. Well, "died" is a nice way of putting it: The koi was eaten by the raccoons that sometimes raided the yard. When I'd returned from Philadelphia, he told me that he had filled in the pond. Our picnic table had been pulled on top of the spot.

Since the day we moved here, I've loved this mouse-ridden, poorly insulated house. It's the only place I've ever lived in that I've owned. After renting apartments where neighbors blasted stereos whenever they pleased and revved their muscle car engines well into the night, the quiet here is nothing short of heavenly. It sits on an acre on the outskirts of Locksburg, two hundred yards from our nearest neighbor and before the woods get denser and turn into game land. The house, with its trees and garden and windows to watch it all, has brought me more joy than anything in my life except for my son. Now, though, it was also the place where a girl had died.

"Mom. I was so scared. I puh-panicked. If the cops found out about the drugs, I could go to jail, on top of the fact that someone d-d-died in our house. The school would take away my scholarship and throw me out, and you'd be embarrassed beyond belief, especially since the n-newspaper did that story on me getting into M.I.T. And—"

"Don't use me as an excuse, Billy. I don't know why you didn't—"

"I wasn't *thinking*! You were coming home soon, and it was light outside, so I couldn't take her anyplace else. I got fuh-fucking scared that I was going to lose everything and I know you say I'm smart but I wasn't thinking, OK? *I can't think the right thing every single time! I can't! I can't!*"

"OK. I know," I said, if only to calm him.

"I fuh-fucked up! And this whole year . . . I thought about what happened. I couldn't get away from it."

I saw my son for what he was, back then and at this moment: not a young man with an incredibly bright future, but a teenager scared out of his wits, in the center of an appalling situation. And now I was involved too, with this young woman's body buried so close to where we sat. A young woman who every police officer within fifty miles has been rabidly searching for.

I asked him more questions and listened to his answers, unlike what the Locksburg cops had done last year. They inquired about when he left the party, then waved him off as he began stuttering during his alibi. The police already had the drug dealer. They had no real interest in anyone else, especially not that smart kid whom the whole town was talking about because of his acceptance to M.I.T. and a bunch of other big-name schools. Truth be told, the local police were out of their league with an investigation into a missing girl. The *Locksburg Leader* suggested as much in an op-ed. A week later the editor's car was ticketed and towed.

As Billy and I spoke, my initial shock turned into an undercurrent of sorrow for Doreen and of dread for my son. Around one a.m. Billy rested his head back against the sofa, exhausted. He closed his eyes. Soon he was breathing deeply.

I sat there watching my sleeping boy and worried. And although I had no real clue about what to do next, at least one thing was certain. When I considered the situation and asked myself how far I'd go to protect my child, the answer always came back the same: For my only son, I'd go as far as I had to go.

I would protect him at all costs.

REED

GREG SAID, "So now Mom is gone. And Little Jimmy could have died too, and that gives me nightmares when I think about it. I'm trying not to hold it against you . . ."

In other words, I thought but did not say, *he is holding it against you.*

I did not put my fingers in my ears but I stopped listening to Greg. When he saw that I was looking elsewhere, he tapped my shoulder and said: "Reed. Do you hear what I'm saying? I don't know if I can risk anything like that happening again. If—"

Little Jimmy came into the room.

Greg went quiet.

Little Jimmy is not like Greg and not like Maggie. Greg is always serious and sometimes frustrated, and Mom said he can be like a chicken trying too hard to squeeze out an oversized egg. He went to college for an accounting degree and when other people would say to him, "Lots of parties at Penn State, huh, Greg?" he would say, "Oh, yeah," in a way that meant he probably did not go to lots of parties at Penn State. When he came back from college, he started dating Maggie Brice, who Mom always said hi to real friendly, but I knew that behind the real friendly hi, she did not like her.

I do not really know what kind of person Maggie was. She never spoke a great deal. She got pregnant, then married Greg, and when she would come over to our house, she would be staring at her cell phone or filing her nails and did not speak a lot to us or to Greg.

Little Jimmy, though, smiles so much. He is interested in many things and likes to explore. When school got out two weeks ago, Greg began dropping him off with Mom and me before Greg went to work. Little Jimmy loves it when I run after him. Sometimes he will do things like turn off all the lights or take a book that he knows I want and run away to get me to chase him. When I do, that makes him laugh, and that makes me happy too. If you listen close, his cackle sounds like Mom's.

Greg stopped and looked at Little Jimmy and said to me: "Maybe now's not a good time to talk, Reed. We've got a lot to clean downstairs. Then I have to go out and run some errands that have to be done by the end of the day."

"I can clean up everything," I said.

"You sure? I mean, I was thinking that might be good for you. Give you something to do. Keep your mind off things."

"Yes," I said, and stood up.

Then Greg turned around to leave my bedroom.

And I saw what was in the pocket of his suit jacket.

I gasped.

I held in my scream because Greg would not like me screaming. But he must have heard the sound I made.

"What?" Greg asked.

I pointed to his pocket. He reached inside.

"Oh Christ. I totally forgot."

35

"You said you were going to give it to Mr. and Mrs. Lombard, the undertakers."

"I was going to give it to them. It slipped my mind."

"Mom said—"

"Yes, you told me. But it was so crazy today, Reed."

Greg pushed it deeper in his pocket as if that could make it go away, but I could see it there and I said: "Give it to me!" louder than I wanted to. Greg took it out of his pocket and handed it to me and even Little Jimmy stopped smiling.

THE STORY OF MISS MOLLY THE DOLLY

I do not like to make things. I would rather watch things instead. But when I was nine we had arts and crafts class in school and the next day was Mom's birthday, so I took two pieces of felt and traced out a pattern and cut them and stitched them together and filled it with cotton balls and made Miss Molly the Dolly. And I handed it to Mom on her birthday.

"Where did you get this, Reed?"

I said: "This is Miss Molly the Dolly. I made her for you in arts and crafts."

Mom took it in her hands and went quiet.

I said: "I did not have any money to buy you something and I am sorry."

She kept staring at it.

"You made this for me?"

Something seemed strange in her voice and I did not know what to say, so I walked away. When I came back a few minutes later, Mom was at the kitchen table holding Miss Molly the Dolly and wiping her eyes.

"I am sorry that you do not like it."

"No!" Mom said. "Oh my gosh, Reed, it's . . . this . . . this is the nicest thing anyone has ever given me in my whole life. Ever."

She stared at it some more and smiled a little and then another tear came down and I said, "If you like it then why are you crying?"

"It's so . . . beautiful."

"I cannot sew well and the mouth is not right and there were kids laughing at it and saying it was ugly with the yarn as hair and Mrs. Vecchio had to tell them to stop."

"Oh, my darling Reed. This is wonderful."

And she hugged me and I waited for that to end and she ran a hand over her face and she said, "Honey, don't let anyone tell you what's nice and what's not. You can do anything you want in this world. I believe that. You need to believe it too. Promise me you'll remember that: that you can do anything."

I said, "I promise to remember that."

"And would you ever break a promise to me?"

"No," I said.

"And would you ever lie?"

"No."

Mom put Miss Molly the Dolly on the mantel and sometimes around the house Mom would ask aloud: "What does Miss Molly the Dolly have to say about this?" and I would say: "Miss Molly the Dolly cannot speak," and Mom would say: "Good. I don't like being interrupted." And when we would leave the house, Mom would call out: "Look after the joint, Molly!" And when Mom became sick a couple years ago, I brought Miss Molly the Dolly to her in the hospital and Mom cried when she saw her and later on Mom said: "Reed. Whenever I go, I want to keep Miss Molly with me forever, OK? I would love to have her right there next to me. Will you make sure?"

I said yes.

She said, "Promise?"

I said yes.

THAT IS THE END OF THE BEGINNING OF
THE STORY OF MISS MOLLY THE DOLLY

I told this all to Greg yesterday. He said he would ask Mr. and Mrs. Lombard to put Miss Molly in the casket with Mom. Now I saw that he did not do that.

"Reed, I don't think Mom was serious. Sometimes you don't understand when people aren't talking literally."

"Mom said it and she meant it and I promised her. And you should never break a promise."

"Maybe . . . maybe you're feeling this way because of what happened. Do you feel guilty or something?"

"I do not feel guilty or something."

I took Miss Molly the Dolly and sat with her and rocked back and forth. After a while Greg said: "Get ready, Reed. You can come with us."

"I want to stay here."

"Reed . . ."

"Let me stay here."

"Are you going to be OK?"

"I am. I will clean the house."

"Are you sure you'll be all right alone?"

"Mom let me stay alone since I was fourteen and now I am twenty. I know how to do everything."

"I mean, do you feel all right?"

"Yes. I want to be by myself."

"You're not going to cook, are you? The neighbors brought food. Don't use the stove."

"I am not going to cook."

"I'll be back in a couple hours, OK?"

"Yes."

"So listen to me: I don't want you to leave this house. Do you understand?"

"I understand," I said, because that part is true. I understood what he was saying. But I did not say I agreed or disagreed.

"Reed. I've got so much to worry about. So I want you to stay here. And if you don't listen to me . . . that's it. I need to be able to trust you. If not, you're going to have to go to that place in Pittsburgh."

A little while later Greg and Little Jimmy left and I walked around the house and realized what he said and I thought of how I hated Pittsburgh and did not want to go there and it frightened me so much that I walked in circles around the sofa.

But I had promised Mom.

And I had promised Mom never to break my promise.

So I took Miss Molly the Dolly and put her in my backpack.

And I went on walking in circles, because I was nervous.

But I had to make a decision.

So I walked in circles around the sofa. Very fast. And when I circled once more, I used the centrifugal force and kept moving, toward the door.

Then all at once I left the house.

LIZ

"OH, BELLE, I'll bet you a dollar!" I said into the phone with a laugh.

"I'll betcha two bucks and a beer, Liz!" she replied in the same way.

We were almost giggling by then, both of us so sure of ourselves. So I said, "Are you near a laptop?"

"Yep. Right here on my desk."

"OK. Check it online. I'll wait."

The tapping of keys. "Son. Of. A. Bunny," she said with the barest hint of a twang.

According to a *Rolling Stone* profile of her, Belle Chapman grew up in Athens, Georgia, and began managing a couple of bar bands when she was eighteen. Within the next three decades she had climbed the ladder to become one of the most powerful producers in the industry. And here she was, joking around with me. "You were right!" she said.

I said: "Not to say I told you so. But, you know, I told you so."

"I can't believe it. It was November 1960. All right, I owe you two bucks and a beer."

Five minutes into the call, after I had untied my tongue, Belle had asked me about my influences. That gave me license to spew out a list of names of musicians I loved and had her saying stuff like "Ohhh, yeah. Wasn't she the best?" and "It's amazing that that album came out in 1961," when I mentioned Etta James's *At Last!* I probably shouldn't have corrected Belle, but almost from the start we had the rapport of friends who can finish each other's sentences and joke around with ease, so I said casually: "I think that was late 1960." That triggered our friendly fight.

"OK, OK," Belle said. "You got me there. Anyway, let me tell you why I called."

I sat down in case my sweaty hand dropped the phone.

Belle said: "Once a year I rent out the Bluebird Cafe in Nashville. You ever been down here?"

"Once, for a very short time," I said, a candidate for overstatement of the year. On my self-funded tour I drove into Nashville to find that the bar where I'd planned to perform had been shuttered by the Board of Health. With all the optimism of a twenty-two-year-old, I opened my guitar case outside the place and began playing on the sidewalk. Thirty minutes later, and eight dollars and nine cents richer, a cop ordered me to move along. Hotels were too expensive for me, so I slept in my car in a Walmart parking lot, then drove out of Nashville less than twelve hours after arriving in town.

Belle said: "Ah, you've got to stay a little while, get to know the place. Anyway, I rent out the Bluebird and bring in a few artists and we all listen, to see and hear how they sound onstage."

"Who's 'we'?"

"Me and my group. Couple of others in the industry. Zach Dell, who I partner with sometimes. You know Zach?"

"I know of him. Heck, everyone knows of him. He's had a great few years. Won a CMA and a couple Grammys, I think."

"Yeah. He's terrific. He brings along some people from the record labels. We sit around, invited guests only, and you play, and we see how it goes. Think you'd be interested in something like that?"

Does a duck have a waterproof ass?

"Sounds great," I said, this one a candidate for understatement of my life. Then, to be sure, I added: "I'm very interested."

"Good," she said. "It's two weeks from tomorrow. Is your schedule open?"

"Let me check: yes."

"That was fast. All right, I'll sign you up. Now here's what I have to say, Liz, so we're on the same page: There are no guarantees or promises or anything. This is just, you know, a semi-casual get-together where you'll play a few songs for us. But your sound is really fresh, and I think you could make some good friends down here. If nothing else, you'll get a longer look-see at Nashville. Afterward, we all head out for a big ol' dinner. It's a fun time."

"I can't wait."

"OK, I'll pass you over to Trish, my assistant. See you in two weeks."

The phone clicked and Trish, at the ready, said: "Hi, Liz. I'll email you the address and the time, but here's the quick version: We're meeting at the Bluebird at eight p.m. on July the eleventh. You should get there two hours early. And . . . hey, hold on a second."

Trish half covered the phone and called out, no doubt into Belle's office: "Belle? Did you want Liz in the studio too?"

"Oh, yeah!" she called out. "Put her back on the line." A *click click*, then:

"Liz? I almost forgot. I liked your tapes. All acoustic is nice. But I want to hear how you sound with some tracks. We got ourselves a studio next door. Can you and your guitar get down here a day or two early?"

"Division Street Studios?"

"That's it."

Sweet little baby Jesus. The place where Ray Charles and Dolly Parton and Johnny Cash all recorded at one time or another. In the past, I would have been ecstatic to merely stand outside the place and snap a selfie. And here I was, being told that I would be inside the studio, playing my music.

"I can be there." I pushed the words out fast in case I began to hyperventilate.

"Good. Let me give you back to Trish."

Another click-over, and Trish said: "This is going to be great. I sit in on the recording sessions so we'll get to work together, Liz. I loved your song 'Buffalo Nickel.' Belle was just playing it."

Did I speak after that? Heck, I must have. But I'm not sure of a single word of it. I know I tried to play it cool and kept my voice from trembling when confirming my email address. Then I listened in silence as Trish gave me some other information, and I thanked her with restrained enthusiasm and hung up.

And there I sat on my threadbare sofa.

Silent.

Unmoving.

Composed.

I had imagined this moment since I was thirteen and thought I'd be leaping up and down and shrieking in joy. Instead, I was thunderstruck. I put the phone on the cracked coffee table. Breathed deeply. Closed my eyes. Reflected on all those years of disappointments and disasters and failures and knew that, even if nothing came from this—*But something would*, I told myself. *Something must*—just the fact that I was asked to record and perform was enough.

I breathed again, and stood calmly, and went to the kitchen for a glass of water.

Then I caught sight of myself in the mirror.

And that's when I jumped up high and screamed loud enough to hurt my own ears: "Yes! Holy *shit*! Yes! Yes! Yes!" And leapt in the air two more times for good measure and strutted into the kitchen, where I wasn't about to drink any crappy *water*, I was going to drink *wine* or *whiskey*! No, *both*!

Well, I didn't have either. But there were a few cans of beer in the fridge.

I cracked open a Keystone Light, slurped the foam that was bubbling out of the can, and shook my head, astounded. All that crap that I had once scorned and derided and ridiculed was actually true: Dreams can come true! Hard work does pay off! Your luck really can turn around in an instant!

And with that, I remembered my beautiful guitar, sitting in my Chevy. I went to get it, to play myself a victory song.

I turned the handle on the front door. The door nearly swung open on its own.

A wall of hot air blew against me.

I backed up a step, then looked outside.

That's when I saw the flames.

My car was on fire.

CARLA

I WOKE TWENTY MINUTES AFTER closing my eyes, remembered the body that was buried in the yard, then stayed up, tormented, for an hour before exhausting myself and falling back to sleep for another twenty minutes. I woke and did the same thing again and again until morning.

At first light I made coffee. Billy padded into the kitchen ten minutes later.

"Wh-what do you think we should do?" he asked.

"I'm thinking it through. As for right now, let's get over to the barn. There's a delivery this afternoon, and the electrician is stopping by to upgrade the fuse box. Let's not change our schedules or do anything suspicious."

We drove there in silence. When we pulled in, Nestor was kneeling in the dirt next to his car, a tire flat from one of the bits of metal that littered the lot. The last time the electrician was there, he grabbed a large toolbox from his van, only to have it flip open and scatter its contents into the dirt. We'd been finding pieces all week.

"Do my benefits cover car repair?"

"I don't pay you benefits."

"So that's a no."

"Yes. That's a no."

46

"Now you tell me."

"Get it patched and give me the bill," I told him. Yet another expense. Save for the pendant around my neck that held my mother's wedding diamond, I'd sold all my jewelry to help finance my plans. I didn't care much. The restaurant was more important to me than any old ring or bracelet. Yet, even with that money and the remortgage, I'd be cutting it close.

The barn sits on two acres inside the Locksburg line and just off well-traveled Route 211, where there are no places to eat for miles. When I first saw the land for sale, I knew the location would be excellent, but the old barn sealed the deal: High rafters and stone walls made it perfect for a comfortable, mid-priced restaurant, something Locksburg desperately needed. The town had a couple greasy spoons and, as its only attempt at appearing upscale, a failing roach trap that masqueraded as a steak house. My restaurant will fill a big void in this backwater of five thousand and the surrounding areas. Better yet, my costs would be kept under control, since I've already contracted to buy meat and vegetables from local farms. That will be a selling point, though I am debating on whether to use the word "locavore," worried that it might be too smarmy a term for the townsfolk, who are suspicious of anything with a strange name or an outsider air.

There was further cause for optimism about my restaurant: The kayaking lodge on the Susquehanna River, which set the locals snickering when they first heard of the plan, was now eyed with envy, as the fifteen cabins were booked a year in advance, and the owners said they may open another for fishing and paddleboarding. And a mile outside of town, a metal shelving company moved into half of an old mill, hiring forty people right off the bat. Rumor has it that a tool-and-die firm had its eye on the other half; they'd opened a plant in Selinsgrove that now employed seventy. All the while, the mayor, as he's done for years, continued to campaign on promises to make our area more attractive to visitors. To anyone who'd listen, he'd deliver blowhard phrases about transitioning from a hard-industry past toward a rustic future, filled with antique shops and bed-and-breakfasts. If it all came together, it would be good news for me: potential diners with money. Yet we all knew the town could go either way. Weeds grew from the cracks in many of the sidewalks, even on the main streets, and there was a constantly increasing number of boarded-up houses that the owners didn't have money to repair and the town didn't have funds to raze. As always, Locksburg was an interesting bet, yet never a sure one.

I've spent every day of the past six months worrying over such issues. Now, however, I had an infinitely bigger worry, and it haunted me throughout the day.

Would I hand over Billy to the Locksburg police, a crew who took their nightsticks to the heads of suspects in the basement holding cell? Could I risk sending Billy to Carroll Valley State Penitentiary? There would be some kind of jail sentence involved, surely, for hiding Doreen's body and keeping it secret for a year. They'd eat a skinny college kid like him alive in there. Everything else would be gone for my son too: M.I.T. His scholarship. His future. The media attention would mark him for life.

As for me, I'd lose the restaurant and my remortgaged house after becoming known as the mother of that boy who buried the missing girl's body. I already had so little to show for my life. Whatever I did have would be gone. And what good would come of any of it? Doreen was dead. Nothing would change that.

This much I decided: I wasn't going to turn Billy in.

I came to see that choice as a giant middle finger to this town. To this world. To any god who would allow an eighteen-year-old girl to die like that, after being raised by a mother who was now serving ninety days in jail for buying meth with the money that the town had raised for Doreen's search. To any god who would give Billy so many disadvantages as a boy, watch him struggle to overcome each one, then put him in this position.

No. God wasn't here, and he wasn't expected to magically appear anytime soon. He was off keeping the weather nice for believers' wedding days. He was securing votes for politicians who'd later embezzle money and inspiring preachers who would soon bed the pool boy.

He wasn't there for me.

He'd never been.

And I wasn't about to ask for his help.

Our delivery was on time but the electrician ran late, so we worked on other things while waiting. In between I would peek over at Billy. In my eyes he was still a boy. Even at nineteen he looked like a high school freshman. He'd always had a slight build, nowhere big enough to fight back against the bullies who once tortured him. Thin black hair that's the same as mine and brown eyes that squinted often, as if he were on the verge of figuring out a serious mathematical equation.

We sanded a section of wooden floor and installed one of the kitchen counters that I bought cheap from a bankrupt restaurant in Harrisburg. And soon, in between stealing glances at Billy, I found that I too was being watched.

"Everything OK?" Nestor asked. He had worked as a contractor for decades and had a great eye for remodeling. Apparently he had a good one for people too. I hadn't realized I'd been acting differently.

"Yes. Why?"

"You look like you're afraid that something might fall on top of your head."

"Just worried about this place. You think we'll be done in time?"

"If we work hard, yeah. It'll come down to the wire, though, even if we pray. You been praying? I told you before, you should."

I shrugged him off. He'd likely be appalled to know that I've never prayed—and never would. When I didn't answer him, Nestor said:

"You sure you're all right?"

Before I could answer, the electrician's truck pulled in, an hour late from his previous call, when he was already forty-five minutes past his scheduled time. I'd gotten him on the cheap and that now seemed to be a mistake. He went to work on the fuse box and finished it fast, making me uneasy: I'm hoping the refrigerators don't kick out on some late night and take a thousand dollars' worth of meat with them.

When the electrician left and we finished our work for the day, Billy and I drove off. On our ride home I said to him:

"We're not leaving Doreen in our yard. I won't have her mother and everyone else spending the rest of their lives wondering what happened to her. That's not right. Her mother is a mess…"

"She is."

"She's still a mother, though. She needs to know."

"I understand."

"So we'll give them Doreen's body."

"How?"

"We'll dig her up. Put her in a place that's farther from here. Then we'll send an anonymous letter to the police. We'll explain to everyone what happened—without telling them who she was with—and where to find her."

"It's been a year," Billy said, and cringed. I did too, thinking about how she must look and smell by now. Her body had no doubt frozen during the frigid winter. The soggy spring would have thawed her and made her body gruesome.

"You got a better idea? I'm all ears."

Billy shook his head.

"So that's our plan. And after we finish, we're never going to talk about this again."

"So wh-when will we do it?"

"Tonight," I said. "So let's get ready now."

REED

I LEFT MY HOUSE and went nine steps before turning around and going back inside to get the key that I had forgotten. It was like an ancient skeleton key from an old movie, and it hung from a foot-long piece of string on a hook in Mom's room. Greg returned the key there after the funeral.

Our house is the only place where I have ever lived but it is not the only place where Mom has ever lived. She grew up in a mansion on the east side of town that had seven bedrooms and five bathrooms and a garage for three cars and a lot of land. When we would pass it, Mom would say, "Ahhh, the old estate." And when we got back to our much smaller house, she would say, "How the mighty have fallen." She would laugh a little, not a cackle, because there was sadness in what she said.

Our family, the Groves, once owned a lot of things in Locksburg. We had a chemical company and some other businesses that closed when the coal mines shut down. Then Mom sold the big mansion and moved to where we are now, a tiny house with my bedroom and Greg's old bedroom upstairs and Mom's bedroom downstairs next to the kitchen. We owned one other place: a mausoleum that the Grove family had built in the 1920s when they were rich. Mom once said, "I was born in a mansion, and when I die, I'll spend eternity in a mansion." She meant the one at the cemetery: It is twice as big as our backyard shed and made of stone.

I would go to the mausoleum with Mom. She would unlock the door with the big key and we would sit inside in the cool air and say hi to Dad as if he were a person right there who you happened to be talking to and not just a body in a space in the wall. "Reed's here with me," she would say. "He's doing well. He looks a lot like you: so tall!" Then she would wipe the dust from the copper plate that had his name and the dates from his birth to his death. Behind that copper plate was Dad's coffin. At the end of the visit, Mom would ask me to go outside so she could talk to Dad alone. I would pace around the mausoleum—it was ten steps by ten steps by ten steps by ten steps—and a few times when I passed by the door, I heard her whisper to Dad that she missed him and she would say: "Look after the boys if you can."

Sometimes Mom and I would walk the three miles home from the cemetery. Almost everyone along the way seemed to know Mom and she would stop to talk to them and it would take hours. If you do not know every single person in Locksburg, you at least know of them or which family they came from. When you do not know a person, you say "Hiya" to them anyway and they say "Hiya" back and ask, "How have you been?" and then you end up talking about the weather.

But on this day I walked down our street to Frederick Avenue and a few people glared at me and instead of saying "Hiya" they stared for a moment then turned away without saying anything. I knew that they must have been thinking about what happened to Mom. There was a story about it in the *Locksburg Leader*.

"Fuckin' murderer!" someone said from a rusted Ford Mustang that was zooming down Moore Street. He stuck his hand out with the middle finger raised. A couple blocks later a white pickup truck came by and the driver yelled: "Who you gonna kill next, imbecile?"

I passed a lot of abandoned houses. They scared me but in the way that you could look at something scary and not have to be a part of it, like a movie that could frighten you, though you could walk away from it at any time. There are a lot of abandoned houses on every street in Locksburg, built when the mines and steel plant were in business and so many people moved here for work. When most of the people moved out, they left the buildings behind. Mom said if we could figure out what to do with all the empty houses, the family could be rich again.

The town once had twenty thousand residents, so that means fifteen thousand are gone, and the rest of the people here always seem to talk about leaving. But I like Locksburg. I like the way that many of the streets are in a grid, and that makes it easy to find anything. I like how the main part of town is only about three miles wide, not so big, so you could never get lost for long. I like how the hills that rise up to the north go green in the spring and summer and seem mysterious, as if another world could be there.

And if I could get back to my house before Greg did, he would never know that I was gone and maybe I would not have to go to Pittsburgh and I could stay in Locksburg with him.

I walked onto the porch of Lombard's Funeral Home and knocked on the shiny, polished door and Mrs. Lombard came and opened it and said, "Hiya, Reed," the same real nice way she did this morning at the funeral when Mr. Lombard rolled Mom's casket into the wall in the space next to Dad's and Mrs. Lombard stood at the back of the mausoleum and directed everyone where to stand.

"Hello, Mrs. Lombard."

"Is something the matter?"

"Yes." I took off my backpack and unzipped it and brought out Miss Molly the Dolly.

"This is Miss Molly the Dolly. Mom once told me she wanted Miss Molly the Dolly to be with her forever and Greg was supposed to give Miss Molly the Dolly to you and Mr. Lombard and one of you would put it in the casket with Mom. But Greg forgot, so now I need you to put Miss Molly the Dolly in there with her."

"Can I . . . ?" she said. She made a motion to Miss Molly the Dolly and I guessed she wanted to hold her, so I handed her to Mrs. Lombard.

"Did you make this, Reed?"

"I did. In the third grade. We have had her ever since."

"She's lovely."

"Can I come with you when you put her in with Mom? I can go with you now but need to get home right after we finish."

I took the old key on the string and handed it to her. "This is the key to the gate of the mausoleum."

Mrs. Lombard said: "Reed. Remember when we rolled the casket in, to that section of the wall? We put the plate on front and screwed it shut. And the casket itself is sealed. Once that happens, we're no longer allowed, legally, to reopen it. We would need a court order . . ."

From the moment she began speaking, I knew she was going to say no. You can hear that in someone's voice, how they start off real nice because they are going to say something that will disappoint you. Mrs. Lombard reached out to put her hand on my shoulder and I moved away because I did not want to be touched.

"Come inside, Reed. Let me get you something to drink."

"I do not like to go inside other people's houses."

"Well, this is also a business. So could you come in if it's where I work?"

"Do you live here?"

"Yes."

"Then it is your house, and what I said remains valid." I was glad to get to use that word, "valid." It is a good word.

She laughed a little, though I could see she tried not to, then she said: "OK. Let's sit out here." She sat on the top step of the porch and patted the spot next to her and I sat there.

"How are you feeling?" she said.

"Not so good."

"That was a foolish thing to ask. Of course not. I meant . . . oh, I don't know what I meant. You'd think, after all these years in this business, I'd be better at it, huh?"

I did not say anything.

"How about this, Reed: We can take Miss Molly over there and put her inside the mausoleum. Then she would be near your mother."

"No," I said. "That is not what I want. And that is not what Mom wanted."

We sat there for a long time. I rocked a little to feel better.

Mrs. Lombard was about as old as Mom, though she was much thinner and her hair was gray and Mom's was brown. And Mom was fat. That is not a bad thing to say because Mom said it about herself a lot.

Mrs. Lombard said: "Reed. Maybe you want to do this because—"

"You are going to ask if I feel guilty, like Greg asked me. I know that people sometimes want to do things not for the reason they say but for other reasons. But sometimes a thing is exactly what it is. Mom asked me to do this and I promised."

"I believe you," Mrs. Lombard said. "But let me ask you: Has anyone said anything . . . unkind to you? About what happened to your mother?"

I did not say anything.

"What happened was an accident, Reed. You understand that, don't you?"

I did understand. So I nodded my head.

"Good. Don't forget that. Things happen. It doesn't mean that anyone's at fault or . . . "

She stopped. Then tried again. "I don't know what to say to you. I wish I were a better talker."

"You are a good talker," I said, and that was true or I would not have said it. She had a voice that made you feel that she cared about you. A good talker is not only someone who knows how to use the right words.

We sat on the steps. I was staring down at the ground. I glanced over once and Mrs. Lombard was staring out on the street in a way that meant that she was not really looking at what she was looking at. Instead she was thinking of something else.

"I had a little boy like you once. Did you know that?"

"I am not a little boy."

"Right. Of course. I meant . . . I had a little boy about the same time as your mother had you. About six months or so apart. You and he looked a lot alike. His name was Timothy. He had a cowlick too and his hair would stick up in the back and it was so cute."

I did not say anything. And I figured something bad must have happened and I do not like to hear or think about bad things. And I did not want to hear what Mrs. Lombard was saying about Timothy. Just like I did not want to hear when Mr. Goodnough, the manager at the supermarket, once told me that he smacked his teenage daughter in the face and then felt horrible about it and did not know what got into him, and when Mrs. Sufflaus, the vice principal at the high school, told me that she thought her husband was going off to be with another woman. People always seem to want to tell me things, and most of the things are not happy. Mom said that is because I am a good listener and she said that listening is the nicest thing you could do for someone. She said that sometimes they were not talking to me at all but to themselves.

I also suspected that Mrs. Lombard was going to say something unhappy because I once heard Mom talking about Mrs. Lombard. Mom had said that Mrs. Lombard had seen enough sorrow in her life and that the Good Lord should bless her.

I sat there next to Mrs. Lombard on the steps of the porch. Then she began to talk.

"Timothy was getting to that age where he was always curious about everything, you know? Sort of like your nephew, Little Jimmy. And Timothy would run around the house and hide and . . ."

Mrs. Lombard paused as if she needed to prepare herself for what came next. Then she went on: "One day we were having some of my cousins over for a summer party. A couple days earlier the sliding door in the kitchen had broken. That door led out to the backyard. The repairman was supposed to be there that morning, but he called and said he got tied up at another job on Verrick Street and he would have to postpone until later. So Dennis—that's Mr. Lombard—he got his toolbox and was working to fix the lock on the sliding door. But then one of my cousins arrived early and wanted to show Dennis his new car, and my cousin's wife asked to see the color I painted our bedroom because she was going to repaint her house. And in the middle of that, some other relatives came and they were loud and happy and moving all over the place. And Dennis was out at the car, and my cousin took him for a ride around the block, and another cousin, she ripped her dress and asked me to help her and . . ."

I did not look at Mrs. Lombard when she stopped speaking. I stayed quiet.

She said: "I thought Dennis was watching Timothy. And Dennis thought I was watching him."

Mrs. Lombard gazed out at the street again. Neither of us said anything for a long time.

"Timothy had gone out to the swimming pool. And by the time . . . I mean, it was only twenty minutes or so. When Dennis and I . . . when we couldn't find him . . . we were fast, searching around. But you only need three or four minutes to . . . and I . . . I, uh, won't go into that day anymore. I am guessing that, uh, I mean . . . everyone's full of gossip in this town. I guess maybe you heard."

"I know something bad happened. But I did not know what it was."

"Timothy is gone but . . . my gosh, Reed. I wanted to explain something to you, and I've maybe ruined it . . . Well, let me say that after it was over . . . no, that's not right. It's never over. But, I mean, a week or two later we—Dennis and I—we searched for someone to blame. First it was the repairman. If he would have shown up on time, none of this would have happened, would it? Heck, we even blamed the customer he was working for—like, what if their stupid problem hadn't made the repairman run late? Then we blamed my cousin with the new car who showed up early. Then the others who took my attention away. Later on, we blamed each other. And then, in the end . . . and this is the worst—my god, Reed, nothing is worse . . . but you blame yourself. And you waste so much time with this blame and this guilt and this remorse. And that's what it is, Reed. It's a waste. It's such a huge, colossal waste. And maybe . . . if you haven't wrecked yourself, you finally accept that it was an accident. You learn that there's no one to blame. You have to let it all go."

I kept staring at the ground.

Mrs. Lombard said: "That's so much easier to say than to do, I know. But accidents . . . they happen. I once heard someone say that 'blame is for God and small children,' and maybe that's right. Blame is . . . useless. It was an accident. There's nothing else to say."

We sat there for a long while, and when I looked at Mrs. Lombard, I was surprised that she was not crying. She seemed too tired to do that. She was only watching the street.

"So, Reed. Do you understand what I said?"

"I do."

"Good," she said softly. "If you ever need someone to talk to about it—about anything—you come over here to see me. Stop by anytime. I mean that. Or you can call me on the phone if that's better for you. OK?"

"OK."

During the time she was speaking, she had been wrapping the string that held the key around her finger—wrapping it around, taking it off, starting again—until I could see that her finger was now red and had marks on it where she had pulled the string tight. Finally she noticed that she had the key in her hand and gave the key back to me.

"I'm sorry that I can't help you with Miss Molly. Maybe . . . you could put her in the ground next to the mausoleum or something. Maybe you could do that?"

I did not say anything for a while.

"Goodbye, Mrs. Lombard," I said when I finally stood up.

"See you later, Reed," she said.

I walked down the street and twenty steps later I turned around to see her there, staring out over Shale Avenue. She saw me turn around and waved at me and I waved back.

Then I kept walking.

LIZ

I RESENTED MY CAR for the too many times that it had broken down and stranded me late at night or right before a show, so there was perhaps a tinge of satisfaction from watching it burn. But I'd sunk a lot of money into that Chevy, and the spite didn't feel that good. Plus, as of forty-five seconds earlier, I'd been planning to drive it to Nashville, where I had a dream about to come true. Most horrifying of all, my prized guitar was in the back seat.

I cried "No no no no no!" as the flames whooshed from the front grille and the open spaces around the hood. Since the fire seemed confined there, I figured that maybe I could put it out with the garden hose. But then a trail of flames raced along the underside of the car and ended at the gas tank, where a couple gallons of regular unleaded ignited in a whump—*boom!* that popped the trunk, shattered the windows, and set the interior alight. I ran forward only to be stopped by a wall of fierce heat that caused some of my hair to curl up and sizzle. I couldn't see the guitar amid the inferno.

Plumes of black smoke polluted the air and reeked of thick oil and burning plastic, no doubt remnants of the dashboard and the cheap Naugahyde seats. Tharp Road, where I live, goes down a few miles to a dead end, and by pure luck some yahoo in a plumber's van was driving toward the river. He slowed to a stop and called out: "Your car's on fire!"

"Ya think?" I tried to make it sound snide but was too upset at what was happening to really stress the scorn.

"Well, yeah!" he said seriously, completely missing my tone.

"You going to sit there or help me, man?"

The guy reached back into the van, got a fire extinguisher, and marched to the car on a mission. Then he sprayed the underside, working his way to the engine and the interior. Within seconds the car was engulfed in a cloud of white. The fire was out.

Both of us stood there listening to the tiny pings and crackles that came from the cooling car.

The guy got on his hands and knees and peered at the undercarriage.

"Fuel line," he said.

"What's that mean?"

"I was down the road when I saw the hood on fire. Then it spread fast, underneath, to the tank. Followed the fuel line. Musta been defective."

"It was just fixed."

"Not too well, it seems."

"And the fuel pump was replaced."

"Yeah. That'll do it. Know Frank Perry over on Richland Street? Same thing happened to him. He replaced the pump on his own, drove the car around the block to test it. Then he shut the car off. Thought it was fine. Went into his house. Took a full ten minutes. Little gas fire starts, drips, then eventually sets the whole thing off. Frank ran out there to try and save the car. Nearly caught on fire himself."

I couldn't respond. Only stared at the shell of the car.

"Frank's sleeve went up when he tried to open the hood. Still has a scar. So, you know, compared to Frank, you're lucky."

"Fuck Frank," I said, even if I didn't know what it meant. Then, when I thought of my beautiful guitar: "Oh, fuck me."

Luke whined that he wouldn't return to Kap's house to tell him about my car fire. When I told him over the phone that I was going no matter what, he became irate.

"Your car was a piece of shit anyway, Liz!" Luke said. "It's your own fault!"

"It's my fault that my car is now a cinder," I said in a tone meant to inform him that he sounded absurd. "And that my guitar is now a pile of ashes."

"So? You shouldn't have put it in the car."

"Are you hearing yourself? I'm the victim here."

"Leave it alone, Liz."

We argued for another ten minutes until I told him that I would go to Kap's house myself and bring the police with me. I had no plan to do that and didn't even have a car to get there, but it got Luke to agree to go, and sooner rather than later. He apparently didn't want to arrive there in the dark. He picked me up in the same borrowed truck and we returned to the place that, a few hours earlier, I'd hoped never to set eyes on again.

Kap stepped from his house as he had the last time. I went over to him before Luke could leave the pickup. I planned to keep my voice in check. Not out of fear but because I wanted to control myself and be clear. Heck, maybe there was a shred of decency underneath the guy's tattooed exterior.

"My car caught fire," I said. "It's completely ruined."

I expected a "What happened?" or "Are you all right?" Instead he glanced at me, then turned away, as if he'd decided that I was uninteresting. For an eternal ten seconds, no one said anything.

"Do you know why?" I said, and learned my lesson: I wouldn't wait for a reply. "The fuel pump and the fuel line burned. I could have died in there."

"You got a point to make?" he said flatly.

"My point is, three hours ago we rode out of here after you said you'd fixed the car."

"Maybe you don't know how to drive. Or maybe you hit something on the road. Ever think of that?"

He turned to walk away.

"You owe me a car!" I said.

"You owe me five hundred and sixty bucks."

"You expect me to pay for almost getting killed?"

"We had an agreement, and you ain't backin' out of it. You got a week to pay me for the work I did. After you pay me, then you got the right to ask me to look at it again."

"You must be kidding."

"Deal's a deal. Now it's time for you to leave."

"OK. I'll be back. With the police."

Everything seemed to stop then. I heard Luke behind me. Some kind of whimper escaped from his throat.

Kap turned around.

"Lady, you bring the cops here and you'll . . ." He stopped, and it was instantly apparent how shrewd he was. He knew better than to threaten me. Especially not in front of another person. Instead, he smirked and said: "Well, let's say I wouldn't recommend that."

"C'mon," Luke said. "You had your say, Liz." I turned around. Luke was staring at Kap, nodding the nod that some men make among themselves, a motion that blames the woman.

"I had my say and now I want another car."

"Heck, you're asking for a refund, and you ain't even paid. How do you know it was the fuel line?" Kap said. "When you come back with my money, bring me a mechanic's report and a report from the fire department and prove it."

"Yeah, sure. I'll go through all that, and when I come back here, you'll find some other excuse, won't you?"

"Honey," he said, a word I hated from strangers, in a tone I loathed from anyone, "you better get off my land if you know what's good for you."

"What? Do you have a gun? I bet the police will be interested in that too."

Rage made him clench his jaw, at least from what I could see underneath his unkempt beard. But again he controlled himself. He turned around, put his back to me, and called out: "Luke?"

"Yeah, Kap?" Luke responded like some eager-to-please mutt.

"Come inside."

"Sure, Kap!"

"I'm not going in there," I said.

"No one asked you to," Kap said.

Luke hurried past me and into the house. I returned to the pickup and leaned against it. There I lamented the loss of my guitar. Even when I got another one—and how to pay for it was an enormous question I'd have to tackle really soon—I'd need time to practice on the new instrument to be ready for the Nashville trip.

I stood outside for close to fifteen minutes and, at first, cursed Luke for taking the keys with him. If I had to get out of there fast, the only way was to run into the woods. After another five minutes I began to worry for Luke, who might at that moment be getting sliced into pieces in the basement. Worse yet, whoever was doing the slicing might soon come for me.

Luke came out of the front door. When he got within ten feet, he tossed me the keys and growled low: "Shut your mouth and drive. Now."

"What about my car?"

"I got it all settled, Liz," he said in a harsh whisper. "Now c'mon. Let's get out of here."

"So?" I said when we turned off the dirt road at Kap's house.

Luke blew air out of his mouth as if he'd survived a car wreck or a knife fight.

"You trying to get me killed? Is that what you're trying to do, Liz?"

I wanted to say, *No, I'm trying to get me to Nashville*, but held off. I didn't want him knowing anything about that. This would be my trip. Alone.

Luke and I had met at Zinger's in Marshalltown, where I was playing an open-mic night, taking the stage before a teenage metal trio and after a lone upright bassist who soloed the same thirty-second refrain for twenty minutes. A couple of Luke's coworkers were rowdy, and, in what I then took as an attempt at chivalry, he hushed them in the middle of my set. Only later did I learn that he wasn't shushing them but wheezing from a bronchial infection, made worse by the cheap, paper-wrapped Phillies Blunt cigars that he smokes and often inhales.

Luke came up to me after the show and handed me a beer that I desperately needed, poured from a pitcher that one of his coworkers had paid for. A week later Luke showed up at another performance, one of six people in the audience. He wasn't my type at all, but he kept coming to my shows, and like a damn fool I kept talking to him because, well, I was more than a little lonesome. And who can blame someone for feeling lonely?

Luke and I sort of settled in to hanging out here and there, and lately he'd taken that to a new level: He began to feel more comfortable criticizing most everything from my hair (sometimes self-braided to save money) to the shoes I wore onstage (Goodwill-bought and pleasingly quirky, I thought). Only a month ago did he finally admit to being in jail for two years for narcotics possession. He swore he had only been holding something for a friend, and I'd bet that in another month he'll feel free enough to admit that he was either selling it himself or buying it for his own consumption. Nashville would be a good breakup point for at least one of us, and that one of us was me.

"I'd hoped you'd stick by me, Luke, since I'm obviously in the right on this one."

He stared out the window with a small smile on his face.

"So what happened in there?"

His smile grew. "I'll tell you exactly what happened. You and me are on the road to making some serious money."

"How?"

"Don't worry about that. Let's get to your place."

"Why?"

"I'll tell you then."

"No. You will tell me now. What happened in Kap's house?"

Luke pulled up his T-shirt and reached into the waistband of his jeans. He took out a plastic bag about the size of a can of soda, filled with what looked like crushed glass.

"This is what happened in there," he said with what sounded like real pride. He gawked at me as if I should be deeply impressed.

"What is it?"

"Crank. Half pound. Pure. Know how much this costs?"

"I don't want to know! What the hell is that doing in my car?"

"This ain't a car. It's a pickup. And it ain't yours."

If I'd been closer to town, I would have gotten out right there on the side of the road. But we were a few miles away from Locksburg, with woods all around and nowhere to pull off.

"So shut up and listen, Liz. This shit costs eight grand. Guess how much I got it for?"

I wasn't going to answer. I was enraged. Still, Luke oozed pride.

"Three grand! Three fuckin' grand. And I can split this up into eight ounces. And I know eight guys who will buy it tonight. Hear that, Liz? I can get a thousand an ounce for this uncut, easy. So that means I take home five grand, clear."

I didn't care.

"So," he said, now talking down to me, singsongy, as if I were a child, "I'll split this up, sell it for cash tonight, and that means I'll be holding it for less than three hours. It's risk-free."

"And if—"

"And then," Luke cut me off, "we pay the money you owe Kap, and that will leave us with, like, a whole lot of cash. Enough to get me out of Locksburg."

"Where did you get the three thousand for it?"

"Kap fronted me the money. He knows I'm good for it."

"Oh, Christ. Now you're deeper in debt with a madman."

"You're in debt with him too."

For yet another time that day, everything stopped.

"Wait. What does that mean? What do you mean, I'm in debt?"

"I mean, you know, with your car," he said, but something in the way he said it made me gather that I was mentioned as a partner in this drug deal.

"Luke. I'm going to speak very clearly here, because you need to understand: When we arrive at my house, I'm getting out. Then you are going to drive off with your drugs. And you are never going to call me or talk to me again."

"Suit yourself," he said. "You're gonna be in debt forever, Liz. While I move out of this shithole place. Good riddance."

There was no talking sense with this guy, so I wouldn't waste any more words.

We were on Harvest Road, a few miles outside of town, when, about two hundred yards directly ahead, a state police cruiser came into view, traveling toward us. My hands froze on the steering wheel. My back straightened. I could sense that Luke was holding his breath. I was too.

The police cruiser passed us.

I let out the air in my lungs.

So did Luke.

I glanced into the rearview mirror. There was a long stretch of open road behind us, so I could see nearly a mile behind. When the cruiser was almost gone from view, I saw it make a wide U-turn out of its lane and into ours.

Luke was gazing into the side-view mirror. He had also seen the cruiser turn around.

"Fuck," he breathed.

"Luke. Whose pickup truck is this?" I asked.

"Too late to worry about that now."

"Is this thing stolen?"

"Not exactly."

The police cruiser was speeding up.

"That was a yes-or-no-type question."

"It's sort of complicated," Luke said.

And there, in that likely stolen pickup that I was driving, next to an ex-con who was holding enough methamphetamine to lock us both in prison for fifteen years, I hoped a silent hope that maybe it was only a coincidence that the cop had turned around.

Then I peered in the rearview mirror in time to see the red and blue lights on the top of the state police car begin flashing.

CARLA

WE WERE WAITING for twilight.

Billy and I spent the early part of the evening talking through the plan and getting together the equipment we would need. About an hour before sunset, Billy went upstairs to try to relax for a short while. I took to pacing the kitchen and the living room, which helped to calm me some. But questions followed me: If we got through this, would I go on living in my house? Would I remain in Locksburg? I couldn't say. Maybe I could get the restaurant up and running, then sell it and the house and move to Philadelphia. Great, I thought, the restaurant wasn't half built and already I was selling it. Even more absurd was the idea of moving to the city.

To those who live in Locksburg and nearby towns, Philadelphia is something like what Paris must seem to those who live in quiet French hamlets or Rome to those settled in tiny Italian villages. The big city is far enough away—a three- to four-hour drive—to feel downright mythic. Yet it's close enough that anyone with a car can get there and back in a day. Everyone in Locksburg has a story that begins: "This one time we went to Philly and . . ." The motor-heads talk about the great parts stores and junkyards there, while the burners fantasize about the pot they can buy from a dealer—always a friend of another friend—who has choice buds that they can bring back, split up, and quadruple their money. My nearest neighbors down the road, the Boyds, still talk about the Saturday night, fifteen years ago, when they went to the city and misread a restaurant menu. Only when the check arrived did they find that the ten-dollar bottle of wine they thought they had been drinking was actually priced at a hundred dollars. "I didn't have my reading glasses!" Ted Boyd says, and Jenny Boyd chimes in: "I wish I knew it was a hundred dollars so I could have savored it!" Over the years they've gotten far more than ninety bucks' worth of conversation from that mistake.

At one time or another, most everyone in Locksburg has threatened to move to Philadelphia. What they don't say is that their threats are usually as empty as air. They're wary of the Blacks and the Hispanics, and enraged at the high prices and the small houses and the crazy drivers and the lack of forests, which few here even venture into anyway, though the woods start less than a mile outside of town. But what they really fear is trying something new. I should know. It would take all my fingers and toes to count the times I've said I'm moving there—and all the hairs on my head to tally the excuses I later made not to go. Some of those excuses were good and real and true. Without a father, Billy needed some semblance of steadiness. And when Billy excelled in his classes, I wasn't going to do anything to jeopardize that by plunking him in a new city and a strange school district. But other excuses weren't worth the exhale that came out when I made them.

And now I wonder what would have happened if I'd have taken Billy away from here. Maybe all those years of playing it safe and staying in place had led to this danger. Maybe this was all my fault.

* * *

73

I watched the shadows in the room grow. Billy and I would need the cover of night, but we didn't want to ride too late: Around a town this small, any car out past midnight was under immediate suspicion of drunk driving or drug running. There were nights that whatever cop was on duty pulled over almost anyone on the road, tailing them for miles to find an excuse to stop the car.

I went to Billy's room. He was in bed, staring at the ceiling.

We moved to this house six months after Eric left, and Billy loved the place as much as I did. The shed was filled with bicycle frames and tires and pedals that he had scavenged and salvaged, then rebuilt into full bikes that he sold to other kids. There were computer monitors and printers and hard drives in the basement from the time he built his own PCs. As for his bedroom, he refused to take anything from the walls once he had put it up, so his room was an artful disaster, a collage of posters taped over postcards tacked on top of comic book pages that were glued on newspaper articles and magazine pictures. He'd said that one day he'd take it all down and relive each year of his past, layer by layer.

"Let's get moving," I said.

"Where are we going to take her?"

"I'll show you when we get there."

"Are you sure it'll be duh-deserted?"

"I'm not sure of anything. I'm only betting it will be."

"If we get caught . . ."

"We won't be—"

"Mom, if we do, tell them everything I told you. I'll tell them the t-truth. That way you won't get in trouble."

"I think it's too late for that, hon. I'm already involved. Anyway, we're not going to get caught. We're going to do this exactly

74

as planned. If we go now, we can be back here in an hour and a half. Maybe less."

"I'm sorry about all this. I should have—"

"Shhh. None of that. Take a shower. Scrub off any fibers or whatever. Then get changed. You found old clothes to wear? Nothing that can be IDed, just in case?"

He nodded and went into the bathroom. While he was in there, I laid out throwaway jeans and a dark pullover sweatshirt on my bed and waited for him to shower with the hope there would be hot water left to scald out the tightness that had crept into my shoulders. When he finished, there was enough to steam the room and tempt me to relax, though my stress returned once I stepped out and thought again about the job ahead. After drying off, I dressed, then donned a hairnet and a black baseball cap.

When I started down the steps, Billy came from his room, dressed much the same, hairnet and cap included. We both checked our cell phones for a final time before placing them on the dining room table and leaving them behind so as not to record our travels. I shoved a small container of Vicks VapoRub into my pocket. Then from under the sink I got the old shower curtain I'd saved a few months earlier for when I'd next need a drop cloth.

Billy bought his car, a Honda Accord, when he turned sixteen. He'd spent a week researching used cars and made a spreadsheet with all pertinent information: reliability, costs of ownership, resale value. Then he scanned sales within a thirty-mile radius and found an Accord for sale in Beaver Springs, underpriced compared to blue book value. He paid cash after talking the owner down an extra two hundred dollars without stuttering. That's my boy. He left nothing to chance. Now neither would I.

We outlined the interior of the trunk with the shower curtain, duct-taping it into place. Then Billy drove the car into the yard and parked it parallel to the house to block our digging from anyone who might look our way. The old koi pond was about thirty yards from the back door, and the yard was mostly shielded by the house. But anyone riding down Route 140 could see behind the house for a moment or two while passing. I'd never brought a car into the yard and it now appeared strange there. This was central Pennsylvania, however, where so many backyards had been turned into ad hoc scrap heaps. No one would notice or care.

I brought over two shovels and a flashlight with fresh batteries for when it became fully dark. We had enough light now, though, to work without it.

"This is the spot. Right?"

Billy may have nodded.

"This is the spot, right?" I repeated.

"Yes."

"How deep?"

"Three or f-four feet."

We began shoveling up the layer of grass and tossing it aside. When we reached soil, we piled that to the other side to put back first, then replant the grass.

We'd gone a foot deep, then two, sometimes moving next to each other, sometimes moving far apart. Soon we'd strike something, and we both became watchful. Billy must have had the same repugnant thought: We didn't want to impale Doreen's body with the shovels.

During the dig, I fantasized that Billy would stop and say: "Got ya! Did you really believe I'd bury a body, Mom?" and break out into a laugh. I swore to myself that if that happened, I wouldn't get angry. The relief would be too immense. No, I'd hug him and say: "I knew all along you were joking! I knew you wouldn't do something like that! Not my Billy!"

But the only sounds were the scraping of the shovels and the grunts we made while lifting dirt.

A car drove down Route 140. We stopped digging and watched it pass, first from the north, then a pause as it passed in front of the house, then for an instant to the south, then out of sight. We returned to digging. A short time later, a police or fire siren went off, somewhere miles off. I almost whimpered. We listened for a full minute. Then, more to myself than to Billy, I said: "It's not coming here. The sound is moving away."

Sweat dripped from my forehead.

I planted the shovel into the hole again. Before I could put my foot on the blade, I felt something underneath. Heard it too: a slight crack. Plastic maybe. I put my shovel aside.

Out on Route 140, another car raced past the house, stereo blaring. Billy, jumpy, turned to look at it.

At the same time, I tugged off my gloves and knelt to reach into the hole to find what I'd hit.

Billy hadn't seen me.

As my bare fingers felt over the ground, Billy turned from watching the road.

And in one swift, unthinking motion, he thrust the rusty point of his shovel down into my hand.

REED

AFTER TALKING to Mrs. Lombard, I walked north, then west for seventeen minutes until I got to Keiser's Hardware Emporium. I have always liked the place because there is so much stuff that you feel like you could get lost inside even though you cannot get lost inside. The store is small and there are products on every wall and many things like rakes and tools hanging from the ceiling. Even better was Mr. Keiser, who had an all-business expression for everyone but would immediately smile when Mom and I walked in. Then he would joke with me and talk to Mom for so long that sometimes he would forget he had other customers and they would complain out loud.

"I think he used to like me," Mom told me once. "Back when I was a heartbreaker."

"I think he still likes you," I said.

"That's sweet," she said. "Maybe the old girl's still got it after all."

"What is 'it'?" I asked.

"Never you mind," she replied.

I went into the store. Mr. Keiser was behind the counter. When he heard the door open, he turned to say hi. Then he saw that it was me and stopped.

"Hello, Mr. Keiser," I said. "How are you?"

He mumbled something that sounded like "All right," then called out: "Ray. There's a customer for you to take care of. I got some things to do." Then he walked away.

Ray, who works at the store, came down an aisle and said: "Hey, man, what can I get ya?"

"Mr. Keiser did not want to talk."

Ray whispered, "Yeah, he's been acting sorta squirrely lately."

I watched Mr. Keiser go into his office. He glanced back at me, then down at the floor, and closed the door. The expression he had was the same as the ones I had seen at the funeral when some people would look at me, then look away real fast to make it seem as if they were not really looking.

"So whaddaya need?" Ray said.

"I want to buy a cordless hand drill. One that also has a reverse feature for taking screws out as well as putting them in."

"Gotcha," he said. He took me to aisle four. "This here's a good one."

He pointed up to the top shelf but he could not reach it, so I took it down, since I was taller. Some kids at school used to call me gawky, a word I do not like, but now being tall was beneficial, which is a better word.

I said: "I will need an extra battery pack for it."

"Right there, brother," he said, and pointed to the next shelf. I took those and a set of drill bits too.

"Ever use a drill before?"

"Yes. I have one at my house."

"Did it break?"

"No."

"Then why are you buying another?"

"The one I have at home has to be plugged in to work. I need a cordless drill for where I am going."

"Where are you going?"

"I would rather not tell you."

"Why not?"

"I would rather not tell you that either."

"Damn, man, that's sorta harsh."

I told him, "I would like to speak with the other man."

"What other man? Keiser?"

"No. You are an Ace cooperative, and the commercials say that Ace is the place with the helpful hardware man. So I would like to speak with the helpful hardware man. Is there a hotline?"

"Aw, that's just a saying. There ain't no one else here but me."

"So it is false advertising. Which is illegal."

"I'm trying to be helpful. I want to know what you're doing so I can recommend the right tools."

"It is private."

"I won't tell anyone. Heck, I think, legally, I ain't allowed to tell anyone. It's exactly like doctor-patient confidentiality except I'm a hardware store worker and you're not sick."

I considered that for a moment. Then I said: "I am going to the cemetery. I will use the drill to remove the plate from the front of the spot in the family mausoleum where my mother's casket was placed. Then I am going to slide the casket out. Then I am going to open the casket and put Miss Molly the Dolly in with Mom, because that is what I promised her I would do. Then I am going to close the casket and slide it back in and screw the plate on and go home before my brother Greg knows that I am gone."

Ray stared at me, blinked a few times, then said: "All right. Suit yourself. If you don't want to tell me, you don't have to tell me. But you don't have to hit me with some bullshit story. Sorry I asked."

If you tell people the truth, most times they will talk over you or not believe you anyway. And if you do not want to tell them the truth, that is easy. Like when Greg said not to leave the house and asked, "Do you understand?" I did understand. That was the question he asked. Just like when he says something and ends it with "Do you hear me?" Of course I hear him. So I nod no matter what else he said, and he takes that as agreement. Some people might call that a lie of omission. I call it a failure to listen properly or to speak accurately. The truth does not depend only on the teller. It depends on the listener too.

I bought the drill and the battery pack and the bits and a flashlight with a credit card that Mom gave me for emergencies. I unwrapped them from the packaging and put them all in my backpack. When I was about to leave, Mr. Keiser peeked out, saw me, then turned away. I went over and knocked on the office door and he said nothing so I knocked again and said: "May I come into your office, Mr. Keiser?"

"I'm, ah, sort of busy, Reed."

"Is that the truth, Mr. Keiser?"

"What do you want?" he said, which is a good example of not answering the question because you probably did not tell the truth.

"I would like to talk to you."

There was no sound for a few seconds until he said: "I only got a minute."

The office was packed with stuff just like the store. There was one desk and on it were a lot of papers and a computer, and on the wall was a calendar and rows of framed pictures, many of them of the Locksburg Bulldogs baseball team, who wore shirts with the store name on the back because Mr. Keiser sponsored them. I played for the Locksburg Bulldogs but did not want to see the pictures because that is not a good memory.

"You did not want to talk to me," I said.

"I'm busy, Reed."

"You did not come to Mom's funeral."

"No. I was . . . busy."

"You are busy a lot."

"I got a business to run. So if—"

"I do not think that you are telling me the truth."

There was some silence before he spoke again.

"What do you want, Reed?"

Mr. Keiser is short and skinny and always wears trousers and a button-down shirt and dress shoes, even though most everyone in town wears jeans and boots. But he is strong enough to lift heavy things into trucks with the contractors and he is what they call no-nonsense and he never seems to smile except for the times when he would see Mom and that is the only time I could tell that he had teeth. They are very clean and white and straight. He must floss.

"Did you love my mom, Mr. Keiser?" I asked.

"I don't think that's something you and I should talk about, Reed. Now, why don't you get home."

"I do not mind. I like it that people loved her."

"A lot of people loved her. She was a good woman. She was nice to everybody, wasn't she?"

"No."

"Really?"

"She did not like Dan Malloy, who used to pick on me."

"Well, no one likes Dan Malloy. He's a jackass, even on a good day."

"And she did not like that priest at St. Stanislaw."

"Ditto on him too."

"There were a couple others."

"Well, ya got me there, Reed."

"She liked you, though."

"I'm a proud man to hear that."

I could tell that Mr. Keiser wanted to say something. He was the kind of person who did not talk a lot to just anyone. I once heard him say to Ray that Ray was paid to work and not to shoot the shit, and I laughed at that one for days. Shoot the shit. That is funny. Just picture it.

"Mom said you two met in high school," I said. "What grade were you in when you moved to Locksburg?"

"Tenth. That's real hard on a kid. You know?"

I did not say anything. I knew that high school could be hard on anyone, so he was telling the truth.

"When I got here, I didn't dare talk to your mom because she was so pretty and your dad was so big. I was intimidated by them. Hell, I was intimidated by everybody. At the time, I didn't think that anyone was ever glad that I moved to town."

"I do not believe that is true."

"I did, back then. But on my second week I was walking down the hallway. Your mom and your dad were talking at her locker and she called out to me: 'What's the matter, new guy, are you too good for us yokels?' and she cackled . . ."

"I loved when she cackled."

"I did too! Then she said: 'Get over here and tell us about you!' And the next thing I knew, I had two new friends. And when you had them as friends, you had everyone as friends. Anyway, that made things easier for me. You have no idea how good that felt."

I did not say anything. I wanted him to keep talking.

"So that's it," Mr. Keiser said, though it seemed like that was not it and like he was stopping himself from saying more. "We were good friends. That's all."

We both stood silent. Then he said: "Did she say something about me?"

Once a year Locksburg has the Locksfest Fair and people set up tables and sell things and sometimes Mom would want to buy something but would walk away from it until the seller would call out: "Hey, wait! Come back here!" and she would walk back and get it for a lower price. She called that a calculated risk and I thought I would try the same on Mr. Keiser, so I moved toward the office door.

"Where the hell are you goin', Reed?"

"You said you were busy."

"I ain't that busy! What did she say about me? Sit down here!"

He moved a stack of papers off a chair in front of his desk and I sat there and he sat on his chair behind the desk.

I said: "What else can you tell me about Mom?"

"I thought you were going to tell *me* something."

"I like to hear about her. Can you tell me what else happened in high school?"

He stayed quiet for a moment. Then he said, "Shut that door," and I realized that I had won the calculated risk. I closed his office door.

84

"If you're thinking we were . . . you know . . . close or something. Me and your mom were never . . ."

"Boyfriend and girlfriend."

"Right! We were never that way. So you get that out of your head right now."

"It is not in my head."

"Well then, good. She was always faithful to your daddy. That's the truth. Those two were always so kind to me. All through school. And then . . ." He stopped, and though most people like to tell me things, I could tell that Mr. Keiser was debating whether to go on. So I took another calculated risk and leaned forward as if I wanted to hear what he had to say. And that seemed to cause him to start to say it. His voice went quieter.

"I signed up for the Navy, two weeks before high school graduation. Figured I'd see the world. And what did the Navy do? Assigned me to Norfolk to clean toilets and mop hallways and . . . ah, to hell with the Navy. But when your mom and dad heard about it, they said they were going to throw me a party. And you have to understand, even though I'd been living in Locksburg a little while, I still felt like an outsider. So every time they did something nice for me, it would make me feel real fine. I said, 'Aw, you don't need to do that,' but they said, 'Yeah we do, sailor!' Reed, do you know where Carson's Outcrop is? That bunch of rocks, up in the hills?"

I nodded.

"Kids still drink up there?"

"I heard they do, yes."

"It was the same in my time. Go up there and drink, make a bonfire. Of course, every so often someone drinks too much and flips their car on the way down the mountain, the imbeciles. Anyway, everyone was going to meet there and have a farewell party for me. I told your mom and dad that I'd drive them there. But on Friday night your dad was needed at the chemical plant for something. I picked up your mom and your dad said he would drive himself up later. So she and I started to drive to the Outcrop."

Mr. Keiser glanced at the door again and then up at the wall, and I could tell that he was no longer talking to me. He now seemed like he was mostly talking to himself.

"It was a Friday night and dark. We were about halfway there when the car sputters and . . . oh, that was a '77 Camaro, shittiest car Detroit ever let on the road. Carburetor had been rebuilt and . . . hell, they don't even make cars with carburetors anymore! But this one was total junk and within a minute the damn car is dead. I pull it over and we decide it might be better to try to walk back to town rather than walk in the dark to the Outcrop. So we start to walk and hope someone will come and pick us up. And . . ."

He looked at the door again, then at me. "I don't know what to tell you, Reed, other than . . . wait. Maybe this is the way to put it: Did you ever have a horrible situation, and you look back on it, and then you think, 'That was actually a fantastic situation'? That's what it was. I was angry that my car was busted and that we were going to have to walk four or five miles but your mom said, 'Oh, this could be fun! C'mon!'

"I've never been a big talker. And I'm not proud of that. What the hell have I been so scared about all these years? Worrying that people might think I was less of a man if I said what I feel? Thinking that only women talked about their emotions? Who the hell cares, Reed? Jesus Christ, who cares? And back then I was worse. I was a runt. Didn't want anyone to know that I was scared of everything. Scared of this town. Scared about going into the Navy. Scared of my own parents, who fought so much and so loud that I couldn't sleep half the night. But there I was with your mom. We got to talking and she asked me about how I felt and what I thought about things. And she wasn't one of those people who'd say, 'Oh, you'll be fine!' No. She really listened. And the next thing I know, I was telling her everything I hid inside me all those years.

"There we were. Walking on this dark road. And talking. And she told me things too and made me see that I wasn't alone in the world. You got no idea how it felt to know I wasn't alone after all. It was like . . . I discovered something. Something big and huge, and the relief was . . . it felt like . . . God.

"And pretty soon, inside my head, I'm praying that a car doesn't come along! Because she and I . . . well, I can say with total honesty: That was the best conversation I ever had in my life. And I shouldn't say this but . . . god damn it, there I go again, stopping myself because I feel embarrassed. But I'll say it: That may have been the best night of my life. Three hours in the dark, walking and talking with your mom. She made me feel good. When before, I wasn't feelin' so good. I was frightened and lonely all my life. And then, for the first time, I wasn't frightened or lonely anymore.

"Anyway, when we were out on Harvest Road, there's that stretch where you can see far ahead, and we could see a car coming a mile away, and your momma moved in front of me and hugged me. We didn't need no more words.

"It was someone from school, who gave us a ride. So we went to the party and I acted all happy and got drunk. And in the firelight I'd sometimes glance over and see your momma and . . . even if the

Navy sent me to some tropic island or to Europe or anywhere, nothing would be as beautiful as seeing that eighteen-year-old young woman in the firelight, sometimes looking over at me and smiling."

It was quiet for a long time. Mr. Keiser sniffed. Then he said, "So you got me talking, Reed. You're good at that, huh?"

I did not say anything.

He exhaled and said, "Well, I went off to the Navy. Got back, your momma and daddy were married. And I met Connie and got married and that was that, until two years ago, when Connie died. Every time your momma came in here, I'd start talking to her but saying nothing. I really wanted to say: 'We're both on our own now. Maybe . . . we could . . . you know?' I damn near rehearsed a speech. But, like the fool I am, I never could say it. Figured there would be plenty of time anyway. So I kept putting it off. And now . . . there ain't no more time."

Mr. Keiser stared at his feet. Then he said, "I'd like to be alone now, Reed. You were right. I ain't got no work to do. I want to be by myself, OK?"

I nodded and got up to go.

"I didn't come to the funeral, Reed. I apologize for that. I really do. But I would have fallen apart. Hell, there's no more lying in me: I did fall apart. I was in the car going to the funeral and I started to cry so much. I pulled over so I wouldn't hurt anyone. Later on I drove up into the hills. Parked my car where my old Camaro broke down. Got out and walked a little. And talked to your mom in my head. I figured that might be better."

"I figure it was too."

"Good."

"You are mad at me because of what happened to Mom. That is why you walked away from me earlier."

He did not say anything.

"It is OK. I know a lot of people hate me."

"I don't hate you, Reed. It's just . . . I'm so sad she's gone."

I put on my backpack and got ready to go. Then I said, "One time when we walked out of your store, Mom was smiling because you talked to her. And she kept smiling as we walked down Rand Avenue. And I said, 'Are you smiling because of Mr. Keiser?' And she said yes. Then she said: 'I'm so glad he moved to town.'"

I left Mr. Keiser's office and closed the door behind me.

LIZ

THE STATE POLICE CAR hit its siren and even from a mile away the sound jolted me in my seat. Luke began scrambling. Within the space of a few seconds, he had tried to push the meth deeper into his underwear, then took it out, then attempted to hide it under the seat, then panicked so much that he froze with the bag in his hand.

What I wanted to scream at him was this: *Luke, what did you do, getting me involved with those illegal narcotics and a motor vehicle that is most likely stolen? A mere two hours ago I was on the cusp of a dream, and now here I am on the threshold of a long prison sentence, for something that is clearly not my fault, and, oh, this seems to be the story of my wretched life!*

Instead I yelled: "You motherfucking *idiot!*"

The cop closed the distance to three-quarters of a mile. I was doing forty-five, the speed limit, and didn't increase it.

"Hit the gas!" Luke yelled.

"Open your window!" I yelled back.

"He'll see us if we throw it!"

Funny how this became an *us* thing, though I guess technically it was. Funny too how my voice went low and slow, in deep and utter seriousness. So low that Luke paid attention immediately when I said:

"Luke. Open your window. Now."

He rolled it down.

I glanced in the rearview. Then ahead.

Raker Road was a hundred yards away. I put on my turn signal.

"You'll never outrun him there!" Luke yelled. "Stay on this road and speed up!" He reached for the steering wheel. I punched his hand. He cried "Ow!" and pulled it back as if he were hurt and offended, instead of minutes away from having a set of steel cuffs snapped on his wrists.

"Quiet down," I said. I was doing the speed limit, driving as if I hadn't seen the cop and as if I were merely on a sightseeing tour of this wooded wonderland. I slowed just before Raker Road.

"He'll follow us! He's already seen us!" Luke said.

"Did I tell you to shut up? Now. Shut. The. Hell. Up." Not quite as profound as I wanted to be, but it got the job done. Luke punched the dashboard and went quiet.

Then I slowly took the ninety-degree turn onto Raker Road. When the cop was out of sight for a few moments, I hit the gas to kick up dust on the gravel road. The tires spun. A giant dirt cloud rose behind the pickup. Then I decelerated.

"We've got five seconds. Get ready to throw that meth over the bridge."

We probably had ten seconds but I was taking no chances. We were fifty yards from the rusted bridge that crossed Raker Creek. After that, the one-lane road went on down to the Susquehanna River.

I drove onto the bridge. Looked in the rearview. The cop hadn't yet made the turn.

"Throw it!" I yelled.

Luke sat paralyzed with fear—of the cop, of the meth, of the money he'd owe Kap, I don't know. He didn't move.

I reached into his lap, snatched the bag of meth, and flung it sidearm out of the window. The bag hit one of the steel girders and ripped open. Meth flew everywhere, then rained into the water below. Whatever fish were there would be speeding up and down Raker Creek for days.

In the rearview, the dirt cloud behind us was billowing. After three seconds, I saw the flashing lights of the state cop car. He'd just made the turn. There was no way he could have seen what I'd thrown.

I drove across the bridge and, at the next clearing, slowed and parked to the side.

The cop pulled behind us. From the speaker atop the car, he barked: "Shut off your vehicle and put your hands on the dashboard!"

The words got Luke moving. He did as he was told. So did I.

"Stay inside your vehicle," the cop said through the speaker. "Don't move."

Luke and I sat in the pickup, hands on the dashboard, as we waited—no doubt for the cop's backup to arrive: There was no way he'd get out to check on a suspicious vehicle on an empty road through the forest.

"Luke," I mumbled, "is there anything else in this car?"

"This ain't a car. It's a pickup," he said.

"Answer me."

"Not that I know of."

"You stole this pickup?"

"We're gonna be OK. You let me do the talking."

I let out a genuine if bitter laugh. "Yeah, then we'll be in jail in an hour. You shut that hole under your nose. I know what to do here."

A minute later, another state police car came from the opposite direction with its lights flashing. It pulled up to our bumper, boxing the pickup in. Then the cop behind us opened his car door and moved slowly to our driver's-side door. The cop's hand gripped his holstered gun. The other cop got out of his car and stood in front of us to the side, keeping an eye on Luke. That cop was jittery and seemed almost eager to pull his pistol.

"Step out of the car, ma'am," the first cop said.

"Is that you, Jeezy?" I said. The dirt cloud was settling, and some was getting in my eyes. There was no way, though, that I was going to move a hand to wipe them.

"Yeah. Hey, Liz. Keep your hands where I can see 'em, OK?"

"Of course."

"Sorry about this but—"

"What the hell is this all about?" I said, trying to sound indignant to the point of innocence. I got out of the truck and kept my hands in front of me.

"This vehicle was reported stolen," Jeezy said. He had been a bouncer at a couple local bars, and I'd seen him often when I performed until two years back, when the state police finally called his number from the waitlist and sent him off to the academy.

"You can't be serious!" I said, and made an exaggerated gawk at Luke. "This is Luke's truck! Isn't it, Luke?"

Despite our past, Jeezy was all business, and I respected him for it.

"Liz, can you do me a favor? Go to the front of the truck, put your hands on the hood, and let the officer check you. Are you carrying any weapons?"

"No, I'm not," I said. "He can check me."

I went around and got a quick pat down; there was nowhere in my jeans and T-shirt to hide much. Jeezy wasn't as friendly to Luke.

"You again, huh?" Jeezy said.

"What do you mean, 'again'?" Luke asked.

"I busted you last year for drunk and disorderly outside Orky's."

Jeezy kicked Luke's legs wide, found that he had no weapons, then stepped back.

"Jeezy," I said. "I don't know what's going on here."

"Why did you turn onto this road, Liz?"

"We were heading down to the river to take a walk, maybe hit Mack's for a burger." I flashed him the cheeriest smile I had in my arsenal. "I saw your lights on. I thought you were chasing someone else! Heck, I was doing the speed limit, wasn't I?"

"Why are you in this truck?"

"Luke picked me up, said he borrowed it. What's the story?"

Jeezy said: "We got a report that this truck was stolen from Harry's body shop."

"That ain't true!" Luke said in a way that meant he was only partly lying. "Call Harry! He'll tell you!"

"Then why did he report it stolen?" Jeezy said.

"Maybe he forgot. He said I could borrow it! I work for him."

"So he said you could take it?" the other cop said.

"I just told you that, didn't I?" Luke said, in a really good attempt at getting a pissed-off cop to take a club upside his head. You almost had to admire his ability to screw things up so consistently.

"Jeezy, maybe you could call this guy—" I began, then Luke cut in.

"Yeah! Call Harry! Do it now, because—"

"Luke?" I said between gritted teeth. "Please. Give me a second here."

I turned back to Jeezy. "Maybe there was a misunderstanding. Luke works for Harry, and Luke here, he's not, shall we say, a world-class communicator. Something might have gotten lost in the translation."

Jeezy took the mic from his shoulder and hit a button.

"Carol? Come in."

After a moment, a staticky "Carol here."

"Patch me through to Harry Conroy, who called in to report the stolen pickup."

"10-4."

As we waited, Jeezy said, "How's the singing, Liz?"

"Good," I said. "Thanks for asking. How you been?"

"Ah, you know. Bought a new house in Lemrock."

"You did? Congratulations! I love that area. Over by the lake?"

"Yeah. It's real nice."

Luke, ever ready to misread a situation and raise the anger level, said, "How long's this gonna take?"

Jeezy eyed me, lowered his voice. "This guy for real?"

I shrugged. Jeezy said, "He your boyfriend?"

"Yeah!" Luke called out. My eyes nearly crossed.

I said: "I needed a ride. My car caught on fire and—"

"Jeezy? Come in," the radio squawked.

"I hear ya, Carol."

"I got Harry. I'll patch him in."

95

"Hello?" a voice came through.

"Harry? We got your truck here."

"Damn, that was quick. Is it in one piece?"

"It is. Guy here says that you lent it to him."

"I ain't lent that truck to nobody. What guy?"

"Guy by the name of Luke Dunn. You're on speaker, so he can hear you."

Luke yelled: "Tell 'em you lent it to me, Harry! You did, remember?"

"Lent it to you? What?"

"You said I could use your truck!"

"That was last friggin' week. I let you borrow it once, for an hour! That wasn't no free ticket to take it anytime you want! How'd you get so stupid?"

Luke didn't have an answer for that. He seemed to think about it, though.

Jeezy said, "So, Harry? What do you want to do? Is it stolen?"

"Can he still hear me? Luke, can you hear me?"

"Yeah."

"You bring that truck back here right now."

"I will! I will!"

"After that, you're fired, you jackass. I never want to see you again."

I could have said the same.

The other cop searched under the seat of the pickup, then the glove compartment and elsewhere. When he found nothing of interest, he nodded to Jeezy, who said we could go. While Luke was getting back in the truck, Jeezy said to me quietly, "Never known you to hang out with guys like that, Liz."

"I know. It's . . ." There was no good explanation so I ended it with "It's a bit of a mess. Thanks, though, Jeezy. Good luck with the new house."

Luke and I drove off. He began to peer over the side of the bridge as we crossed it. "Stare straight ahead, Luke," I commanded. Those were the only words that came from my mouth. Ten minutes later I got out at my house and slammed the truck door behind me. Luke drove away.

I went inside and sat on the sofa, nearly breathless with the idea that I had been moments away from spending fifteen years in a jail cell. I gulped the remaining two cans of Keystone Light in the refrigerator in record time.

An hour later I was still on the sofa when a knock sounded at my front door. I opened it. Luke tried to maneuver his way inside. I stood in the threshold and didn't move.

"Can I come in?" he said.

"No, Luke. Go home."

"Just for a minute? I gotta take a piss. I walked all the way from Harry's place."

"No. And if I have to say it again, I'll call the cops. They won't be too happy to hear your name again."

"You know who else isn't going to be too happy? Kap. He's not going to be too happy at all. We have to figure some things out, Liz. Fast."

"There is no *we* anymore, Luke."

"That's not what *he* thinks. How much do you owe him for the car?"

"He owes me!"

"Now you're the one who needs to listen: When I was doing time in Carroll Valley prison? Some guy owed Kap a cigarette. The guy said Kap gave him the smoke. Kap said he sold it to him. Kap's part of this gang, so he wasn't about to be challenged. Know what happened? Kap shanked the guy in the eye. You hear me? Stabbed him in the eye socket with a sharpened piece of metal. For a single cigarette. Kap said the guy had given his word, so it was a matter of principle. Now that he's outside, he's a top member of a biker group. He's their mechanic, and, believe me, even those guys are scared of him. They'll do anything he says."

"Then why did you get me mixed up with this maniac?"

"You wanted your car fixed cheap! You said you didn't care who did it as long as it got done!"

"I never, ever want to talk to you again."

"You don't want to see me anymore, Liz? Fine. Seriously. I'm fine with that. But Kap will come after us. You and me both. That's guaranteed."

"I'm leaving town, then."

"With what? Gonna steal a car? Or drive that?" He pointed to the burnt shell of my Chevy in front of the house.

Well, he had me there.

Luke went on, "Because if you do steal a car, do yourself a favor: Sell it and use the money to pay off Kap. He's got no qualms about hunting us down. Or about finding your dad and taking it out on him if you leave Locksburg."

The fear in Luke's eyes was palpable.

Luke said: "You owe him what? Five hundred something?"

"Five hundred and sixty, he says."

"And now . . . we're in deep for three grand more because of the meth that you threw out of the window."

"What did you want me to do? We'd be in jail right now if—"

"Listen, Liz. You're really smart about a lot of things. But you need to understand this: We owe Kap $3,560. And we need to get him that money or we're royally fucked. He doesn't care about excuses or explanations. He only wants what he wants."

I needed more money than that. A decent tenor guitar would set me back at least five hundred dollars. And how much more? Maybe another thousand to travel to Nashville and stay at the cheapest hotel? And how about a car? When I added it up, the total felt overwhelming.

"You got anything at all you can sell?" Luke said. "Seriously, anything?"

I shook my head.

"Do you?" I asked.

He shook his.

"So what's all this mean?"

"This means, if we don't find a way to pay Kap back, we're gettin' bullets shot into our heads."

CARLA

WHEN I REALIZED that Billy was thrusting the shovel down, I pulled away as fast as possible, probably saving my hand from being severed at the wrist. Instead the blade tore through two of my fingers.

A bone snapped. I inhaled so deeply that no cry could come out. Billy gasped, though, and jerked the shovel back, far too late. He threw it aside and knelt next to me. I could hear only some of his apologies. I was groaning in agony while pressing my lips together to try to keep quiet. The sound came out as a low moan from the center of my throat.

"I duh-didn't see you!" Bill said. "I was watching the road and automatically . . . !"

I rocked back and forth, holding my hand. Blood streamed down my arm and wet my sweatshirt.

Billy helped me to my feet and hurried me to the house. He turned on the faucet. I put my hand underneath. The water ran clear before it met my fingers, then circled the drain a rich red. I've worked in kitchens all my adult life and have seen countless cuts, most of them caused by cooking knives that sliced cleanly. This was a jagged mess. I moved my hand out of the stream to get a better view.

Half of my pinky finger was almost detached. About an inch of it drooped over to the side, hanging on by a thin flap of skin. A piece of bone poked white through the bloody flesh. The finger-nail was shaved off too. The finger next to it would need plenty of stitches but would fare better. Though the meaty part was gashed open down to the webbing, at least the bone was intact.

"Go upstairs," I told Billy through clenched teeth. "Get the gauze and medical tape that's under the sink. Alcohol too." He hurried. I called after him: "And painkillers!"

I let the water run over my fingers until he returned.

"Why was your hand there?" he asked. "I was duh-digging, then looked away for one second, out at the road, and—"

"I thought you had stopped. I saw something in the hole. Doesn't matter. Give me that dish towel."

I wrapped my hand. Blood soaked the cloth.

"You need to get to the huh-hospital."

"Later. Now listen. Tape the gauze around my fingers, then bind them together tight. Try to . . . put the one finger back into place."

Billy was all action. He stripped five long sections of tape from the roll and hung them over the edge of the counter, then prepared the gauze. I clamped my jaw shut and poured rubbing alcohol over my fingers. Then I presented my hand to Billy and tried not to shriek when he moved my pinky. I felt him piece it together, fitting the top back on the stump before he wrapped it.

He taped the fingers separately, then bound them to each other. When I pulled my hand back to examine his work, my entire arm throbbed. I nodded at the bottle of Advil. Billy shook out two, and I motioned for two extra. Opened my mouth. He deposited the four in and poured me a glass of water. I swallowed them and longed for a belt of whiskey. But not yet. There was too much left to do.

"I'll refill the hole," he said.

"No. We're almost done. We need to keep going."

"Your hand . . ."

"My hand's the least of our worries. Wait here for a minute. Sit down."

I went upstairs. My hand would be in more agony soon. For now, I had to use the energy and adrenaline that pumped through me. With one hand I pulled the sweatshirt over my head, then took another from the hamper. I pulled the new one on and eased it past my injured fingers.

When I came downstairs, Billy got up and we returned to the yard. We stepped around the car and surprised two raccoons that were at the side of the hole, about to move inside. In some way that was more horrible than my hand, the idea of them feeding on Doreen. Billy swung a shovel and they ran off into the dark.

At the hole, I switched on the flashlight and found what I'd hit with my shovel: a syringe.

"It was Doreen's," Billy said. "I threw it in there too."

"Take it out. Put it to the side. Then you'll need to finish digging. I'm sorry. I can't help with that now."

As Billy dug I took a bedsheet and spread it on the lawn ten feet from the hole.

"I . . . She . . ." Billy started to stutter. Finally he said: "Here she is."

I aimed the flashlight in the hole. Doreen was buried as if sleeping on her side. Her shoulder rose from the dirt, the highest part of her. She was wearing a red Locksburg Bulldogs T-shirt. Billy switched from shovel to broom and swept the dirt from the body with the stiff bristles. She wore jeans and sneakers, with not much skin exposed. Mercifully, her face was turned and shielded by her matted hair.

Billy used the shovel to loosen the soil around her back and hips. When the upper part of the blade pressed against her, her entire body shifted.

All at once, Billy gagged and stepped away.

I'd never smelled anything like it before, yet I had. Or maybe I'd never smelled such a combination: like feces mixed with rotten meat and, worse yet, a few drops of sickeningly sweet perfume. It was unholy. We'd ignored earlier hints of the scent. Now the movement of her body had released something, and the odor came at us in a wave.

With my good hand I took the jar of Vicks and passed it to Billy. He opened it, ran his finger inside, and wiped a thick line under his nose. I did the same.

Billy shoveled some more, then got on his knees. As if he were cupping water in his hands, he tossed dirt from the hole. Here and there, fat worms wriggled. He may not have seen them. His eyes were mostly shut as he worked, his head turned away from the hole to breathe in fresher air.

"Let's take her legs and pull her out," I said after a minute. "We'll place her on the sheet. Then we'll roll her up and get her in the car, OK?"

He didn't answer, or maybe he only nodded. Still, he'd heard. He reached down and took one of her sneakers.

I said: "Billy. You'll need to hold her by the ankle, not by her sneaker. Her shoe will come off. Her jeans will too if you just grab those. She's . . . smaller now. If we do it right the first time, we won't have to do it again. I know it's not pleasant. We have to, though."

103

Again no answer. But he put his gloves back on and gripped her at the ankle. I grasped the other ankle.

On the count of three, we leaned back. I felt the bone inside her shift and had the vile thought: *What if we pull her leg off her body?* Billy was already frightened into silence. Who knows how he might react if something so hideous happened.

We couldn't move her and let go.

Billy took the shovel, placed the blade parallel with her back, and pushed it into the soil. While it was there, he turned it from side to side to loosen the dirt around her body. Then he took dirt out with his hands. After another minute we pulled her legs again. She slid toward us, free of the hole.

"Keep going. Don't stop."

We moved the body toward the sheet, placed her in the center, and let go.

"Let's c-cover her," Billy said.

"Throw that syringe in there. And anything else that's hers." I shone the light in the hole—empty except for the stench, which was winning the battle over the Vicks sweating off my skin.

"Did she have a purse?"

"No. She had the drugs in her pocket, in a small case."

"Make sure it's there."

Billy dropped the syringe on the sheet, then bent and tapped her pocket.

"It is."

"OK. Let's wrap her up."

I shone the light around the sheet, a final check for anything we missed.

The beam of light passed over Doreen's face for only half a second, and that image was instantly seared into my mind and threatened to drive me mad. What I saw: Hundreds of insects had nested on her and, stirred by the movement of her body, began crawling over her hair, making it move. Then something, maybe a thousand-legger, scuttled from her nostril and another from between her lips. I switched off the light fast so as not to see any more.

I turned to the side and vomited. My dinner and the water and the Advil jetted out and splashed on the grass.

Billy too had seen her decomposing face. He whimpered like a child.

A long string of spit hung from my lower lip as I doubled over, hands on knees. I spat and spat until it broke loose and followed the rest of my puke to the ground. When I got up I motioned to Billy to take the other end of the sheet. We covered Doreen over and wrapped her body the best we could.

"Lift on three," I said.

I held tight to the bunched-up sheet with my good hand and with the thumb and forefinger of the injured one. Her body was lighter than I expected. The MISSING posters that hung around town marked her weight as 120. She had shrunken to 75 at least. I bit my bottom lip as my hand ached, and we lifted high and got her into the trunk. Billy slammed it shut.

We stood there breathing heavily, as if the worst part were over. As if that were the end rather than just the start of what we needed to do. Crickets sounded in the summer night. Something moved in the brush. Probably the raccoons, waiting for a chance to return.

"Wh-what about the h-hole?" Billy asked.

"Fill it when we get back. Let's go."

The key jittered in Billy's hand as he guided it to the ignition. After two tries he got the key in and turned. He hit the gas too hard. The engine surged.

"Turn the car off."

"You're kidding."

"You need to relax."

"I won't relax fuh-for a hundred y-years."

"Calm yourself as much as you can. We can't get pulled over. Not tonight."

I took an alcohol wipe from the container on the front seat. Removed my gloves and cleaned my hands, then wiped away the snot and puke and Vicks from around my mouth. Billy did the same, dropping the used wipes out of the window to be picked up later.

"Breathe," I told him. "For one full minute."

My vision spun, my head woozy from blood loss and fatigue. I didn't know how I'd make it. We had a ride and a hike still ahead of us.

This is your son. Don't fail him. That thought shamed me into having strength.

"Let's go."

Billy drove the Honda out of the backyard, ever so slowly. We surely had the same idea: If the car got stuck there in the soft soil, how would we get it free, and if we couldn't, what would we do with Doreen?

Billy eased the car from the back lawn around the side of the house.

We moved into our driveway.

A police car pulled in from the other direction.

REED

I LEFT KEISER'S Hardware Emporium with my backpack filled with the tools that I bought. I retied my shoes because Locksburg cemetery was on the other side of town and it would be a long walk. I would also have to go a few extra blocks because I did not want to walk by Truman Memorial Baseball Field and would have to walk around it. That place brings back memories that are not happy.

It would be dark in a little while and the sun was making the biggest shadows. Sometimes I would walk backward to watch my shadow. I was walking backward and made it eleven steps. That was my record. I did not want to do any more than that because I might walk into something or fall. So I turned around.

Then I stopped walking altogether.

On the corner ahead was a police car. Dan Malloy was inside it and looking the other way. I began to step back in the direction I came and hoped that he did not see me. Then the police car started. It came down the street next to me.

"Yo! Reedy Reed! What's going on, man?" Dan said through the window of the police car.

I kept walking. The more I tried to slow down, the more I seemed to speed up. Dan rode alongside me, sometimes looking ahead, then back to me.

"Where you going, dude?" he said.

"I . . ." Nothing came out.

"Cat got your tongue? Or maybe a pussycat?"

He laughed at that. I did not say anything.

"I'm talking to you, man," he said.

I kept going. By then I was at the corner of Pulaski and Washington Streets and Dan pulled the police car up on the sidewalk and said: "Stop right there, Reed," and I did.

Dan got out of the car and hitched up his police pants and adjusted his belt. He glared at me. I looked across the street. A woman was watching what was happening. Then she turned away and closed her door.

"Why you runnin' from me, Reed?"

"I was not running. I was walking fast."

"OK, smart-ass. Why were you walking fast away from me?"

I did not say anything. I crossed my arms and hugged tight because sometimes that helps.

"Dude! I'm just talking to you! Don't get all scared! Jeez!"

He slapped me on the shoulder and held on and shook me, then smiled real wide, but it was not a smile that I liked.

There are many reasons not to like Dan Malloy. One of the biggest reasons is that the things he says do not match the real meanings of the words. He will say: "There's my best friend Reed!" even though we are not nor have ever been best friends. His actions too do not match. He will hold out a hand to shake and when I put out my hand he will pull his away. He has always been this way to me, especially in high school. He was two grades ahead and sometimes in the hallway he would see me and smack a book out of my hand and say real loud: "Oh, so sorry!" when it was obvious that he was not so sorry. Once he stood in front of the lavatory door when I was trying to get inside and said: "Oh no, Reed, this bathroom is broken!" even though there was not an OUT OF ORDER sign on it and even though other people were coming in and out of the lavatory. I really had to go pee, because I had drunk too much apple juice, and every time I tried to move around Dan, he would step in front of me. When he would not let me in, I ran down the hallway to another bathroom and did not make it in time.

Then I had a Big Fit.

I wet myself and tried to clean it and missed my class and sat in a stall in the bathroom. I was so angry at everything that had happened that I rocked back and forth and put my fingers in my ears and tried to calm myself but then some kids came in and kept laughing and knocking on the door of the stall and that made me smack myself on the forehead with the palm of my hand to stop all that was happening inside my head but that did not help too much so I tried for more pain to distract me. When Mr. Bello, the janitor, came in and unlocked the stall door, I was screaming and whacking my head so hard on the lavatory wall that my head began to bleed. I had some Big Fits in grade school but that was the first time in high school.

This day, Dan was standing next to me on the corner and I was looking away and he said: "So how you been, my man?"

"OK."

"That's not what I heard. Your mom died, huh?"

I did not say anything.

"Well, I'm sorry to hear that," Dan said, and he did not sound sorry to hear that at all.

"I need to go," I said.

"Where you going?"

"I have things to do."

"Ha. What kinda things? Bagging groceries?"

I stood there. I was not sure what to do.

"Dan, I have to—"

"You should call me 'Officer,'" he said.

I did not say anything.

"Damn, I'm only joking with ya, Reedy Reed! Man, you are one serious motherfucker."

We stood there for a while. He glanced around as if to see if anyone was watching him.

"What's in the bag?" he said.

"This is a backpack."

"No shit, Sherlock. What's in it?"

"I have a rechargeable drill and an extra battery pack and some drill bits and a flashlight."

"Are you working for someone?"

"No."

"Nothing else in there? No weapons or anything?"

"No."

He circled behind me and unzipped the backpack and peeked inside then zipped it back up so hard that I almost lost my balance.

"I didn't even need to check. I know you don't lie."

I did not say anything.

"You ever been in a police car?"

I shook my head.

"Well, it's your lucky day! It's the dead of summer. Not much is going on. Get in, Reed. I'll take you for a ride."

He was acting like this was a happy thing. It was not.

"I have to go," I said.

"C'mon, I'll drive you home."

Home was only two blocks away and in the direction of the cemetery, so that would not make me late to do what I wanted to do. Still, I did not want to get into the police car.

"I can walk home," I said as Dan stood there with his hand on the back door, waiting for me to get in.

"Dude, your mom died. I'm trying to be nice and do you a favor. What's your problem? C'mon, now," he said, in a way that implied I should not say no to him. I went and got in the back of the police car and Dan shut the door.

Dan's father was named Jack and he was a police officer too. I did not like him either. To me and Greg, Mom would say, "You two stay away from that peckerwood." Dan was two years ahead of me in school but three or four years older because he was absent from school for a year and had to stay back a grade. He told everyone he was absent because he got in an accident on his bike and broke his arm and jaw and some other things, but I overheard people say that his dad beat him so badly that Dan could not go to school for a while. I was not going to ask Dan about that. After high school Dan's dad got him onto the local police force and now Dan cruises around Locksburg, and every time he is on duty, I try not to let him see me.

"So, are you enjoying it back there?" Dan asked when we pulled away from the curb.

I did not say anything.

"Feel how slippery the seat is? Know what I do? I spray down that fake leather with polish at the start of my shift. Then when you cuff someone with their hands behind their back, and you take a turn real hard, they slide over and bash into the door."

He turned the corner hard and I slid and grabbed the door handle to stop. I have a cut on my forearm that I got a few days ago and I bumped it and that hurt.

"See!" Dan said. "Or I go straight and speed up, then hit the brakes. Last week, some guy almost put his head through the partition. Fucker deserved it."

"My house is—"

"I know where it is. Chill. What, you don't like hanging out? What else you got to do?"

It was getting very humid in the police car with no open windows in the back and the partition in front of me.

"Seriously, man. I'm being a hundred percent serious here: What do you do all day when you ain't bagging groceries?"

"I do a lot of things."

"Like what?"

I could have told him that I help plant and weed and water the garden and take care of the house and I cook some things very well and make coffee and do errands for nice neighbors and do not ask them for money. But Dan was driving faster and that made me nervous so I could not answer.

Dan said: "I mean, you ain't one of those *Rain Man* autistic guys. You ain't supersmart with numbers or anything, are you?"

I shook my head because I was not too good with math. He looked in the rearview mirror.

"Yeah, that must suck, you know? Like, you don't get any of the benefits. You're, like, more retarded than autistic, huh? Is there a difference?"

Dan had taken the turn to Brice Avenue, which was going farther away from my house. I wanted to tell him to drive me home, because I do not like being in a fast car that was so hot in back. Then all at once he made a hard turn on Edgewood Avenue and I slid across the seat because I was hugging my arms and I banged against the door.

"Holy shit, I didn't mean that, Reed! Honest!"

When I feel a Big Fit coming on, I try to control it by focusing on what is bothering me and dealing with that. But a lot of things were bothering me and I could not focus on just one. Among them: I did not want to be around Dan. And I did not want to be in this car. And this car was going fast. And it was hot. And the worst thing was that when Dan finally did slow down, he had stopped in front of Truman Memorial Baseball Field. And I do not like it there.

I hugged my arms harder and pressed the cut that was on my forearm and started to hum, because sometimes that helps too.

"Remember this place, Reed?"

I had tried not to walk past the field and had tried not to think about it. But there we were and Dan began to talk about the baseball team and soon I put my fingers in my ears so I would not have to hear him.

THE STORY OF MY TIME ON
THE LOCKSBURG BULLDOGS

I was a member of our high school baseball team, the Bulldogs. I did not want to be a member of the Bulldogs. But there is a requirement that every student must play a team sport for at least one year. I did not want to play football or soccer or volleyball, so I chose baseball. I could catch the ball in practice but not in the game and I could not hit the ball with the bat because the ball went too fast and it seemed like it would hurt me. Then Dan Malloy joined the team and that made things worse. The Locksburg Bulldogs usually won lots of games, but that year the team was really bad. We were so short of players that we could barely field a team, so everyone was required to play each game. We lost the first two home games to the Pine Mountain Saints and the Marshalltown Knights without scoring a run.

At our baseball field, spectators sat on two bleachers that were pushed together near our dugout and you could see and hear those people who were watching. Back then, Mom was working as a receptionist at Locksburg General Hospital and had to stay there until six, which was when our games started. So she would arrive halfway through the game and watch from the bleachers and call out: "Come on, Reed! You can do it!" And when I would not do it, she would say: "No problem, hon! You'll get 'em next time! Good effort!"

At the third home game we played the Shamokin Indians, who were our main rivals. I got up to bat. Mom was not there yet. After the second strike Dan's dad, Jack Malloy, called out from the stands: "Jesus Christ! Just swing the fuckin' bat!" Then he groaned and made a hissing, frustrated sound when I did not swing at the third strike. From then on everything changed. The rest of the players started to be meaner to me and I could hear parents in the stands exhale real loud when I would get up or when I would miss catching the ball in the field. Before that day the other players would sometimes pat me on the back or wish me luck, but after that day some would go to the men's room or turn away when I stepped up to the plate.

At the next game I went to bat and Dan's dad said, "Oh, this'll be great," and threw his soda cup to the ground when I struck out without swinging at the ball. When Mom would show up later, Dan's dad would not say anything.

I wanted to stop going to the games but Mom would say: "We're not quitters, Reed." I wanted to tell Mom that I was sick with a stomachache but she made me promise never to lie so I did not.

The games made me feel worse and worse every time and I was glad when the season was ending. For the last game we played Shamokin again and the score was close. Jack Malloy was in the stands, and once I saw him point at me and whisper something to another dad, who nodded and frowned. When I went up to bat, Jack Malloy said loudly, "Well, we're screwed now with this kid, ain't we?" and a couple people laughed and some made sounds of agreement.

Jack Malloy did not realize that Mom had gotten there a minute earlier. She was standing to the side of the bleachers where no one had seen her.

Mom said out loud: "What did you just say?"

And everything went silent. Even the other team stopped moving.

"I asked you a question!" Mom snapped.

"Time out!" the umpire said, then moved toward the stands. "Ma'am?" he said to Mom.

But Mom walked over and stood in front of the bleachers and stared right at Dan's dad. "I'm talking to you, Jack Malloy. What did you say about my son?"

Jack Malloy sort of mumbled and turned his face away.

"You going to look me in the eye, you coward?"

And it went more silent.

Mom stood there.

Then Mom said: "Someone told me you'd said something about Reed before, but I didn't believe 'em. I told 'em, 'No man would say something mean to a kid playing baseball.'"

Mom stared at the rest of the parents: "And none of you stuck up for my boy? Everyone here is a coward too?"

All of them looked away: at the field or at their hands or into the air.

Mom stood there and no one spoke.

She stared at them for an extra-long time. I saw that my teammates were examining their cleats or inspecting their gloves, anything not to watch what was going on.

Then Mom put her back to the parents and looked at me and said: "You go on, Reed. Hit it out of the park."

The umpire walked back to his place behind the catcher and I stood at the plate. And if this were a movie, what would have happened was that I would have hit a grand slam and won the game. But life is not a movie, no matter how badly you want it to be or how badly it deserves to be. And the pitcher pitched and I swung the bat and missed. And he pitched again and I swung the bat and missed. And when he threw the ball the third time, I tried so hard to hit it that I swung and missed and lost my balance and fell on my hands and knees on the ground.

The umpire came over and tried to put a hand under my arm to lift me up.

"*No!*" someone shouted. The umpire jumped as if a sharp fork had been stuck into his rear end. He took his hand off me.

It was Mom who had shouted. I turned and looked at her from down on the ground and she said: "You get up on your own, Reed. You show 'em how it's done."

I wiped the dirt from my face then nodded.

And I got onto my knees.

Then I got to my feet.

And then I was standing.

I brushed at my pants.

"Good man," Mom said.

And I walked back to the dugout.

For the rest of the game, no one said anything from the stands. They did not cheer or groan or call out. We lost 6 to 4. At the end, we players stood in a line to slap hands and say, "Good game. Good game," to the other team. Then I went to use the restroom behind the snack bar.

I did not know that Mom had gone back there too.

Mom was weeping.

I had seen Mom cry a few times before but never like this. She had an arm on the wall of the building, and her head was leaning into it, and she was sobbing and her chest was moving up and down.

I knew that Mom's crying had something to do with me.

All at once I had a thought that I had never had in my life. But it was a thought that was big and unexpected and felt true. And my thought was this: *Maybe things would be better for Mom if I was not here anymore.*

I thought: *Things would be better for Greg too.*

I walked away before Mom could see me and went into the woods and kept going. After a little while I heard "Reed! Where are you, Reed?" as people called out for me. Truman Memorial Baseball Field is at the end of town and the woods there go on all the way up to the game lands and I cannot say for certain where I was going;

all I knew is that my mom was crying because of me and I did not want her to cry anymore.

I walked for a few miles until it got dark and chilly, so I sat against a tree and fell asleep, and when the sun was coming up, a dog was sniffing me. Then a man with a yellow vest called out, "I found him!" and they brought me to the police station. Mom had been out searching for me too, and when she came to the station, she ran up and hugged me. I was scared that maybe she or Greg would be angry but they were not angry and even Greg patted me on the back and Mom said: "Oh, Reed. Oh my god. I don't know what I would have done if I'd have lost you," and she was crying again, but this time they were a different kind of tears.

THAT IS THE END OF THE STORY OF
MY TIME ON THE LOCKSBURG BULLDOGS

All of that was on my mind when I was in the back of the police car. Dan said: "Remember that day when your mom told off my dad? Man, that was something. No one, and I mean no one, ever said shit like that to my dad before. He was in a bad mood for days. Let me tell you, I freakin' admired her for it. She was a tough old bird. She had more balls than most guys I know."

Dan's police radio crackled. A voice coming from it said: "Dan, get over to Carla Louden's house on Route 140. You copy?"

I could hardly hear anything. I was remembering all that happened at the baseball field to make Mom cry and be sad, and I was in this police car where I did not want to be after going very fast on the road and that was scary and had me shaking.

I started to recognize the signs of a Big Fit.

I did everything that my counselor taught me to stop it. Dan was saying something into the radio. When he hung it up he said: "OK, you gotta get out of the car, Reed."

I heard him with my fingers in my ears but barely. I was rocking back and forth and could not stop. Dan turned around and yelled: "You hear me, you fuckin' imbecile? Get out."

My body would not stop rocking.

Dan said: "You really are fucked-up, aren't you?"

I did not say anything.

"You're so fucked-up, you killed your own mother. Now get out of my car."

Then all at once came the Big Fit.

One second it was not there and the next second it was there. Everything in me that could stop it seemed to shut down.

I smashed my head against the door window of the police car.

I smashed it again.

I smashed it again.

Dan was screaming: "What are you doing? Stop that, Reed! Stop that! Stop that!"

I smashed my head again.

LIZ

I was so tired that I couldn't sleep. My day had been spent nearly being jailed, falling deeper into debt, and watching my dream start to slip away. I was hours past exhaustion. Yet when I closed my eyes I remained awake, dwelling on all that had happened and listening to every creak my rented old house made, wondering if the sound came from Kap or one of his biker pals breaking in to force me to pay up or else.

Sometime about four a.m. I dozed, only to wake at nine that morning and give up any chance of falling back asleep. So I prepared to visit my dad. I picked a bunch of flowers from the side of the house. I liked to keep them in Dad's room to show whoever came in that Dad wasn't one of those residents who received no visitors. Someone cared for this guy, even if it was only me.

Hillview Living Center isn't a horrible place, considering the circumstances. It's fairly new, and I recognize many of the nurses from town. It was built on a plot of land about two miles outside of Locksburg, and though they offer a shuttle into town for the more mobile residents, I can't shake the feeling that the place was designed to hide away the old. I walked over to the shuttle stop and caught a ride to Hillview.

Dad was sitting at a table in the community room. In front of him was a mound of coins, all of it change that the nurses would dig from their purses and lend to him to examine.

Dad smiled the semi-unsure smile that he gives to anyone coming his way. I can usually tell within a minute if he's having a good day: He can sometimes get frustrated or unsettled with the brain fog that his Parkinson's can bring on. Today he seemed cheerful and alert, and there was recognition in his eyes when he saw me.

"Hello!" he said.

"Hi, Dad!" I said, and kissed him on the cheek.

"Where's your mother?" he asked. "Wait," he said before I could answer. His tone went quieter. "Cancer. Breast cancer."

"Right. That's how she died."

"I remember. It was in the spring."

"April. Twenty years ago."

"We loved her."

"Oh gosh, yes, we did," I said, and we both smiled. Sometimes our conversations about Mom could go weepy, but not now.

"How are you, honey?" he said.

"Good. You?"

"I'm fine. Have you gotten checked for breast cancer too? It runs in the family."

"I did. About six months ago. They had free screenings at Locksburg General Hospital. I saw Callie there. The nurse. She said to me, 'Tell your dad I said hi, Liz!'"

I slipped my name in there for courtesy's sake. When Dad has to ask my name, it both embarrasses him and saddens me.

"How is Callie?"

"Good. She's getting married to some guy she met in Lee Mountain."

"That's nice."

"Dad, I put a bunch of flowers in your room. I went there first and they told me you were in here."

"Can you stay?"

"Absolutely I can. As long as you want."

"Do you have any more coins, Liz?" he said. "We could look at them together."

When I was eighteen and considering whether to chase my dream, I had real reservations about leaving my father alone. He was still several years away from retirement at the highway department, where he spent frigid winters salting roads and broiling summers laying down blacktop. The aches and pains of age were starting to wear him down. On the night of my high school graduation, I was telling him how nervous I was about my future. He listened to my fears, then became sincere and said:

"Liz, I've never told you to shut up before."

"Yes you have. A million times."

"Well, I never really meant it."

"Sure you did. I—"

"Just shut up and listen to me: Get away from Locksburg. Focus on your music. Your music, it's . . ." He stopped for a moment. He was never a man to overshare emotions, and I could tell he was searching for a way to articulate what he wanted to say. "It's lovely, Liz. *You're* lovely. When I hear you sing I . . . oh God . . . I'm sorry I don't have better words."

"Those are wonderful words," I said, and hugged him.

Two weeks later he helped me move to Philadelphia. During my years away we'd talk on the phone often. I'd tell him of the shows I played, and he'd update me on his coin collection and on Locksburg gossip. Once or twice a year he'd surprise me with a visit that I knew he couldn't afford. Sometimes I'd send him an old coin that I'd found in a pawnshop, then skip lunch for a week to pay for it.

A few years ago he started to mention a friend he sometimes went to dinner with. Imogen was her name.

They'd met at church.

"Outside of religious hymns, I'm not much of a music person," Imogen said when we first met. I had come home for Christmas, and we were at the dinner table while Dad was in the kitchen. "But your dad says your little songs are nice."

It was that word, "little," that grated against my ear like a long fingernail scratching a chalkboard. My dad would never call my songs "little," or "nice," for that matter. But Imogen had a way of throwing in stray words that sounded derisive even when delivered in a faux-pleasant tone. I let it go, as well as the dozen other remarks that she delivered during the three days I'd returned to Locksburg.

Looking back, I think the signs of Dad's illness were there, and I hate myself for dismissing them. Dad had locked himself out of the house once. After letting him in, we discovered that his keys were in his pocket. His unsteadiness and memory lapses I took as the result of stress or simple forgetfulness, and I told myself that, when I came back in the summer, I'd take him to a doctor for a checkup.

A month after Christmas, Imogen and Dad went to City Hall to marry on her birthday. He told me that it had been his idea, but his voice didn't sound so certain. Soon she was answering the phone whenever I called, usually to inform me that my father was busy and couldn't talk. A year and a half later, he was a resident at Hillview. I found out only when I called home and she told me of his recent diagnosis. She was now living in our house with Chas, her son from her first marriage, who had moved in.

Soon after, I returned to Locksburg and rented the old house where I'm still at. During the first week I stopped over to my childhood home to pick up some of my old things. Imogen was coming out of the front door. I said hello and told her why I'd come. She shook her head.

"I'm sorry but not now," she said. "Next time you want to stop by, please call first."

"This is the house I grew up in," I said. "I don't have to call anybody."

"You haven't lived here for ten years, hon. Things have changed. This is now my house, and you're not allowed inside without my permission."

"What's the matter, Mom?" Chas said, locking the door behind him. He was a doughy, Baby Huey type, full of a haughtiness that annoyed me from the first time I heard his pissy voice. More annoying were the shirts he wore, which were always an inch too short so that they rode up and exposed the bottom of his hairy belly.

"Nothing, Chas," Imogen said. Then both of them drove off in what had been Dad's car.

I called a lawyer friend from my days in Philly, who said there were lots of options, none of them good. "You can fight her, sure," the lawyer said. "It'll cost you, though. And she'll drag it out. Or sell everything in the house and hide the money. I mean, how much are we talking? What's a house like that worth in Blocksburg?"

"Locksburg," I corrected. And though the lawyer was doing me a favor by giving me free advice, I couldn't help but be irked by her metro attitude toward small-town people. Money is different here than in the city. Thirty bucks in this town can be the difference between two weeks' worth of heat during a frigid winter or hearing your pipes burst. Yet in Philly clubs I'd seen people spend that much on a single drink and leave half of it unfinished.

I said: "It's a beautiful old place. Three stories. There aren't many of those in Locksburg. But it's not about the money, it's—"

She finished: "About the principle. Right. Well, in this case, the principle will cost you a couple thousand dollars to retain an attorney and file the papers. And Pennsylvania courts look kindly on old ladies with ill husbands, so you're already at a disadvantage."

From then on I did my best to avoid Imogen. She rarely visited my father. When she did, a nurse told me, Dad tended to grow uneasy. Once, the nurse had walked in to find Imogen roughly grabbing my father's wrist, then blamed him for being aggressive.

Here and there I've gleaned some information about Imogen. She was from Springer, a town smaller than Locksburg, about a half hour away. Why she'd traveled here to go to church, I soon found out: Someone told me that there were no single older men there, and Imogen had likely been prowling around.

Maybe illness had clouded my dad's judgment. Or maybe he'd just been lonely.

And who can blame someone for feeling lonely?

* * *

I was so broke that I didn't have any coins to share with Dad, so we went through the ones that were already on the table. Within minutes we were having a delightful time—so delightful that I easily held off thoughts about the mess I was in. Still more gratifying was Dad. The doctors tell you not to get too caught up in a patient's moments of near-normal lucidity, for they won't last. But I couldn't help it. Dad and I were checking out coins like we did when I was a girl, all while talking more than we had in months.

"Dad, I haven't told anyone this, but . . . I got an invitation to perform at a showcase in Nashville."

"When?"

"Two weeks."

"So you'll have a record deal in two weeks and one day."

"Oh, don't I wish," I said. "I just needed to tell somebody. It's all bottled up inside me."

"When are you leaving?"

Now, there was a good question.

"I . . . I can't be sure. I'm in a bit of a bind at the moment. But I'll find a way. I've got to."

"Money problems?"

"Yeah."

"Well," he said, "then it's finally time for Liberty."

"Hmmm?"

He picked up a dime from the pile.

"The Seated Liberty dime."

"Sorry, Pop. That's a Roosevelt dime. From 1986."

"*Our* Seated Liberty dime."

"It's the nurse's dime. We have to give it back."

He said: "Are you . . . what's that word . . . ?"

126

"What word?"

"Stupid."

"What are you saying, Pop?" Maybe his period of clarity was ending.

"I am asking you, Liz, if you're being stupid on purpose. Because normally you're the smartest cookie in the oven."

"I don't understand."

"Our Liberty dime. Eighteen fifty-six."

"Oh! From your collection! Is that what you're talking about?"

"Did I stutter? Yes, our Seated Liberty dime. *Your* Seated Liberty dime."

"It's not mine. It's yours. The best coin you own."

"I bought it on the day you were born. Went straight from the hospital over to the coin dealer."

"I remember you telling me that."

"I bought it for you. Coins usually . . . what's that word? For when things go up in price. Over time . . ."

"'Appreciate'?"

"Right. Coins usually appreciate at double the pace of inflation. Sometimes much faster. So I bought it thinking I'd surprise you and give it to you on your wedding day."

"I'm not getting married anytime soon."

"Good. That guy . . . what's his name?"

"Luke?"

"Yeah. Luke. He's a . . . what's that word?"

"What word?"

"Dick."

"Yeah, he is. He's out of the picture."

127

"Good. Then use the Seated Liberty dime for your trip."

"We love that dime."

"Now you're being extra stupid. It's only a piece of metal. Use it for your dream."

"But, Dad . . ."

"Liz, I've never told you to shut up before . . ."

"Yes you have."

"Good. Then you're used to it. So shut up and listen: Sell the dime. I bought it for nine hundred dollars. Last time I checked, it was worth four thousand."

"Dad. Are you sure?"

"The dime's not mine anymore. It's yours, Liz. It's always been yours. I was going to surprise you . . ."

"You have!"

"Take it over to . . . what is his name? The coin dealer? Jeez, I used to know that . . ."

"Ed."

"Right. Ed. The coin dealer. Take that dime to Ed. He'll give you a good price."

I spent over an hour telling and retelling my dad the story of my phone call from Belle Chapman and her invitation and of my car going up in flames. I didn't mention Luke and the rest; no need to worry Dad with that. After a while I could see Dad growing tired. I walked him back to his room.

I opened the door. Imogen was there, rooting through the bureau drawer. She had just taken Dad's wristwatch and was handing it to Chas.

"Oh!" she said, caught in the act and trying to fake nonchalance. "Hello, Roy. Hello, Liz."

"That's Dad's watch," I said.

"I told Chas he can use it. He's got—"

"My mother gave that watch to Dad."

The flowers that I'd brought were sticking out of the wastebasket.

"And I brought those flowers for him."

"Sorry," she said with no sorrow. "I have hay fever. So, Roy? How have you been feeling?"

Dad was staring off, paying little attention. He wasn't the alert man he had been fifteen minutes earlier. He moved past Imogen and sat on the bed.

"I'm tired," he said.

Imogen grimaced at me as if that were my fault. "Of course you are. You need to relax. Lay down. We were leaving," she said, though they'd apparently just arrived.

I walked over to Chas to take the watch from him. He put it on his wrist, daring me to try for it. I had no problem doing that, but not when Dad was there. I wouldn't want to risk upsetting him. Instead, I shot Chas a look. Out of the corner of my eye, I saw Imogen lift Dad's feet and push them onto the bed.

"Please be careful!" I barked at that careless bitch.

I helped Dad cover up; then, when Imogen and Chas stepped out of the room with mumbled goodbyes, followed them into the hallway.

"You leave that watch here," I said.

The two ignored me and went out of the side door into the parking lot.

"Did you hear me?" I called while following them.

"Hon, I don't want to leave that watch here in case someone steals it. Chas is going to borrow it for a church social we're going to in Springer. It's not your business."

"Dad's been here for a while and no one has stolen that watch. He needs it."

"There are plenty of clocks around."

I reached for the watch. Chas held his arm high.

I said: "Do you want me to call the police?"

"Be my guest," Imogen said. "I'm his wife. I'm allowed to protect his possessions."

She was right, at least legally. I tried another angle.

"There are things in that house that are mine. Dad wants me to have them. I'm coming over right now to get them," I said, though how I'd get there without a car was a good question. To walk would take hours.

"Well, we won't be there. We're going over to Springer for the social."

Imogen and Chas got into the car. Then Imogen rolled down the window.

"Next week, I'm putting the house up for sale."

"What? Dad didn't—"

"I was coming here to tell him, but you exhausted him."

"You can't sell it! I'll—"

"I'm moving back to Springer. And your father's happy here."

"Listen to me. Dad has some things there that are mine."

"What things?"

Maybe she knew about his coins, maybe she didn't. But I couldn't risk mentioning them.

"Keepsakes."

"Well, I'll be having a yard sale next month, to sell all that old stuff. Whatever you want, just let me know. You'll get a discount."

"You don't understand. These things are mine."

"*You* don't understand," Chas chimed in, as annoying as ever. "It's her house. Everything in it is hers. So buzz off."

Then they drove away.

I walked a full circle of the parking lot, my mouth hanging open in horrified amazement. I kept shaking my head, then muttering, "She can't do this!" though I guess she *could* do it—and *was* doing it. I made my way back inside and looked in on Dad. He was asleep.

I sat in a chair. Over the intercom came an announcement that the shuttle into town would be leaving in ten minutes. I walked over and kissed Dad on the forehead. Then I went to the bureau and opened the drawer to see if Imogen and Chas had lifted anything else of Dad's. His wallet was there, as was his key ring. I shut the drawer and walked across the room to leave.

Then I stopped, nearly frozen in place.

I said to myself: "No, you can't."

Shook my head.

In a different voice I said to myself: "Yes, you can."

I stood there some more.

Then I went back over to the drawer and took out the key ring. On it were two keys:

One key for the front door of his house.

The other key for the lockbox where he kept his coins.

I stared at it.

The intercom called out that the shuttle was leaving in five minutes.

I stared some more.

Then I put the key ring in my pocket.

CARLA

BILLY HIT THE BRAKE hard when he saw the police car pulling into our driveway. I jolted in my seat, then went still, like some tiny animal in fear of being discovered and devoured.

Billy tried to speak. Nothing but half sounds came out. His hands gripped the steering wheel as if he were entertaining some wild idea of hitting the gas and racing past the cop.

"Put the car in park, Billy."

He didn't. I asked again, then reached over and did it myself.

"Are you cuh-cuh . . ." He couldn't get hold of a word and for once I was glad. I didn't want him talking himself into a panic.

"If the police knew about this, they'd have sent ten cars," I said. I couldn't be sure of that, but just saying it made it feel true. "And they'd have their guns drawn."

I breathed deep and opened the door to get over there fast so the cop wouldn't come to us. "I'll see what he wants," I said. "Don't move."

I went to the cruiser. Dan Malloy was there. The cop usually had a smart-ass comment to deliver or a leery eye to gaze at you. But now he was turned around and babbling to someone. I bent down to find that Reed Grove was sitting in the back seat, hugging himself and rocking back and forth. In the light that was left in the sky, I could see that Reed's face was beet red. There were welts on his forehead.

"Calm down, Reed. Calm down. Calm down," Dan was repeating in a fearful voice.

"What's the matter?"

"He had, like, a breakdown. He was whacking his head against the window."

"He's having an anxiety attack."

"I didn't do anything!" Dan said. For a guy like him, it was practically a confession that he did do something—and not something good. Maybe he'd goaded Reed into some sort of meltdown. I wouldn't put it past him. The guy was an incompetent jerk who reveled in power, like his dad had been. And worse than his father, Dan was little more than a smart-ass kid, far too immature for the job, and he was the only one who didn't seem to know it.

"Unlock the door," I said. He did, and I slid into the back next to Reed.

"Reed? It's Carla. Remember me? You and your mom used to eat at the Coal Miner Diner when I was a waitress there."

Reed nodded. Sniffed.

"I didn't do anything to him!" Dan chimed in. "Did I, Reed?"

"Be quiet for a second," I said in a tone that even he could translate as *Shut your mouth, dickhead.*

"Reed. Can I get you something? A glass of water?"

"Pancakes."

"You want pancakes?"

"No. That is what I used to eat at the diner. And you put chocolate chips on them for me even though they were not on the menu. That is why Mom and I used to want you as our waitress."

134

"Yes! I remember that too! So do you want some water now?"

He shook his head. Then Reed motioned to my bandaged hand.

"Did you hurt yourself?"

"Yes. I got cut."

"Are you OK?"

"Yes. Thank you for asking, Reed. That's very nice of you. How about you? How are you feeling?"

"I had a big fit. It is going away, though."

"Good. What do you need now?" I asked.

"To go home."

I looked to Dan. He nodded eagerly.

"OK, Dan will drive you."

"Can you take me home?" Reed asked me. He pointed over to Billy's car. Dan looked there too, as if he were seeing the car for the first time.

"Oh, honey, I wish I could . . ."

I tried to fashion a fast excuse; there was no way I could risk letting him into our car.

Dan interrupted: "Carla, you need to get over to that restaurant you're building. Now."

"Why? And why are you here in my driveway?"

Dan said: "I was cruising Reed around. To show him the police car. Then he freaked out, right when Chief Kriner called. I couldn't just leave Reed on the street. So I let him stay in the car to calm him down while I drove over here."

"So what about my restaurant?"

"There was some kind of smoke or fire or something. The chief tried to call you, but you weren't answering your phone. That's why he told me to come check your house."

135

"OK," I said. "Thanks. I'll go to the barn. You take Reed home."

That would get Dan out of my driveway and away from my bigger problem, which was a dead girl in the trunk of my son's car, not fifty feet away.

I patted Reed on the arm, then left the cruiser. Dan backed out into the road. Then he opened the passenger-side door and called: "Who's that driving? Billy? Tell him to follow me. I'll escort you to the restaurant."

"You don't have to . . ."

"It's on the way," Dan said. "The chief ordered me to bring you there."

He shut his window, ending any debate.

I didn't know what was happening over at the barn, and at this moment couldn't care. But Dan flicked on the red-and-blues and waited for us. I got into Billy's car.

"Wh-what the hell?"

"There's something going on over at the restaurant. He was told to escort us there. Follow him."

"Maybe wuh-we can drive away or—"

"Don't do anything suspicious. Drive. We'll find a way to get out of there fast."

We sped along Route 140 behind the police cruiser. Doreen's body had been in our car for only ten minutes, yet the stench of damp decay was already seeping from the trunk. The odor seemed to be attaching to us, leaching into our clothes, invading our noses, making our eyes water. We opened our windows all the way.

When we got to the barn, Dan waited for us to pull into the parking lot. When we did, he drove off, hopefully to take Reed home.

The town fire truck rumbled to a start. It left the lot, followed by four or five other cars, no doubt the volunteer firefighters. The only vehicles remaining were the police chief's cruiser and Nestor's pickup. Billy parked as far from them as he could.

"Stay here."

Billy tried to say "OK." It took five or six syllables. He gave up and nodded instead.

Before I could get out, Billy grabbed my shoulder and yanked me back inside. He pointed to my head. The hairnets. We took them off and tossed them in the back seat with the hats. Then I got out and hustled over to Chief Kriner.

"Where ya been, Carla?" Kriner said. "I called your cell phone four or five times."

"I must have lost it in the house. What happened here?"

"Fire in your fuse box," Kriner said. "Your guy, Nestor, put it out with the extinguisher. Then he called the fire department."

"How bad is the damage?"

"You'll need to replace the box, maybe some wiring. Otherwise you're good. The fire chief opened the windows to air the place out. Go inside for a gander."

"I will. But that might have to wait until tomorrow. I hurt my hand pretty bad. I need to get home."

"What happened?" Kriner asked as I tried to walk away. Normally I liked the chatty central Pennsylvania residents. They could talk about the corn crop or the deer hunting or the school board election for half an hour, then answer a question about it with another twenty-minute tirade that cursed the agriculture department or the game commission or the local government. But I needed to get out of there fast, so I said only: "Cooking accident."

He waited for a story. I didn't offer any. Then he motioned to Nestor, who was sitting in the police car. "He sucked in some smoke. I'm taking him to the hospital, just to be safe."

I nodded and went around to Nestor and leaned down to talk to him through the window.

"What were you doing here, Nestor? It's getting really late."

"Working," he said.

"I can't pay you for it."

"I know," he said. "But if I go home, I sit around and it's hard not to drink. Plus it's quiet here. So I can pray."

He'd mentioned prayer often, and though I'm not a church-goer, I live in central Pennsylvania, a place where to badmouth religion is to lose your friends and piss off large swaths of your family. Prayer, to me, has always seemed like a way to avoid action, and to keep from looking hard at tough truths. But in Locksburg, you keep such doubts to yourself and bury any derision.

"Well, I hope you're praying for the restaurant to succeed."

"I pray for a lot of things. You should try it."

"Maybe I will," I said, knowing I wouldn't.

"I'm serious. I can tell, something's been bothering you." When I didn't respond, he said: "Give it a chance. You don't pray to change God's mind. You pray to change your own."

I nodded out of politeness. "Anyway, Nestor, you saved the place from burning down. Thank you. Now get to the hospital."

I glanced across the parking lot. Chief Kriner had walked over to Billy's car while I'd been talking to Nestor. And there, the chief of police stopped and leaned against the trunk, his ass eighteen inches from the body of the girl he'd spent a year searching for.

Billy got out and began trying to talk to him. I held my good hand high and called: "Chief! Can you come here?" I held tight to each syllable to keep my voice under control. I was nearly crawling out of my skin with apprehension. "There's, uh, something I want to show you!"

I had nothing to show him, but I had every reason to get him away from there. Kriner moved himself off the car. Billy exhaled so deeply that he seemed to shrink. From thirty yards away I could see the sweat glittering on Billy's forehead.

Kriner stopped and sniffed the air. He got moving after a long moment, and when he came over to me, I pointed to the barn windows, adding a little drama to shift his attention to the building. He sniffed again and scrunched his nose.

I told him: "Um, I'll leave the windows open all night, to get any smoke out. Can you tell whatever officer is on duty to watch the place in case anyone comes up here?"

"Yep," he said.

"I'm going to leave the windows open."

"You said that already."

"Sorry. I'm a little shook up."

"Course you are. You've had a hell of a night. Coulda been worse, though."

A mad cackle almost burst from my mouth.

Kriner said: "Before you open your restaurant, you need to check the field around here. Someone probably hit a deer on Conover, then it came up here to die. You smell that?"

I acted as if I were taking a whiff, then shook my head no.

"Well, I can," he said, then sauntered away. "Dead deer."

Kriner got into his police car. As he and Nestor drove out of the lot, Nestor gave me a wave.

Months later, in court, Nestor would testify that he saw that the back tire of Billy's car was low on air. Nestor would tell the judge that, when he got to the hospital, he tried to call me, to warn us that maybe there was a screw or a nail in the tire and tell us that we needed to be careful.

But of course we never got that call.

I'd left my cell phone at home.

REED

DAN OPENED the back windows of the police car and the air blew in and cooled my skin.

"Feelin' OK, Reed?" he asked as we drove away from the restaurant that was not yet a restaurant. I could tell that he did not care if I felt OK. He was asking to make himself feel OK. But I nodded because it was true: I was feeling better, though my head hurt some. Dan looked in the rearview mirror and saw me nod.

"Attaboy," he said. "Let me tell you, Reed: You scared the heck out of me there for a minute. Smackin' your noggin. You're more fucked-up than I thought. You . . ."

Dan kept talking and I stopped listening. Dan did not seem to me to be a very perceptive policeman. At Carla's house he had been talking so much that he did not notice that Carla was wearing a sweatshirt in the summer or a hairnet under her hat, which was very strange. I would have asked her why she was wearing those things or why she and her son were pulling the car from behind their house if I had not been fighting the Big Fit.

"I'm talking to you, nimrod!" Dan shouted.

I looked up.

"I asked: How's your brother doing these days?"

Dan only wants to know bad things about people so he can use it against them later or tell those bad things to someone else. If you said, *I am doing well*, and told him something nice, he would not care. He was not concerned with Greg, but I did not want to lie and say Greg was doing fine because Greg was not always doing fine since Maggie left town and since Mom died.

"Greg enjoys his work a lot," I said, because that was true. When he would drop off Little Jimmy at our house, he seemed happy enough to go in to work and sometimes he would call to say he would be late because he would go out for beers with his work friends. Little Jimmy and I liked when that happened. Little Jimmy and I would play hide-and-seek or he would run away and I would chase him down to the creek.

"How's he doing after you killed your mom?"

I waited some time before I said: "I would not like to talk anymore. I would like to go home."

"Yeah, man, that's fine. I don't want you freakin' out or anything. I can be quiet."

And ten seconds later Dan proved he could not be quiet because he began talking again, about how great it was being a police officer and how if he were the chief he would clean up our town and about how the rest of the Locksburg police officers were losers. Dan was meaner than every other person I have ever met, but he was like every other person I have ever met because he liked to talk to me a lot, though he was mostly trying to convince himself of something that he already believed to be true.

"They're too soft!" Dan said about the other officers. "Bunch of pussies, you know?"

I did not say anything.

"This town needs some law and order. Put me in charge, I'd make this place squeaky-clean. People would move here from all over. I mean— There! Jeez, you see this shit? This is exactly what I'm talkin' about! Look!"

Dan pointed to a man who was walking on the side of the road. The man was probably tall but he was stooped so that his neck and head were hanging low. When the man saw the police car, he turned around and walked the other way. He was making movements with his hands as if he were arguing with himself. I am not good at telling a person's age, but he was older than Mom had been, and his hair was white and his dark brown skin made his hair appear even whiter.

"Da fuck is this coon doing?" Dan said.

Dan pulled next to the man and brought down the passenger-side window and said: "Hey, old timer. What are you doing out here, shufflin' on the road all alone?"

"I'm good," the man said.

"Yeah, but that's not what I asked. I said—"

The man walked away, and that made Dan angrier than he normally is, and he is normally very angry.

We were on Carbon Road, which is just before Locksburg becomes more crowded. There were some houses out here, most of them remodeled shacks where coal miners and their families used to live.

The old man turned down a dirt driveway. Forty yards away was a house. I thought Dan was going to let the man go home, but Dan was mad at the way that the man had ignored him.

"Hey! Where you going?" Dan called to him.

The old man was talking to himself. Dan pulled the police car into the driveway, then cut him off. The old man started to walk around the car. Dan slammed the transmission into park and got out.

"I said stop!" Dan said, although he was saying stop for the first time and the implication was that he had said stop before, which he had not. I like that word: "implication."

Dan went over and stood in the man's path. The man tried to move around him. Dan kept blocking him until the man turned and walked back the way he came. He went so close to the car that I could have touched him out of the open window if I had wanted to. Dan ran around the car and blocked the man, who turned yet again and walked toward the house.

The man rambled and kept moving his arms and seemed frustrated. Dan got in front of him and said: "Not another move! Sir, you need to listen to me right now." The man tried to walk past him. Dan grabbed the man's arm, pulled it behind the man's back, and pushed him down on the hood of the car. The man did not seem very strong but Dan was breathing hard after he did it.

"That hurts that hurts that hurts!" the man said at first, then he started to whimper.

The front door to the house was thrown open and another man stormed out. He was younger but just as tall and I guessed he was the older man's son.

"What the hell you doin'?" the younger man said as he went down the front two steps and toward Dan.

"Stay over there, sir!" Dan said. At the same time Dan reached for his handcuffs, which were on his belt.

"Da heck is goin' on?" the younger man said. "He's seventy-eight years old!"

"Sir, stand back, please."

"Stand back? You come onto my land and push my father around? Why don't *you* stand back? Who the hell are you?"

"I'm an officer with the Locksburg Police Department. And you—"

"You're a piece of shit is who you are. Hurtin' an old man. What is wrong with you?"

The older man grunted and tried to get away from Dan. Dan pulled the man's arm up higher to bring him pain and stop him from moving. The older man let out another sound that made me sad to hear.

"*You're hurting him!*" the younger man screamed. "Leave him go!"

A woman came out of the house. She was about the age of the younger man. She saw what was happening and screamed too.

"You're gonna break his arm!" she screamed. "Stop that!"

"He needs to stop resisting!" Dan said. Then he yelled at the older man: "Stop resisting!"

The woman said: "He gets senile! And he had a couple drinks! Leave him alone!"

"Then he's intoxicated and resisting arrest!"

"Arrest? What the hell?" the younger man yelled, and moved closer.

Dan was screaming at them to shut up and the older man began to scream too and struggle and the woman came down the steps and she was throwing up her hands and so much was going on at one time that it felt like an outside version of what happens inside my head when I have a Big Fit.

"He's seventy-eight!" the woman screamed.

"You can't do that!" the younger man shouted.

"Step away!" Dan yelled.

And the older man cried and growled and struggled and Dan pulled his arm back harder and went for the other arm.

Then the younger man bellowed: "*Stop hurting him!*"

The man charged forward and pushed Dan on the shoulder. But Dan moved and the younger man's pushing hand slipped up and hit Dan's face. Dan let go of the older man, who fell to the ground.

So much was happening and no one was listening. It was escalating. I used to like that word, but not now. What we needed here was a better word: "de-escalation." Even I could see that if everyone relaxed and stopped talking or maybe went away, everything might be OK.

But I knew that Dan was not going to back down.

And I knew that the younger man was not going to back down either.

And I knew that meant bad things were about to happen.

LIZ

LUKE WAS SITTING on my front steps when I returned from visiting my dad at Hillview Living Center.

"Why aren't you at work, Luke?" I asked, knowing the answer.

"Uh, I got fired, remember?"

"Oh right! That was after you almost got me arrested for drug possession and grand theft auto! How could I forget?"

"I'm sorry for all that. That wasn't like me."

"Yeah, you're usually worse," I said. "So what do you want?"

"I want to know if I'm going to die."

"The answer is yes. We're all going to die, Luke. Didn't anyone ever teach you that?"

"But am I going to die soon?"

I was going to say something like *In a cosmic sense, our entire life is but the batting of an eye.* But good sarcasm would be lost on him. So I went with "I sure hope not."

"Have you figured out a way to pay back Kap?"

I walked past Luke and unlocked my front door.

"Come in," I called to him. "And close the door behind you."

I went to the kitchen, filled two glasses with barely cool water from the tap, and motioned for Luke to take the seat opposite me.

I said: "I want to ask you some questions, and I want honest answers, you hear me?"

"You got anything else to drink besides water?"

"And I want you to shut up if you're not answering the questions. Got it?"

His brow wrinkled, but he apparently thought the better of talking back. He sipped his water.

"Luke, have you ever broken into a house before?"

He glanced around the room, as if I had offended him deeply and he was searching for a witness to this insult.

"Who do you think I am, Liz? Some petty thief? You're an insulting bitch sometimes, you know that?"

I went silent. Stared at him.

"Why?" he said.

"Answer the question."

"Only losers do breaking and entering."

I went silent again.

"Well, you know, maybe once, when I was a kid."

In other words, he'd probably broken into several houses over the past few years.

He said: "Why are you asking?"

There was no way of getting around it: I'd have to tell him my thoughts.

"My dad collected coins. Most of them were only low-grade. He bought them cheap, just as a hobby and mainly for the history. They're worth around five bucks each."

"How many does he have?"

"Maybe two hundred or so. They're worth about a thousand dollars, total. And that's if anyone is buying. And that's if you could sell all two hundred together, which you probably can't. But there's one special coin. A rare Seated Liberty dime."

"How much is that worth?"

"About four thousand dollars."

Luke's eyes went wider.

I said: "I've told you before about my dad's second wife, Imogen, and her son, Chas."

"You said they're dirtbags."

"I would never say that about anyone."

"Yes you would. You said—"

"OK, maybe I did. But that's beside the point. And the point is this: My dad said he wants me to have that special dime. But Imogen won't let me into the house."

"That bitch!" Luke spat.

"And that dime is mine."

"Of course it is!" He nodded extra eagerly, to drive the point home.

"My dad bought it for me when I was born."

"That's really nice!"

"And, sure, I could file some kind of lawsuit against Imogen. But that would take months or years. And I need that money now."

"Yes, you do!"

"And even if I won a lawsuit, Imogen could sell the dime before then or say she lost it."

"Right! She totally would."

"I'd almost be doing this for my dad as much as for me."

"You'd be a great daughter."

"It's not like I'd be stealing."

"It's *absolutely* not stealing! *She's* the one who's stealing!"

It didn't seem right that Luke and I were agreeing so much, but I ignored that for the moment.

"So where is the dime?" he asked.

"In the office of my dad's house."

"How can we get in? Is there an open window or something?"

I had initially planned to talk this idea out, then talk myself into it. But Luke jumped ahead and . . . ah, who was I fooling. I couldn't blame it on anyone else but me. This is what I wanted to do.

I took my dad's keys from my pocket and held them in front of Luke.

"Well, well, well," he said. "That makes breaking in, like, easier."

We spent a half hour discussing the plan. Along the way it became a certainty rather than a proposal.

Luke said: "One time, out at Trevor Falls, this guy came into his garage when we were hotwiring his car."

"I thought you said you never did this before?"

"It was sort of on the up-and-up."

"How can stealing a guy's car be on the up-and-up?"

"His ex-wife told us about it. So that car was kinda hers at one point."

I was through trying to speak logically to him.

Luke said: "What I'm saying is we have to make sure no one is home."

"Imogen said they were going over to Springer."

"When?"

"Now."

"As in *right now* now?"

"That's what 'now' means. She was leaving from Hillview to go to there."

"Then let's get to your dad's place. Now."

"You mean *right now* now?"

"That's what 'now' means. We can get that coin before she comes back home. This is the perfect time."

"What do we need?"

"Do they have a dog?"

"No."

"A burglar alarm?"

"Not that I know of."

"Then all we need is the key. This is what we're going to do: We're going to walk over there, casual. Then we're going upstairs and taking the coin. Then we're leaving. It's foolproof."

"Nothing's foolproof, Luke."

"Pah," he said. "If we're in that house for more than five minutes, I'll eat my own shit."

On our walk, Luke took on the attitude of a professional, pompous as he offered advice and gave suggestions.

"The secret is not to be distracted. We're going in for what we need and that's all. Don't take anything else. And be quiet. Don't say anything that doesn't need to be said. Most important: If anything goes wrong, don't panic."

I turned a corner and Luke said: "Why are you going this way? I thought your old house was down the other way."

"Please tell me you have a quarter."

"What are you—"

I pointed across the street. One of the few remaining pay phones in Locksburg.

"Who do you need to call? Come on, we got stuff to do!"

"Luke, seriously, shut up and give me a quarter."

He dug deep in his pocket and found one, along with a lot of lint. I shook the lint off and put the quarter in the phone. Dialed the number of my dad's house. After ten rings I hung up. The pay phone coughed the quarter back into the slot. Luke practically lunged for it.

"I called there. No one answered."

"Ohhh!" he said. "Smart!"

I started to have second thoughts about bringing Luke. But I'd need someone there for a lot of reasons: as a lookout, as a helper in case we needed to force open a door or something, as . . . well, those excuses were exaggerated. The real reason I needed someone with me was because I was frightened about this. I'd always been the good girl. But now I needed to do something bad, and it was a foreign concept to me. My hands were already trembling. I'd barely gotten the quarter into the pay phone.

We made our way across town on foot, the humid summer streets mostly empty. When my old house was in sight, I stopped to survey the block and see if anyone was watching us. After a moment I was recalling the past. In many ways I loathed Locksburg. But my youth and memories were here, and to see my old home flooded me with emotions.

The place is a tall, three-story brick house that rises still higher by being set at the top of a small rise, giving it a good view of the town. My grandfather bought it when he was a young man with money from his management job at the coal mining company. Back in the day it was the perfect residence for an up-and-coming executive. By the time my dad inherited it and the coal mines had closed, it was a white elephant that no one wanted but us, on a block that had as many abandoned houses as occupied ones.

This was the street where I biked on summer nights until my mother would step out onto the porch and call "Liz! Dinner!" to the block and I'd make my way home. When she died, my dad attempted to downsize to a smaller house, but there were no buyers for the place. So we stayed. I didn't mind. I adored the house. It felt like my own castle.

This was the block where my father sprinted along at least twice a year to chase down the school bus and hand me my breakfast through a window when I ran late and left the house without eating. And the house where, a year to the day after my mother died, I woke to a muffled sound and peeked into my father's room to see him weeping with a small framed photo of her in his hand, then crept back to my room to shed tears of my own.

More happily, it was the street where I missed Halloween due to a night's stay in Locksburg General Hospital when my tonsils became inflamed. The next night my father told me to stop sulking and dress in my costume. Then he took me from door to door. Later I found out that he had bought boxes of candy and called in every favor from the neighbors. They opened their doors to my day-late trick-or-treating and filled my bag to the breaking point with the full-size chocolate bars that my dad had given them.

"Ready?" Luke said.

His voice brought me to attention. I felt the key in my pocket and took a final view around the deserted street.

"In and out, right?" I said to Luke.

And of course the shithead giggled at the phrase.

"Oh yeah," he huh-huhed. "In and out."

He was probably grinning. I didn't bother looking.

We walked up the steps to the porch like we were on a mission. The key slid in and unlocked the door with no resistance. We entered immediately and closed the squeaky door behind us. I peeked into the parlor: It now was practically a forest. Imogen had dozens of houseplants there.

"Hello!" I called.

Luke nearly leaped out of his skin. He went to put a hand over my mouth and I shook him off. Shot him an expression that said, *Do not touch me again.* Then I yelled: "Anyone here? The door was open!"

We listened for a count of five. No response.

I went for the stairs.

Luke had said not to look around the place. That was impossible. Memories slammed back into me, and anger too, at the things that Imogen had changed: She'd taken down our family photographs and replaced them with tasteless Thomas Kinkade prints that made me sneer. A Picasso-esque painting of a guitar, which I'd made in high school and which my dad had proudly framed, had been removed and replaced with a needlepoint that read: *I have found the Lord!*

"I didn't know he was lost," I mumbled, and looked to Luke for a cheap laugh. I turned around. I was halfway up the stairs and he wasn't behind me.

"Where are you?" I whispered loudly.

"Seeing what else is down here!" he said from the living room. "Bunch a fuckin' plants! Maybe she's growing weed!"

"You said we were here only for the coin! That was your first rule!"

"Yeah, but . . . you know."

"No, I don't 'you know'!"

"Sometimes you gotta break the rules."

I exhaled in disgust.

Luke followed me up the first set of stairs, then across the hallway. The walls there too were filled with new things, all of them tacky and clichéd. A needlepoint showed a smiling face and a steaming turkey, with the saying *The way to a man's heart is threw his stomach!* Apparently the maker hadn't realized the error. A second needlepoint declared: *Act as if ye have faith, and faith shall be given to ye!!!* Those three exclamation points irked me more than the other mistake.

By the time we had climbed the second set of stairs, I'd had enough: I wanted to flee the house immediately after getting the coin.

Luke and I entered Dad's old office. Dad had had ten framed sets of coins on the walls. Now there were only five. I'd bet that Imogen had sold them or given them to Chas.

My heart started to sink.

If she had found and sold the Seated Liberty dime, I felt like I'd collapse on the floor and cry. For years, Dad had the coin alone in a frame on the wall. When he'd begun to get unsteady, he accidentally knocked it off the wall and broke the frame. We put the coin in the lockbox, promising to reframe it later, and never got around to it. The lockbox was a heavy metal case that would pose no serious challenge to a seasoned thief. But it gave Dad and me some confidence that we could secure things of value, and it was well hidden, pushed far underneath his desk. You'd need to be searching to find it.

The lockbox was still there. I pulled it out.

I put the key into the lock, turned it, and opened the lid. Inside were a stack of old receipts. A few rolls of quarters. Some silver certificates barely worth the denomination.

I moved them all aside.

Underneath them, the Seated Liberty dime.

I picked it up. Examined the coin through the small, round plastic container, which was about three times the size of the dime.

"Yeah, baby," Luke breathed. "That's it, right?"

"Yes."

We stared in silence. Then I whispered, "Let's go."

"What else is worth taking?" Luke motioned to the frames on the wall.

"They're worth maybe a hundred each."

"Let's get 'em."

"You said to take only the dime."

"Yeah, but—"

"No. We can't carry those across town. Someone will see."

He opened his mouth to argue. Then stopped.

Downstairs: a squeaking noise.

We went silent.

I think both Luke and I tried to convince ourselves that we hadn't heard what we'd heard, which was the unlocking and opening of the front door.

But then the front door thumped shut, and it was certain.

Someone was now in the house with us.

CARLA

BILLY AND I pulled out of the restaurant parking lot and onto Conover Road. It was impossible to get used to the smell that was coming from the trunk. Each new inhale made my stomach churn. I wanted Billy to drive faster, to bring more air through the open windows, but the risk was too great. Slow and steady had to be our strategy wherever we drove.

"We need to get to the river," I said.

"We're not putting her in the wuh-water, are—"

"No. Close to there, though."

"Then the fuh-fastest way is through town."

"Let's take the second fastest way."

"Route 211?"

"Yeah," I said. "Take it. And please, go easy. When you're nervous, you tend to drive too fast. Do the speed limit."

Route 211 would circle us around Locksburg. Then we could get on Tharp Road and take it toward the Susquehanna to finish what we started.

I put my head back, closed my eyes, and felt the air rush over me. It was a sensation I hadn't experienced in years—I'm so rarely a passenger in a car—and a feeling that, as we moved across the secondary roads and closer to wooded land, brought me back to my teenage years. Kids who grew up in cities had the avenues and the clubs. Those who lived by the ocean had the beaches and the waves.

When you lived in a place like Locksburg, you had the forests and the hills.

When my friends and I were teenagers, we cruised the back roads for hours, tuning in any classic rock station that we could find on the radio and singing over the static. We'd sometimes stop to wade into icy-cold streams or to park and hike into the woods. There are still times, when the weather and the daylight and the music all collide just right, when I can recapture a wisp of those emotions. The nostalgia can almost break my heart.

Back then we could drive for twenty minutes without seeing another car. Some of the other kids loved the remoteness and longed to be away from people. But the empty roads made me melancholy: They meant that no one wanted to come to this part of the world. They meant that anything important was happening elsewhere, far from where we lived.

Eventually we'd tire of wasting gas and we would park up at Carson's Outcrop or by Laurel Lake. There we'd pretend to enjoy the warm beer or Boone's Farm wine that we forced ourselves to swallow, then turned away while we shuddered at the taste.

On one of those Friday nights near the end of my senior year, a random party formed at the Outcrop. Someone started a bonfire. About twenty of my classmates stood around drinking cheap alcohol that their older siblings or friends bought on our behalf after we begged them enough to break the law. More than a few of us were already devising excuses to tell our parents, who'd later ask where we had been, and if we'd been drinking, and why our clothes smelled of smoke.

The boys were in an argument that was growing from low mumbles to heated comments. Brian Brick had said something about how he'd never once been to a city.

"Drive to fuckin' New York, then, man, and quit your bitchin'," one of the guys said.

"I wasn't bitchin'; I was only sayin' that we should all go."

Someone asked him if he was afraid of the gays or the Blacks there and said that maybe he liked them both, and a bunch of the guys snickered. That turned into a cacophony of razzing and arguing and swearing before Brian said that he should drive there tonight if only to shut them up.

The girls had long dismissed Brian as an also-ran to the other guys. He seemed to always have his head somewhere else, and his clumsiness made him the butt of derision and teasing and the target of legs that stretched out to trip him. He was tolerated only because he had a car and knew enough to help the other guys fix theirs on the cheap. I never minded him much, and there at the Outcrop I found his stand heroic. I'd seen too many movies about the misunderstood boy and the damn-everyone-else girl who had the guts to take his side.

"I told you he has no balls," one of the guys declared. Someone chucked a beer can near Brian's feet.

Freakin' men, I thought, with their out-of-nowhere aggression and their inane wagers and their meaningless pride. There was nothing so stupid that they wouldn't attempt, nothing so tender that they couldn't ruin. I understood so little about them. And I didn't think they understood themselves, or cared to. In some ways that was worse.

As they jeered Brian, he sipped his can of Old Milwaukee and stared into the fire, probably hoping they'd stop. When they didn't, he said: "Screw you guys, all right?"

"You brought it up, asshole."

"So now I'm dropping it."

"Because you're a pussy."

"Oh, am I?" he challenged. "Put up or shut up."

"I will."

"How much?" he said.

"Twenty bucks."

"That won't pay for gas."

"It's not about the money. You said you were going to do it. So do it, fuckface."

"I'll bet twenty too," someone else said. "You'll never go."

"I didn't say I'd do it alone. I said a group of us should go together."

"It's after nine o'clock. You wouldn't get there until, like, two a.m. even if you left right now. Stupid."

"OK, you're right," Brian said.

"There he goes, chickening out."

Brian regarded the girls, though none said anything. As much as they sometimes disagreed with the guys, they'd never take a stand against them and risk their wrath.

"I'd go," I said.

The talk around the fire stopped. That got me self-conscious, so I said: "We should all go. I've never been to New York before. It could be epic." I thought it romantic, saying that aloud. Or maybe I thought it was what a romantic would say, which was what I wanted to be.

I should have expected the next comment from some wiseass: "There you go, Brian! Forty bucks and a hand job from Carla!"

"Patty's coming too," I said, and nodded to my only real friend there. That was news to her. Then I looked over at the group. "Come on. Let's go. Everybody."

The guys quieted, either because of my challenge or because they thought I was strange. My mother and I had moved into Locksburg from Ashland a few years earlier and I was still considered the new girl, with a bit of mystery remaining around me.

I turned to Brian and raised my eyebrows.

"Let's go," he said, almost a question.

I grabbed Patty by the hand and pulled. The three of us walked toward Brian's Chevy Nova.

For some weird reason I expected cheers from those we were leaving behind. Or maybe I thought they'd follow us. All we got was silence. Bunch of losers.

"Are we really going to do this?" Patty asked.

Some guy in the crowd must have thought the same. He yelled: "You have to take a picture! Three of you in the city!"

We piled into the rusted Nova and slowly moved down the switchbacks of the hills.

"You OK to drive?" I asked Brian.

"Yeah. I barely had one beer."

"Are you really going to do this?"

"Why not? What else have I got to do? I'll drop you at home if you want."

"I don't want. Patty, we'll take you home, though. I didn't mean to drag you into this. Sorry."

"No. If you're going, I'm going."

We wondered aloud if we would actually make the trip and speculated how long it would take. Then, twenty-five minutes into the ride, Brian took an on-ramp to the interstate and we realized we were no longer debating but actually setting out on the journey. I unfolded Brian's paper map across our laps—the three of us were squeezed into the front bench seat—and Brian clicked on the dome light. At a rest stop we got bottles of Pepsi from a vending machine. Then we returned to the car, where Patty took the back seat and Brian drove on.

The further we went, the more our energy increased. We talked nonstop, cutting each other off, telling secrets, relating old stories. An hour later we moved out of small-town Pennsylvania and into more populated areas. Two hours beyond that and we were driving past suburbs that had double the number of people in a quarter mile than we had in our entire county.

Then, some four hours after setting out, we sped by a green sign: NEW YORK CITY, 31 MILES. My god, how I remember seeing the glow in the dark distance: an immense, otherworldly dome of light. It was both frightening and exhilarating.

A short while later we caught our first glimpse of Manhattan and its skyscrapers.

"There," I said, breathless. Brian's mouth fell open. Patty leaned forward from the back seat. We three small-town rubes, approaching a new universe.

"It's so . . . big," Brian said. He hadn't taken his eyes from it.

"It's like life," Patty said, and somehow that made sense.

The city rose up as we rushed toward it. We became quiet and solemn. Reverent, almost. And scared shitless. Then we entered the Lincoln Tunnel, nearly blinded by its white fluorescent lights. Minutes later, we surfaced in Manhattan.

Brian said, "I don't know where to go."

At a stoplight, I wheeled down the window and called out to an old man walking a dog: "Excuse me sir. I'm sorry. We've never—"

"Where are you going?" he said.

"Times Square?"

"You asking or telling?"

"Uh, asking. Or telling. I'm not sure."

He huffed in impatience and pointed. "Up there, left on Tenth Avenue, then to Forty-Second."

We drove off. Patty said: "He's walking his dog at two o'clock in the morning."

"I guess people do that here," Brian said. "Isn't it great?"

Everything about the place was so foreign that I remember being pleasantly surprised that I could read the street signs. I almost expected them to be in another language.

Minutes later, we were overwhelmed by the blinking bulbs and the giant crowds and the ceaseless noise as we drove right through Times Square, a place brighter at night than Locksburg had ever been on any day.

"I can't be sure this isn't a dream," Patty said. "It feels totally unreal. In a really good way."

Brian kept his hands gripped on the steering wheel. Eight blocks away we stopped for a car that was pulling out of a spot. "Go in there!" I told Brian, and we parked.

Every instant was now alive, filled either with delight or anxiety or confusion or a mixture of all those and more. If I were envious of those who lived in such a thrilling place, I knew that, for this moment, I had at least one thing they didn't: I now had the experience of seeing this city for the first time.

We got out of the car, and even the asphalt felt different under my sneakers. We walked up the street, close together, and memorized the cross streets where we had parked. Then we watched a guy playing drums on a bucket. Then stared up at the buildings, which were so high that we became dizzy. Throughout the night I imagined how we must look from above, as if I were both living my life and watching it, a participant and a spectator.

We spent two hours walking the city. It was the closest thing to real magic that I had ever felt. My stomach leapt again and again. First, we waded into the wild river that was Times Square, amazed that so many people could be there, and rafted along with them. Then, at about four a.m., we found ourselves on some nearly deserted blocks by the East River. I bought a disposable camera at a tiny convenience store and asked a passing group of club girls to take our picture with the Empire State Building behind us. Then we moved on.

Patty said, "Do you think, if you lived here, you'd get tired of it someday?"

Brian said, "Maybe. But it would probably take a long, long time."

We walked back to the car, relieved that it was still there and impressed with ourselves for finding it. I took a picture of Brian sitting on his hood, the city street visible behind him. Before we could get in the car, Patty said, "Come here." And on the sidewalk the three of us hugged. She said: "We are so awesome. We are."

We went quiet for much of the ride home, shell-shocked that something like this could exist in the same world as the one we lived in. We stopped for take-out coffee just as sunlight arrived to make what we'd done feel more unreal.

We booed when seeing the sign that read: LOCKSBURG, 24 MILES. Within an hour, the three of us were home, lying to our parents about where we'd been—I think each of us said we'd fallen asleep at the other's house—and crawling into bed to sleep until another night came around.

These days Patty manages the deli counter at Weis Supermarket. I see her there at least once a month and we'll sometimes rehash old times or share local chatter. Every so often she'll host a Tupperware party or a Tastefully Simple demonstration and I'll go to drink white wine and laugh with her other friends and buy a few things that I don't need. Then, later in the night, I'll seek out the photograph that she keeps framed on a wall in the dining room: the three of us as teenagers, by the Empire State Building. If Patty and I find ourselves alone and drunk enough, we'll raise a glass toward the picture and drink to Brian and wonder aloud where he is now.

At the end of that summer, Brian was preparing to attend Millersville University, a state college where he had planned to study education and follow his father into middle school teaching. A week before Brian was to leave, he stopped at my house and knocked on the front door.

"Hiya, Brian. What's up?"

"Hey. You wanna take a ride?" he said.

Except for our only adventure, we'd never been close, so the request surprised me. Yet I went, and ten minutes later we were making our way into the hills, windows open to catch the cool forest air.

"So did you get your roommate at Millersville?" I asked as we drove.

"I'm not going to Millersville."

"Why not?"

"I gotta . . . I mean . . . I'm going to New York instead. Remember how it felt there?"

"Whoa, whoa, whoa, Brian. That was a fun time, yeah. But you can't give up college."

"I can go to college in New York."

"Did you apply?"

"No. But I found this guy there who needs a roommate. I can get a job, and work, and take classes. There's a lot of colleges there. I can—"

"What are your parents going to say?"

"I don't care what they say. It's my life."

I tried to talk him out of it. Our conversation only went in circles. He had already made his decision and wouldn't be swayed.

When we were high up in the hills, he pulled over at a lookout. We went to sit on the hood and there he said: "Why don't you come with me?"

"You can't be serious."

"I don't mean, like, boyfriend and girlfriend. I mean . . . together. We can share the bedroom. I'll sleep on the floor."

My gosh, the stupidity of youth, when we think everything is possible except growing old. Yet I don't say that only about Brian. For a moment I seriously considered the offer. Recalling New York made my stomach flutter, and I imagined going there with him.

"I . . . I can't right now. My mom . . . she's not in good health. She needs me. But . . . are you serious? Are you really doing this?"

"I already sent a letter to Millersville canceling my acceptance. I did that so I wouldn't turn back."

"You're so . . . brave," I said. "I don't think I've called anyone that in my life."

"Promise me you'll be brave too. If you can't leave now, promise that you'll get out of Locksburg someday."

"I promise," I said. I meant the words then, just as I am ashamed of them now. "I'll be out of here soon. You'll see."

We drove off in silence. After a while he said, "The only thing I'm going to miss is these hills."

I made him promise to write, which he did, twice. Both letters were full of exclamation points and wild stories about things I didn't really understand, like the 6 Train and the *Village Voice* and a play he went to at a fourth-floor walk-up theater with a work friend who was also an actress. After the second letter, I'm not sure which of us stopped writing: Either he did because he was too busy, or I did because I was embarrassed that my letters contained nothing outside of town gossip and lame news. In that way, he made me see myself.

Brian ended that second letter with "If you want to come, the offer is still open," though I could sense that he didn't mean it as much as he once did. He was finding his own way now. He didn't need me.

Brian never returned to Locksburg—at least, not that I know of. And in the summers, like now, when the breeze coming off the woods feels humid and peaty and thick, I stare into the hills and think of him and hope that he has never tired of the city.

The steering wheel on Billy's car started to vibrate. That brought me back into the present.

"What's the matter?" I asked when I opened my eyes.

"I duh-don't know."

"Feels like the tire."

Up ahead was Orky's, a roadhouse biker bar that was legendary in Locksburg for hosting a stabbing or bar-clearing brawl at least once a month. I don't know how true those rumors were, but they were enough to keep all but the roughest townies away. The parking lot closest to the front door was filled. Four or five spots next to the road were empty, with no one hanging around. We could park there for a minute to check the car.

"Pull into that lot," I said.

"Are you crazy?"

"You can either pull in there or we can break down on the road. Your choice."

Billy drove into the cindered lot and took one of the open spaces. We both got out and walked around the back to find that the rear driver's-side tire was low on air. Billy took off his hat, wiped his brow, then placed his hat on the trunk as he got on his knees to give the tire a closer examination.

"There muh-may be a nail in there or something. I cuh-can't really see."

"How bad is it?"

"I don't know. I think we cuh-can ride on it for a while. Maybe t-ten miles."

"We'll have to," I said. "Let's go. Fast."

We got in the car just as three motorcycles rumbled down Route 211 and pulled into the lot. Billy put the car in reverse, noticed that he'd left his hat on the trunk, then stopped. He opened his door to go get the hat as a motorcycle pulled in next to him. His door connected with the handlebars. The rider wobbled and the bike pitched over on its side. The guy barely missed having it fall onto his leg.

Billy cried out. I did too, concerned for the rider. The guy, though, was all fight. He bolted over to Billy's open window.

"Da fuck, man?"

"You pulled . . . you . . . I didn't . . ." Billy was stuttering and babbling and apologizing, and the guy was having none of it. He continued screaming as he lifted the bike back to a standing position and examined it.

"See that? Scraped the paint off! This bike has never been dumped before! Never! Open your door, jackass!"

"We're sorry," I said. "You pulled in fast—"

"Gimme your insurance card," he said.

I opened the glove compartment and dug through some papers. Nothing.

"Where is it, Billy?"

"I don't know. I have another card in my wuh-wallet. But that's . . ."

I already knew where his wallet was: at home, where we had left all our personal items so that we wouldn't accidentally drop them when we disposed of Doreen's body.

169

"Listen," I said to the guy. "We have insurance. But the card's at home."

"Oh, sure. I'll believe that one."

Two other bikers walked over, dressed the same: denim jackets, jeans.

"What happened?" one guy asked.

The first guy said: "This idiot opened the door right as I was pulling in."

The third guy said: "Call the cops, man. You're in the right. The guy who opens the door is always at fault. That's the law."

"Please," I said. "We'll pay for everything."

"Damn right you will."

"Call the cops," the third guy repeated.

I said: "We need to go."

"Don't let 'em leave, Zig. Once they pull out of this lot, you've got no proof. Their word against yours. Then you're screwed."

"That's five hundred in damages at least," the guy named Zig said. "What do you have on you?"

"I duh-don't have any money with me," Billy said.

"That's too bad," Zig said. "You ain't goin' nowhere unless you pay for the damages to that bike."

"We have to leave," I said, sounding more desperate than I'd wanted. "Now."

Then, cat quick, Zig reached inside and pulled the key from the ignition.

"This car ain't going anywhere," he said as he shoved the key in his pocket.

REED

DAN REGAINED HIS BALANCE after nearly falling when the younger Black man pushed him.

The younger man went to one knee and helped the older man up. Dan took a step back. When the two of them got to their feet, Dan barked, "Both of you, hands on the car!"

Neither followed Dan's order. The younger man put his arm around the older man and said: "You OK, Dad?"

"My wrist hurts," the older man said.

"We'll get you fixed up."

"You need to follow my orders!" Dan said.

The two men turned to walk away. When Dan saw that, he reached over and pulled the younger man's hand off the older man's shoulder. The younger man spun around, pointed a finger at Dan's face, and growled: "Go ahead. Touch me again."

"Or what?" Dan said.

"You'll be pickin' up your teeth with broken fingers."

They stared at each other.

"I've seen you before in town!" the woman said. "Always staring at people. You're the one who's a troublemaker!"

I was sitting in the back seat of the police car, the window open, ten feet from where this was happening. I felt like I should say something but I did not know what to say and I did not think anyone would hear me anyway because all of a sudden there was a lot of loud talking and accusing.

"Sir," Dan said, "you need to stop interfering and let me do my job."

"What's your job? Harassing an old man?"

"I was concerned with his well-being, then you came out and pushed me. That's assault. So now you need to put your hands on the police car."

"Don't do it, Freddy!" the woman called out.

"Ma'am, you should keep quiet," Dan said.

"Shut up!" she said. "You came onto our land and pushed around my father-in-law and—"

"Come on, Dad," the man said. Again he put his arm around his father. "We're going inside."

Dan looked at me. I did not want him to do that. He was already angry that someone was questioning his authority and not listening to him, and then he saw that someone else—me—was watching this happen. That made him more adamant, I think, as if he had to prove himself. At one time I liked the word "adamant" but not now. I also did not like the word "inevitable," but when you take a bad person like Dan and give him a lot of power, that is what situations like this become.

Dan pushed the man's hand off the other man's shoulder. He tried to turn the younger man's arm behind his back but the younger man twisted free.

All at once a lot of things happened at the same time.

The woman yelled things at Dan, like "Get the hell out of here!" and "You piece of shit!" as the younger man spun around to face Dan and said, "Motherfucker!" as his hand turned into a fist that he pulled back as if he were going to punch Dan while the older man said, "What the hell's he doin'?" and he too turned around and stepped toward Dan, then Dan took a step back and yelled: "Stop moving! Both of you! Stop moving now!"

And they did not stop moving.

And then Dan put his hand down to his side.

And Dan pulled his gun from his holster.

He aimed it at the younger man's chest.

Up until then Dan sounded different than he normally did. He was using a police-speak that maybe he thought made him sound more professional like the police on TV who are not real police but actors who play police. Yet once Dan's gun was in his hands, he started to talk as he normally did, and I did not like that at all.

"Go ahead, fucker!" Dan said, and moved the gun to point it at the younger man's face. Then he fast pointed it at the older man's face and said: "You too! Go ahead!"

He moved the gun back and forth between the two of them.

The woman screamed a whole bunch of words that ran together. Dan said to her: "Shut up, bitch!"

"Who the hell—" the younger man said. His mouth opened a little and the lines on his forehead grew deeper in the kind of expression you make when you cannot believe that something is happening even though it really is happening.

"Hands on the car, I said!" Dan screamed. His hand holding the gun shook a little.

Except for Dan's shaking hands, no one was moving, and in some way that was scarier than if there was a full-fledged fight in progress. Everything was focused on the gun, and that was treacherous, and that is rarely if ever a good word.

Then I had an idea: I would go and stand between the man and Dan. If I did that, Dan would not shoot him.

So I reached out of the window and opened the car door handle from outside. Then I got out.

In all that was happening, Dan must have forgotten that I was there. When I opened the door, he turned his head to look at me. When he did, the younger man lunged forward. He swung his hand hard and punched the gun. The gun flew out of Dan's hand.

It sailed through the air.

And it landed at my feet.

They all turned to look at me.

I was not sure what to do.

But I knew that everyone there was angry and I did not think anyone there should have it.

So I bent down and picked up the gun.

LIZ

LUKE AND I FROZE when we heard the front door of the house shut.

Then Luke reached over my shoulder and snatched the Seated Liberty dime from my hand. He popped it into his mouth.

I spun around just in time to watch his Adam's apple slide. Then he forced the coin down. He'd swallowed the dime, protective hard-plastic cover and all.

"What the hell . . . ?"

Luke silently gulped to make sure it wasn't coming back up, then whispered into my ear: "That way, if we get caught, they can't find it on us."

In some way there was logic in that move. But I didn't want to think of the bedpan that would have to be used tomorrow to get the coin back. Not with all the greasy meat and deep-fried food that Luke ate these days.

"Hello?" a woman's voice called up the stairs. "Is anyone here?"

We stayed still. Whoever was down there started to sing. And god help me, it was "Baby, We Won!"

"*Follow your dreeeeeeams!*" the woman warbled. "*Things aren't as bad as they seeemmmm!*"

If rolling my eyes could make a sound, we'd have been discovered in seconds.

At first the singing was clear. Then the sound became muffled. Whoever was down there was first in the parlor, then had moved to the dining room. Then she must have walked into the kitchen.

"Who is it?" Luke whispered.

"I don't know," I said. "It's not Imogen. That wasn't her voice."

Luke went to my father's desk and picked up the heavy metal trophy that my dad had won years ago on the highway department's bowling team. Luke turned it upside down so that the marble base was at the top. He held it like a hammer and whacked the marble against his open palm, testing its weight.

"No!" I whisper-shouted between my teeth. "Put that down!"

Luke flashed an expression I'd never seen on his face before. It was part malice, part hate. He growled: "Shut the fuck up, Liz."

"What are you doing with that?"

"I'm on parole. I ain't going back to jail."

I reached for the trophy to pull it out of his hand. Luke held it high above his head.

"Don't fuck with me," he said. "Or I'll brain you too."

"What do you mean, 'too'? Luke, if you hurt anyone, I'll . . . I'll scream."

"Go ahead and scream," he said, "and I'll bust your head wide open."

It's been said that you don't really know a man until you see him under pressure. Well, we were under pressure, and I saw a side of Luke he'd never shown to me before. Up until then I had judged him as a minor-league loser, mostly harmless. Now, though, we were cornered, and he was as panicked and as shifty as a rat.

The singing grew louder. Whoever was downstairs was now coming up the first staircase.

"The first time I saw yooooooou! That was when I kneeeeeewwww!"

Christ, she almost deserved to be beaten for singing that shitty song.

There was no lock on the office door. She'd be able to come right in and find us. Luke positioned himself to the side of the door, hand raised high, ready to batter whoever entered.

I peered around my father's old office for someplace for us to hide or maybe something to hit Luke with and stop him from what he might do.

But I found something better.

On the floor, underneath the window, was a large wooden box. "Oh please oh please oh please," I repeated as I went over and threw open the lid. Inside, a rope ladder. I exhaled in humongous relief that it was there.

In a fire, large houses in Locksburg were death traps no matter how quickly rescuers could arrive. Most of these wooden homes were built decades before any real safety features, and the wind coming off the hills could stoke a spark into an inferno in minutes. My father was a stickler for safety. Our second- and third-floor rooms all had fire ladders.

Luke was standing by the door. Judging by the sound of the singing, whoever was on the second floor was in the front room.

"We are in loooove! Flying higher than a doooove!"

"Come over here!" I whispered.

"What's that?"

"Escape ladder!"

I eased open the window and slid it as high as it would go. Then I motioned to Luke to grab the other side of the rolled-up rope ladder. We lifted it from the box and heaved it out of the window. I looked down. Two feet of ladder lay on the ground. Its path avoided the second-floor window, which was placed farther right. No one would see us from inside the house when we descended.

The top of the ladder was bolted into the floor. I pulled and found it secure. Then I stood and put a hand on the windowsill. This would be tricky, especially in a hurry. I took an extra second to consider how to safely move out of the window. In that instant, though, Luke shoved me aside and threw a leg over the sill. So much for ladies first.

"What the hell, Luke?"

"Let me go down before you. I've got the coin, right? I'll, uh, go knock on the front door and get her to answer. That way you can take your time."

It was as clear as crystal: Luke was lying. Hell, he was barely trying to cover it up. He was going to get down that ladder and run off, leaving me behind. Then, as he always swore he'd do, he'd leave Locksburg. Somewhere in the next day or two, he'd shit out the Liberty dime, sell it for four grand, and start his miserable life over in a less miserable place. In the meantime, I'd be mired in this town where, even if I did get out of the house and avoid arrest for breaking and entering, I'd still be the one stuck deep in debt to Kap.

"Wait, Luke!" I whispered.

He didn't even consider me.

Luke straddled the windowsill, one leg in, one leg out. He found a rung with the foot that was outside and stepped onto it.

"No!" I said to this prick who was about to take off with my father's coin. But there was nothing I could do and he knew it. He grinned.

The singing grew louder. She moved into the refrain the way a steak knife saws through gristle.

"Our hearts beat as oooonnnnne! This love has only just beguuuunn!"

Whoever was out there was now on the stairs to the third floor.

Luke grabbed hold of the sill and swung his other leg out of the window.

In Luke's defense, he was understandably panicked, not only from the fact that we were committing a crime and were seconds away from being caught, but also because he had just looked out of the window and realized how high up three stories actually was. On top of that, neither of us had taken Fire Safety: Advanced Ladder Techniques anytime recently. So I didn't laugh when I saw the worried expression on Luke's face as he shimmied his body out of the window.

Nor did I snicker when I saw him appear so unsteady on the rope ladder. As a matter of fact, I reached for his hand when I understood that he was in danger of falling.

But any help I could offer was too late. All of Luke's weight had already shifted, and that made the rope ladder more unstable. When Luke started to fall, there was still a chance he might be OK. That chance was lost when he tilted backward and his foot tangled. Luke's foot held on just long enough for it to turn his body around and have him pitch over headfirst, arms flailing.

And headfirst is how Luke landed on the concrete patio, forty feet down.

CARLA

"YEAH MAN, that's the way it's done!" one of the bikers cheered when Zig snatched our car key. Zig now wore a self-satisfied expression that masked only half of the anger he had shown since his motor-cycle connected with our car door.

"I'm telling you, call the cops," the other biker said.

Zig said: "I'm not getting them involved unless I have to." He peered into our car and said: "Now, if you want your keys, you gotta pay for the damage you done." He sniffed and said, "And I ain't taking your car unless I have to. This thing stinks."

I said: "I told you, we don't have anything."

"Then you better call somebody to bring you something."

I almost considered that until I realized I didn't have a cell phone either.

"Luh-look," Billy said. "I wuh-will give you our address and ph-phone number."

"What if you give me a fake one? You could write anything down."

"I guh-give you my word."

"Remember, Zig," one of his friends said. "Once they leave this lot, you're screwed."

"You fucked up the best bike I ever had," Zig said to Billy.

"And I'm s-s-sorry. I know wuh-we . . ."

Billy's ability to speak coherently was nearing its end. I recognized his limits. During his worst bouts of frustration, he wasn't able to force out a single word, and he was close to that point now. The night already had both of us more stressed than we'd ever been, from digging up a decomposed body, to being surprised by the police, and now to this.

One of the bikers snickered.

"Luh-listen . . ." Billy said.

"We're lul-lul-listening!" one of them said. "Ya stutterin' prick!"

The other biker laughed. "That's from a movie!" he said.

"What is?"

"'Ya stutterin' prick!' Who said that? Remember the movie?"

I saw the expression on Billy's face change. He tried to right himself, to get back on track, and couldn't. Then Billy pushed open the car door. I grabbed at him but he was too quick.

"Uh-oh! He's mad now!" one of the bikers laughed. If we were in a different situation, there might have been some humor in seeing all five foot eight, 140 pounds of Billy standing up to three guys who each had over a hundred pounds and six inches in height on him.

Billy closed the car door. One of the guys hooted.

With a surprising calm, Billy reached for the pocket where Zig had put the car key.

"He's going for your cock, man! Watch out!" one of Zig's friends said.

Zig stepped back. Billy went for the key a second time.

"If you touch me again, I'm gonna tune you up. And my word is my bond, little man," Zig warned.

I got out of the car. But by the time I circled it, Billy had again reached for Zig's pocket. Zig had an *Oh well* expression when he threw a meaty, open-handed smack that was horrible to hear when it connected with Billy's face. Billy staggered against the car. No one was laughing anymore.

In some way, I hoped, things would now be calmer. Billy would stop what he was doing, maybe get back in the car. And Zig would have a little satisfaction from hitting him, maybe draining some of his anger.

What a damn fool I was.

Instead of calming, Billy surged past his breaking point. He launched himself at Zig. He left his feet when diving for him. As he did, his hands went for Zig's throat. Zig rocked back when Billy's full weight slammed into him. Billy had both hands around Zig's neck when Zig roundhoused a right into the side of Billy's face. It had no effect. Billy kept holding on. I screamed. Both of the other bikers rushed forward and tore Billy off their friend. They threw him to the ground. Enraged, Billy raced to get to his feet. Then Zig kicked his stomach with a steel-tipped boot. That took the wind from Billy's lungs. He collapsed.

No one seemed to know what to do. And I realized this could go either way: These three guys could walk away now—there was real wariness in their eyes, after seeing Billy's rage—or they could kick him some more. In that case he would be battered in seconds.

"No fightin' in the parking lot!" someone yelled. "Take that shit somewhere else!"

All heads turned to see a woman with an apron standing in the bar's doorway.

"I'm calling the cops!" she said, and disappeared as fast as she had emerged.

The three guys looked at each other as if debating a next move.

I couldn't take any chances—not that they might go back to beating Billy, and not that the police might show up at any minute.

"Here!" I said, and reached behind my neck. My bandaged hand ached. But the thumb was good enough that, with it and my other hand, I could unhook the latch of my necklace. Then I held it out like some trembling, madcap jeweler.

"This chain is gold. And that diamond . . . it was my mother's engagement ring. A half carat. It's worth eight hundred dollars at least."

I stepped forward. Held it out. Zig raised a hand and I carefully laid it in his palm.

"No!" Billy said in a pained voice. He rolled to his side, attempted to get up. "Don't, Mom."

"It's OK, Billy," I said. It was far from OK, of course. But this needed to end now.

Zig took a long look, then put the pendant and chain into the chest pocket of his denim jacket.

"C'mon," Zig said to the other two. "Let's roll."

He dug into his jeans pocket and took out our car keys. In a final insult, he tossed them on the ground next to Billy.

The three men moved to their bikes, kick-started them, and roared away as I helped Billy to his feet as best I could with one hand.

"Can you drive?" I asked. He didn't answer, only took the keys and got in.

We pulled out of the lot and rode down Route 211 in silence. I glanced over once to see dust and sweat and snot on Billy's reddened face. He was good at hiding any pain, though. I reached over to brush something from his shirt. He shrugged off my touch.

"You gave him your mom's diamond."

"Yes."

"Why?"

"There was no other way. We needed to get out of there."

"It's because of me. All of this is b-because of me."

I didn't know how to respond. If Billy had problems getting words out, I had problems using them. The older I've gotten, the more I say only what needs to be said, if I can help it. I sometimes fool myself into thinking my terseness is a product of my work. After all, it's tough to hold an in-depth conversation when you're working the dinner rush, juggling five tables, and have a party of twelve come in unannounced, all with questions about how a dish is prepared and three of them asking for special orders and two of their noisy brats complaining about the temperature or the seating. That aside, I have an innate fear of saying the wrong thing, and that's usually enough to keep me quiet. But then a tear rolled down Billy's cheek, leaving a line behind in the dirt there, and I knew I had to say something.

I said: "Billy. We've never been one of those TV families. We don't tell each other every feeling or sit down for dinner every night. Your father . . . well, I try not to bad-mouth him, but he was a . . . disappointment. He wasn't the person I first thought he was. But you've never disappointed me. I knew you were a winner from the moment the nurse put you in my arms. That pendant? That thing means nothing, zero, compared to you. I've been telling myself the restaurant would be my big redemption. But I'm already redeemed. I've got you."

After a bit he said, "Thank you."

"I mean it. I know we don't say it a lot, but you're my son, and I love you more than anything. More than everything I've ever had combined."

"I love you too, Mom."

We drove for a mile, then he said: "Are we going to be able to do this tonight?"

"I don't think we have a choice."

"So where are we taking her?"

"Turn up here, onto Tharp Road. It's only a couple miles. Let's get this thing over with."

REED

EVERYONE STOPPED SCREAMING. The quiet came so fast and was so complete that it surprised me. All of a sudden I could hear birds chirping; one was a red-breasted nuthatch. I went to summer explorers camp and we studied songbirds, and when I did a presentation on that bird, the other kids giggled. Later, Greg told me that nuthatch was sort of like a word for testicles and that was why everyone was laughing. Or it could mean that someone is a weirdo or a jerk. It is a funny word and I . . .

"Reed, put that gun down," Dan said, breaking the silence and snapping me out of that memory of the nuthatch.

I had held a gun one time before, when Greg worked a summer at the firing range at the Locksburg Gun Club. He taught me how to be safe and how to load a pistol and how to remove the clip. I took a single shot at a target, then put the gun down and never tried again. Greg got angry that he had spent so much time teaching me and I did not like the gun or shooting it. Dan's gun fit right in my hand and was heavier than I expected and I did not like it either.

Dan took a step in my direction.

I said, "Do not come near me, Dan." And he stopped coming near me.

Dan is a nuthatch.

I did not mean to think that, but it made me giggle too.

Dan said, "You have to give me that gun, Reed."

Dan looked at me as if I would do something with the gun. He looked at me as if I would do something with the gun because he was the kind of person who would do something with the gun. He was engaged in a process called projecting. I usually like that word, "projecting."

He stepped forward again as if he were tiptoeing. I said, "Stop," and he did. He listened to me because I had the gun.

"Don't give him that gun," the woman said.

"Right," the younger man said.

"Mm-hmm," the older man agreed.

"See?" Dan said. "They want the gun. They want to hurt me with it."

I did not think they wanted to hurt Dan with it, but I did know that no one should have the gun, not even me. I thought that it would be best to throw it into the woods, but then Dan would go and get it. Then I thought maybe I could run away but I cannot run very fast and Dan would catch me. What I wished was that there was another policeman here like Chief Kriner, who I do not believe thought highly of Dan and who was, people said, pretty straightforward, not like Dan, who was the opposite of straightforward, whatever that word would be. I do not know what word that would be but I bet it is an interesting word.

"I'd be fine with y'all just, you know, getting the fuck out of here," the younger man said.

"Then we are getting the fuck out of here," I said.

I got in the back seat of the police car and slid to the middle so Dan could not reach in and grab me.

"What are you doing, Reed?" he said.

"Take me to the police station."

"Give me the gun first."

"I will give you the gun when you take me to the police station."

"You can't walk into the station carrying a gun."

"I will give it back to you in the parking lot."

"If you don't return my weapon, that's a felony."

"I do not care."

"I'd go, jerk," the old man said.

Dan raised his middle finger at them. "I'm not done with you," he said. Then he got into the driver's seat and we drove away.

"OK, we're out of there. Now give me back the gun," Dan said when we got back on the road.

"You can have it in the parking lot."

He went quiet as if he were thinking, and as if thinking was not something he was so good at. Then he nodded to himself and said to me: "In high school, they said you never told a lie. Is that true?"

"Mom made me promise never to lie," I said.

"All right, then. You give me that gun in the parking lot. And you never, ever tell anyone about what happened. You promise?"

If that would get me to the police station and keep Dan from going back right now to that house while he was still mad, I think that was a fair deal.

"I promise," I said.

"You'll never say anything about what happened back there, right?"

"I promise," I said.

"So if the chief—"

"Dan, I would appreciate it if you would stop talking. It makes me nervous." I could feel my hand getting sweaty on the gun and did not want to have it slip.

"All right Reed, I'll stop talking. But you need to—"

"Shut up, Dan," I said. And he finally did, after an excruciatingly long time. It was not really excruciating but I like that word and do not get much of a chance to use it.

A few minutes later we pulled into the police station parking lot.

Greg's car was there.

"Now give me the gun, Reed," Dan said.

I opened the door. Dan opened his and fast-walked over to me. When I got out I handed him the gun. He immediately shoved it into his holster, then spun around to see if anyone had seen us. But no one did; the lot was small and the police station was smaller than the lot. There was a door and two windows and no one was looking outside.

"Now get out of here and remember your promise."

"That car is Greg's. My brother."

"What's he here for? All right, go in."

We went inside the station. There was room for four desks, and even those barely fit in the space. Behind one of the desks was Chief Kriner. In front of the desk was Greg and Little Jimmy.

Chief Kriner had been on the phone. He put it down.

"Well, there he is. Told ya we'd find him," Chief Kriner said, and laughed. Then Chief Kriner looked at Dan and stopped laughing. He gave him the kind of expression that Mom used to give me that said, *You know you are in trouble.*

Little Jimmy stood up and ran over and hugged me and that made me smile.

"Look!" Little Jimmy said, and showed me a pair of handcuffs.

"The little rascal stole them from me when I wasn't watching," Kriner said. He was saying something else but I was looking at Greg, who was staring at me with anger.

"Where were you, Reed?" Greg said.

"I was out walking and—"

"And I found him!" Dan chimed in. "He was lost, so I picked him up and brought him here. Ain't that right Reed?"

"Yes, you brought me here."

"OK, then. So he ain't lost no more," Chief Kriner said. "You can take him home, Greg."

Greg got up, shook Kriner's hand, and thanked him. Little Jimmy was taking things off one of the desks and Greg yelled, "Stop that!" in a way that meant he was not as angry at Little Jimmy as he was at someone else, and that someone else was me.

"Wait a second," Chief Kriner said to me. "How long were you with Officer Dan?"

"For a little while," I said.

"How long's a little while? More than an hour?"

Dan said: "Yeah, he was with me and—"

"I'm talking to Reed, Dan," Kriner said.

"Yes," I said. "More than an hour."

Chief Kriner said to Dan: "I just got a phone call. Guy over on Carbon Road. He's coming in to file a complaint. Said you pushed around his father, then pulled a gun on an unarmed family."

"That's a lie!" Dan said. "The guy . . . that old guy . . . he was on the road, all kinds of crazy. I nearly hit him with my car! I tried to take him home. Then a couple other people came out screaming! You know how those people get!"

"What people?"

"Out on Carbon Road. They hate the police."

"They said you pulled your weapon."

"That's another lie!"

Kriner said to me, "Were you there, Reed?"

"Yes, I was there."

"What happened?"

"I was in the back of Dan's car."

"All right. Go on."

"And there was a lot going on outside it. I looked at the front of the car. There is a police radio and a radio that plays music too. I did not think police cars had those."

"See?" Dan said. "He was checking out other stuff. He got scared when all of them were screaming. They were belligerent and you know they lie! They'll all lie together to get a cop in trouble. So it's their word against mine."

"Did your gun ever leave your holster?"

"Never!" Dan said, and looked down at it, as if that proved something.

Kriner stared at me.

I did not say anything.

Greg said: "It's been a long day. Can we go?"

Kriner said: "OK. But I may need to talk to you again, Reed. You got anything else to say?"

I shook my head.

Greg opened the door to leave.

But before we left, I stepped over to Kriner's desk.

From my pocket I took the clip of bullets that I had removed from Dan's gun when I was sitting in the back seat of the police car.

When I put the clip on the desk, everyone there stopped and stared at it. Little Jimmy stepped over to touch it. Greg pulled him back.

"Dan, give me your weapon," Chief Kriner said.

"That ain't mine!"

Kriner said: "Dan. Surrender your weapon. That's an order."

Dan took his gun from his holster. He handed it to Kriner, who turned it upside down to see that there was no clip in it.

"You said your weapon never left your holster. So how did Reed get your clip?"

"I . . . I . . ." Dan said, as if he were stalling for time to figure out what to say.

Kriner opened the drawer of his desk and put Dan's gun in there, along with the clip.

"You're relieved of duty," Kriner said to Dan, and held out his hand. "Your badge."

"This is crazy! Who you gonna believe? I don't have to say anything to you!"

"I'm not asking you to say anything to me. I'm ordering you to give me your badge."

Dan cursed and complained and argued, all while Kriner stood with his hand out. Finally, Dan handed him the badge. Then he said he was going home to file a stack of complaints with the Fraternal Order of Police and said that Kriner would be sorry. Then he brushed past us and slammed the door behind him. I heard his car race out of the parking lot.

"OK," Kriner said to us. "I have to go back out on patrol, since he's off the street. Reed, I am going to need you to come in tomorrow so we can talk, OK?"

"I'll bring him in," Greg said.

"Good. Now I have a whole lot of calls to make before I head out. Have a good night, gentlemen."

Little Jimmy climbed in the back of Greg's car.

"Good night," I said to him. Then I said the same to Greg.

"Where do you think you're going? Get in the car, Reed!"

"I have something to do."

Greg was livid. I like that word too, even if I do not like to see someone that way.

"This is what you'll do! You'll get in my car and go the hell home! Do you know what happened tonight? I went to the house and you weren't there. So Little Jimmy and I rode around for an hour, worried sick. I had to come here to ask the cops to search for you."

"I was with a cop. Though he is not a cop anymore. Not after tonight. I—"

"You said you were going to stay home."

"I did not say that. I said—"

Greg slammed his hand down on the car.

"Jesus Christ, no more splitting words and telling me what you meant! I can't—"

Greg inhaled. Ran his hand through his hair. And I knew he was calming himself because he wanted to say something important. And I knew what that something important was.

"Reed. I'm sorry. I can't do this anymore. I can't."

He turned around, then faced me, then exhaled. He said: "I've got so much going on. I can't risk it. Not with what happened to Mom. Not with you leaving the house, and then I have to go out searching for you. I just can't. I think . . . Listen, I'm being honest with you: This Pittsburgh place seems really nice. We'll visit it. And if you don't like it, we'll find another. I promise you that. But you need to be somewhere where they can . . . handle you. I think it would be really good for you, and I'm not just saying that. I think you'd be less . . . lonely."

I was going to say, "I am not lonely," but I did not want to say something only to say it, and I did not want to say something that was untrue. I did not know if I was lonely or if I was not lonely. I had never thought about that. After this was over, I would have to consider it.

"I knew you were going to send me there," I said.

"I'm sorry."

"And I believe you. I know that you are sorry, Greg."

We stared at each other. It was quiet in that parking lot.

Greg finally said: "You asked me before why Maggie left me."

I did not say anything.

Greg said: "She told me I worried too much. It made me . . . too tense. Do you think that's true?"

I said: "I do."

"She wanted me to be a different person."

I said: "I think you should be the person you are. I like you for that, Greg."

"Really?"

"Perhaps a majority of the time, yes."

194

He laughed. "Thank you for being honest. I like that about you, Reed."

I hiked my backpack higher up on my shoulders and turned around to leave.

"Reeeeed," Greg said in that drawn-out way he says my name when he's tired. "Get in the car."

"I have something to do," I said.

"I'm asking you to get in the car," he said. "Please."

"You can no longer say, 'Reed, if you do not listen to me, I will send you to Pittsburgh,' because now you are sending me to Pittsburgh anyway," I said. "So I am going to do something that I need to do and you cannot stop me."

Little Jimmy must have tired himself out by touching everything in the police station. He was asleep in the back seat. I was going to wave to him or knock on the window but I did not want to wake him.

"I am going, Greg."

If we were brothers like some of those I have seen in movies and in real life, I think Greg would have asked, *Where are you going?* and maybe tried to help me. Or maybe if I were a better brother I would have trusted him enough to tell him about my plan and ask for his help. But we were not good brothers like that. Greg stood there staring at me. He appeared dumbfounded, which is a really interesting word. Does it mean that you were found being dumb, or that your life is founded on your dumbness? I will have to look it up.

I said to Greg: "I will be home in a little while."

And then I left the parking lot.

LIZ

I WAS THANKFUL that I hadn't eaten much all day. Because when I saw—and just as horrible, heard—Luke hit the concrete headfirst, I gagged. But with an empty stomach, nothing came up.

The *whack-thwap!* of his head and, a millisecond later, the rest of his body was far louder than I imagined it would be. Though, granted, before that moment I hadn't imagined it at all.

I pulled myself back inside the window and bit onto the palm of my hand to keep my mouth from screaming. Then I looked out again, hoping that I had mis-seen what I saw. On second view, it was worse. Thick red blood was pooling all around him.

Whoever was coming up the stairs heard it too. She rushed down to the second floor and threw open a window to look outside. She screeched. Then, maybe twenty seconds later, she had sped downstairs and out onto the patio. There the woman let out a shriek, something along the lines of "Owwwwahhhhh!"

With a mad, mindless giggle I thought: *Well, at least she's not singing that tacky pop-country song anymore.*

The woman saw the rope ladder and followed it up with her eyes. I pulled my head back inside before she could see me. It was time to get the hell out of the house. I bolted to the steps and raced down two flights. Sometime during that, the woman stopped her wordless shrieks and started on: "Hellllp! He's dead! He's dead!"

I threw open the front door, peered around the block, and, seeing no one, stepped out. When I got on the sidewalk, I forced myself to walk slowly in case anyone saw me. And someone, somewhere, would be looking soon. The woman's wails were getting louder.

I took a left to the more deserted part of the block, then, fifty yards on, turned a hard right to get out of sight of my old house. After another fifty yards, I took a left. By then I was well clear of the place, though I was shaking enough so that my knees nearly buckled.

From the other side of town, an ambulance siren sounded out. *Take your time*, I thought. *There's no reason to rush.*

I sat on my sofa, unsure of how to feel besides horrible. I hadn't liked Luke but I hadn't wanted him dead. To see how he ended up shook me so much that I nearly lost my way on the walk home. It was good luck, at least, that there were few people out.

An hour later, all at once, I freaked, screaming aloud in my house: "Luke, you asshole! You had to swallow that coin, didn't you? Then you had to die! Idiot!" I paced for a while and brought down a dozen more curses on him—sorry to speak ill of the dead—and didn't bother to quiet myself. There was no need, with the nearest neighbor so far away.

I fell asleep on the sofa and remained there through the night. At nine the next morning, a knock on the front door woke me. Police chief Kriner was standing on the small porch. I panicked but struggled not to show it. He took off his hat. I swallowed hard and steeled myself for whatever he had to say.

"Hiya, Liz."

"Hiya, Chief. What's up?"

"Can I come in?"

"Why?" I said, acting perplexed. In search of an innocent expression, I raised my eyebrows extra high.

"Let me come in so we can talk," he said. I stepped aside and motioned to a chair.

"Luke Dunn. He was your boyfriend, right?"

"Yes, he is," I said, paying attention to verb tense for the first time since high school.

"I'm afraid I've got some bad news," Kriner said. "He died."

I shook my head no. "He can't be dead," I said, and wondered how Meryl Streep would handle this act and what words a good screenwriter would put in her mouth. "We were together yesterday."

"What time was that?"

"About three."

"And then what?"

"He was here. We took a little walk. Then he went home. Did he . . . was it . . . natural causes?" I widened my eyes, just short of overplaying the emotions.

"So he was here at three o'clock." Kriner took out a small pad of paper. Licked the end of his pencil—I still don't know why people do that—and began jotting down some notes.

"Right. Then we took a walk. Then he left."

"And had you seen him since?"

"No. Can you tell me what happened?"

"Luke was at your father's house. Your old house. And he—"

Now was a good time to interject: "My old house? Why?"

"Apparently, he was there to rob the place. Did he say anything to you?"

I let my mouth drop open, then stared at the ceiling as if I were recalling yesterday. At the same time, I tried not to let my final view of Luke enter my mind lest I gag at the memory.

"I was at Hillview yesterday. To see my dad. Oh my god. I . . ."

"What?"

"I remember telling Luke how my dad used to collect coins. You don't think . . . ?"

Kriner scribbled some more.

"Did someone shoot him?" I asked. A fair question for these parts.

Kriner said: "He fell out of a window. Imogen . . . do you call her your stepmother?"

"No," I said, though *Fuck no* would have been more appropriate.

"Imogen went out of town. She called a friend to come over and water her plants. Luke must have heard her and tried to climb out of the window. He fell, and I'm afraid that's how he died."

"That must have been . . . horrible."

"Can I ask: Where were you yesterday?"

"I went to see my father for a few hours, then came back here. Luke was waiting on my porch, so we hung out for a while, then he left. Tell you the truth, we argued and sort of broke up. It's been a long timing coming."

"Maybe that's why he decided to steal from your dad."

"Maybe," I said and shrugged.

Kriner asked another twenty minutes' worth of questions before slapping the notebook shut to signal that he was finished.

Before he stood he said: "Oh. The woman who was watering the plants: She said she didn't see anyone else in the house. But I'm wondering if maybe Luke had a friend in on it. Do you know if he was going to meet anyone after he left here?"

He was only going to meet his maker, I thought but didn't say. Instead, I frowned as if I were thinking, then shook my head.

"He didn't have many friends," I said. "So, no."

Kriner said: "My guess is that he thought your dad had something of value, then went there to steal it."

"Did you . . . find anything on him?"

"No. He had a single quarter in his pocket, but it wasn't a rare coin or anything. There were unlocked windows at the house. He probably entered through one of those and shut it behind him."

I nodded as dumbly as I could, which was pretty dumbly.

"Luke also had an extensive criminal record, so this seems pretty open-and-shut."

"I . . . I mean, he told me he'd had some troubles, but I didn't know . . ."

"A half dozen breaking-and-entering convictions; a few other crimes too," he said. "Anyway, I'm sorry about this, Liz. It's the worst part of my job. It truly is."

A minute later his hat was back on his head and his ass was back in his police cruiser.

I spent the rest of the day trying to figure out ways to buy a new guitar and to get it and me to Nashville, all the while blocking out the images of Luke's smashed head that sometimes invaded my thoughts. I wandered around my house, appraising the tattered furniture, the outmoded television, and my few other possessions, all of them bought secondhand or gotten at no cost from sympathetic neighbors eager to give away their junk. Even if I could find a buyer, nothing was worth much.

I'm well aware that life isn't just about the objects you own, but, my god, when you look around and realize that you have so little, it's hard not to think that you've somehow failed. I considered calling Belle Chapman and asking if she would pay for a flight to Nashville. Yet, even if I could get that to happen, I'd still be deep in debt to Kap, and I couldn't risk having him go after my father when I left town.

Nothing is impossible! a snide and cynical voice mocked me inside my head. I didn't even have the energy to tell it to shut the hell up.

Six or seven hours later, another knock on the door: Kriner, for the second time that day. I invited him in, and his hat came off once again. Someone must have seen me, I thought. I'm going to jail.

Kriner said: "I'm real sorry to disturb you another time, Liz. But I've been on the phone all day, trying to track down Luke's family. Well, what's left of his family. His parents died in a car wreck years back."

"He told me. Drunk driving."

"Luke only had an aunt. She hated him, it seems."

Go figure, I thought.

Kriner said: "She said he broke into her house twice. Stole pretty much everything she had of value. She never wanted to see him again."

"OK. I can't say I know of anyone else."

"The aunt said there are no relatives besides her."

"So . . . ?"

"Well, in this case, in Pennsylvania, if there are no other relatives, the body can legally be released to a common-law spouse."

"But he wasn't married."

"I meant you. If you passed the interview, you'd be considered his companion, and that would give you the right to claim the body."

"No, I'm sorry. But . . ."

"I understand," he said. "But I did want to ask before I released his body for a pauper's burial."

Kriner got up and moved toward the door.

"Wait!"

"Hmm?"

"Maybe . . . maybe I should?" I said, more to myself than to Kriner.

The chief nodded. "It would be the Christian thing to do."

"Of course," I said. "I should take care of him. I'm sorry. I wasn't thinking."

"It's all right. I know you've been shaken up by all this."

"Yes, I have been," I said. "So when . . . I mean, who gives that kind of interview? For someone to be named a companion?"

"Well, in this case, me."

"Oh. When can we do it?"

"You just passed," he said. "So you're good with this?"

"Yes," I said. "I'll claim the body."

CARLA

WE DROVE ALONG Route 211 and approached the turn at Tharp Road. We were on the edge of Locksburg. There were only a few houses, spaced far apart. Once we passed them, we'd be in forested land until the road ran to the river.

Beyond the turn, Tharp Road became a straightaway. Billy pressed the gas pedal; the engine revved and worked harder. We tried to ignore it. The sound didn't go away.

"It's the tire," he said.

The steering wheel shook. Then a dismal sound: the slap-flop, blubbering thuds of a flattened tire echoing off whatever we passed and bouncing back through the open windows to our ears.

"This has got to be a j-j-oke," he said.

"Pull over. We can fix it."

"Where, Mom?" he said. "At somebody's house?"

"Billy, be calm. Do you have a spare tire?" I asked.

"Yeah. It's under the dead buh-buh-body in the trunk. Let's take her out, then pull away the p-plastic and get the spare tire underneath and we're fucked. We're totally mother-fuh-fuh-fucking fucked!"

Sparks in the side-view mirror caught my eye. The wheel was running on the rim. We were barely doing twenty miles an hour on that dark road, with metal loudly grinding on asphalt.

"Can we call . . ." he said, then shook his head when he no doubt remembered that we had no cell phones.

The steering wheel vibrated hard in Billy's hands.

"Mom . . ."

"I know."

"The sparks are f-flying. They're getting worse . . ."

"Keep driving."

It was the only thing I could think to say—and the best thing I could think to do. I closed my eyes and breathed in like I did when I jogged and willed some solution to present itself. My mind came back blank. If I had been a praying person, I'd have pleaded with God. We needed some kind of miracle.

I opened my eyes. Someone with a backpack was up ahead, walking in the center of the road. Whoever it was heard the racket and turned around to see us coming. Then he moved to the side of the road to let us pass him.

"Who the heck is that?" Billy said.

I knew who it was.

"Pull up next to the guy."

Billy did.

"Hiya, Reed," I said when we were alongside him.

REED

I LEFT GREG in the police department parking lot and got back to walking. It took twenty minutes to get to Tharp Road. The cemetery was about two miles farther down there, toward the river. Mom and I had walked that way plenty of times.

I adjusted my backpack and kept going. The night was cool and the crickets and all the other night bugs were loud and melodic. I heard that word once and loved it: "melodic."

Soon a racket began, something human-made that was not melodic at all. It was Carla and Billy's car coming from behind me. It pulled next to me and Carla said hiya and I said hiya back. Then I said: "You were wearing a hairnet earlier. I was wondering why."

"That's, uh, a long story, Reed."

"And a sweatshirt, which is good to wear when it is chillier but it was not good to wear earlier when it was hot out. Why was that?"

"Uh-huh" was what she said, which was not an answer. She said: "What are you doing out here?"

I did not want to tell her, so I said: "That is a long story too." I thought that was a good way to respond.

"Touché," Carla said.

"That is French."

"*Oui.*"

205

"So is that."

"Correct."

"That is not."

"Reed, could you call your brother? We sort of have a problem here. We have a flat tire."

I looked back. "You do not have a flat tire. You have no tire."

"Correct again."

I said: "Open your trunk. You can put your spare tire on. I can help. I have done that before."

Billy made a sound like something dry was stuck in his throat.

"We, uh . . . we don't have a spare," she said.

"What do you mean?"

"The spare got flat too. It's being repaired."

"You should have gotten another spare to keep while the spare was being repaired."

"Well, you know, when it rains, it pours."

"No, it does not. Not always. Sometimes it only mists and that is not pouring. A few weeks ago it was drizzling for about twenty minutes, then it stopped altogether, so it never poured."

"Do you have a cell phone, Reed? Maybe you could call your brother? And maybe he could lend us his spare?"

"They are not all interchangeable," I said. "Do you know that? Different cars have different kinds of rims."

"Oh."

"Greg has a Ford. You have a Honda. It will not work."

"Oh."

"You see that car?" I said, and pointed across the road to the last house that was there before the road ran through the woods.

"Yes."

"It is a Honda too. Do you know what that means?"

"What?"

"Tonight is your lucky night."

Billy made that sound again.

"Pull over there," I said, and they did. I like when people listen to me.

They went into the driveway. There were two other cars there. One was a shiny Honda. The other was a burned-out frame of a Chevrolet.

There were lights on in the house. I thought that whoever was inside would have heard the car and come out, but they did not. So I went up to the front door and knocked to ask them if Carla could use their Honda's spare tire.

Right after I knocked, there was a *thunk* sound.

Then a woman opened the door. It was Liz Moyer. She worked as the receptionist at my old high school and also played guitar and sang in the local bars. She was holding a fireplace poker.

I peered past her. A man was lying on the floor. The back of his head was bleeding.

Liz said, "Yeah?"

I said, "Is this a bad time?"

LIZ

I WENT TO LUKE'S APARTMENT. I had been there once before and vowed never to return. At the time, he swore that he had cleaned the place, yet it reeked as if someone had spilled beer on the floor, then soaked it up with the moldy throw rug there. As expected, dirty dishes were piled high in the sink and buzzing flies circled them, perhaps frightened of landing on such a mess.

"You couldn't wash those?" I had asked then.

"I didn't think you'd go in the kitchen."

"Luke, it's a studio apartment. The kitchen is in the living room."

"I mean, I didn't think you'd go over there," he said, as if that explained it perfectly.

This time the place smelled worse, like an overused porta potty on a humid day. The landlord had already learned of Luke's demise, and though I arrived with excuses at the ready—*I'm Luke's legal next of kin! Call Chief Kriner if you don't believe me!*—none were needed. The landlord let me in with no resistance. Before walking away she said: "Whatever you don't clean up is going in the dumpster. I need to find another tenant."

Plates and piles of soiled clothes aside, Luke didn't have much else. A mattress and box spring, sans sheets and frame, were pushed in the corner. A sagging sofa sat in front of a large, tubed television that was perched atop a pair of milk crates. I went through every space, even the sliding silverware drawer—his was filled with plastic fast-food utensils instead of metal forks and spoons—and found nothing worth more than $3.99.

I'd been searching for cash or anything worth selling. If I were forced at gunpoint to say something kind about Luke, I'd say this: *He wasn't lying about being broke.* I had a hope of finding enough money to pay for his cremation. Now I resigned myself to the fact that I'd have to do it on credit.

I walked to Locksburg cemetery. There, a couple of white buildings sat on the south side of the property: one for grounds-keeping, the other the business office and crematorium. A surprisingly young woman in a sharp suit greeted me at the front office desk.

"Good morning," she said. "How can I help you?"

"My boyfriend," I said, and confused myself a little before realizing that I was talking about Luke. "He died. And, uh, I'd like to talk to someone about a cremation."

"I'm so sorry to hear," she said. "Were you planning to have the ceremony here? We have a small chapel."

"Yes, I know. I was here a few years ago when an old neighbor passed away. I'd like to do it here."

"So when would you like the service?"

I looked around. Then to her name tag. "Stacey. To be completely honest, I'd like it to be as soon and as cheap as possible."

If I struck her as tactless, she didn't let on. Instead, she clicked a few keys on a laptop and said, "The day after next? From one to two?"

"I don't think I'll need the full hour. He has no family. And he was, well, sort of friendless."

"OK. How about one to one thirty?"

"Is that the cheapest option?"

"I mean, I have an opening tomorrow morning in the chapel at nine. That's probably too soon for you—"

"Perfect."

"OK, then. How about remembrance cards? They can be printed—"

"No."

She tried to sell me on a special urn, a rental casket, and a burial plot for the ashes. I said no so many times, I got a kink in my neck from shaking it.

"You work on commission, huh?" I asked after shooting down an extra charge for a music package that would play in the viewing room.

"Is it obvious?"

"Kinda sorta," I said, and for the first time we shared a smile.

She took a form and began filing it out with the necessary information. Near the end she said, "Does the deceased have any gold fillings in his teeth? Or anything else metal, such as implants? Things like that will be destroyed or completely melted down in the cremation, so they might need to be removed."

"No, he doesn't," I said.

"OK, then, we're finished with the questions. Now about the service . . ."

I said: "I need the least expensive service, along with some kind of payment plan, because I am currently—and, with luck, temporarily—broke."

She slid forward some papers on which small print informed me of a 19 percent annual interest rate and of an agreement that the cemetery would hold the ashes until the balance was paid in full.

I signed them all, along with a release for Luke's body from the Locksburg General Hospital morgue, where he was currently cooling. Twenty minutes later I walked out $987.50 deeper in debt.

The next morning I got up at seven and picked out a dark sleeveless dress for the cremation ceremony. I chose flat shoes, considering I had two miles to walk there. I swung an oversized, grandma-style handbag over my shoulder, left my wristwatch behind, and wore no jewelry other than a pair of small, inexpensive earrings.

Stacey greeted me solemnly with a brief handshake, and I played the part of grieving girlfriend as best I could: saying little, nodding along.

At nine she opened the chapel. A heavy cardboard casket was placed on a stainless steel table that was atop what looked like a monorail. The track traveled over to the wall. With a push of a button, the casket would move along as the doors on the wall opened, taking the body into the crematorium.

"He's . . . ?" I said and nodded to the casket.

"Yes," she said. "We moved him from Locksburg General this morning."

Plastic plants were propped alongside the casket in a vain attempt to make the space seem filled. Fake lilies were on the cardboard lid. I sat on one of the chairs, put my handbag down, and tried to appear sad.

At 9:05, Stacey checked her watch.

I said: "He had only a few friends, and I don't think they could make it on such short notice." In truth, I'd told no one about the service. Heck, I wouldn't even know whom to inform.

"I understand," Stacey said. Whether she did or not, I can't say for sure. But she sounded sincere. She was built for this business.

I got up from the chair and walked to the casket. It wasn't tapered or shaped like a coffin. It was no more than a box you'd get from a front-door delivery, albeit one big enough to hold a man.

And all at once I got surprisingly choked up. Maybe a little for Luke, but mostly for the existential ideas that came into my head and the absolute absurdity that this is how we all end up, sooner or later. Whether it be lying in a rotunda in a stately marble building or in a box at a cheap, small-town crematorium, not one of us gets out of life alive.

I felt some water gather in my eyes and tried to well it into tears. It didn't work, so I put my hand over my forehead as if I were holding back my emotions.

"Can I have some time alone?" I asked Stacey.

"Of course. Of course," she said. "I'll be in the office if you need me."

I nodded and she left.

The door closed behind her.

Twelve hours after leaving the crematorium, I parked my new used Honda next to the charred shell of my old Chevy and went into my house to pack. I'd just come from visiting my dad at Hillview. We spent an hour together, and the tears I couldn't find for Luke turned on full blast when my dad and I were in his room and I told him goodbye, at least for a short while.

At home, I pulled from under my bed the two large canvas duffel bags that had been with me throughout my travels. I bought those when I was eighteen, at the army surplus store that had once been on Queen Street. Even now, at thirty, I barely owned enough to fill them: In one, I put all the clothes that I wanted; in the other, a few framed photos, a bunch of books, a couple of keepsakes.

I walked into the bathroom to get my toiletries.

I opened the shower curtain. Kap was standing there.

I didn't have breath to scream. He reached out and grabbed a handful of my dress at the shoulder. I struggled and pushed him but he was far too large and strong. He shoved me back against the wall and growled, "Remember me?"

Finally I got some air in my lungs and said: "Yeah, you're not the forgettable type."

Kap threw open the bathroom door with one hand, holding on to me with the other, and went out into the living room. He yanked me along behind him.

"Now listen," he said. "I'm here for my money. And I ain't hurtin' you unless you fuck with me, you understand?" He didn't wait for an answer. He walked forward, pulling me along like a big kid with a well-worn rag doll.

We were passing the fireplace when someone knocked at the front door.

That surprised Kap. He loosened his grip. I pulled away. And in one motion I grabbed the fireplace poker and swung it at the back of his head.

The poker practically bounced off his skull. Kap yelped and staggered, almost ready to fall.

So I swung again at his head.

His hands popped up to protect himself.

Then I held the iron like a Louisville Slugger and whacked him hard at the kneecap.

That brought the big man down.

Nearly bent the damn fireplace poker too.

CARLA

REED CAME DOWN from the house. As he did, the other Honda bleep-bleeped and the doors unlocked. Reed opened the trunk, then went around and lifted out the spare tire.

"What did they say?" I asked Reed.

"She said we could use the spare tire."

"That's nice of her."

"Yes."

Reed rolled the tire over to us. Then Billy, Reed, and I inspected the back wheel of Billy's car under the beam of a flashlight. A few remaining scraps of tire stuck to the rim. They were still smoking. The car itself leaned to one side. If there was any good part of all this, it was that the burning rubber covered most of the scent of the rotting body.

"Well, let's g-get this duh-done," Billy said.

Reed said: "Open your trunk."

I said: "Why? We have the spare!"

"We need your jack."

"It got buh-broken!" Billy said, too fast and too loud. He brought it down a notch when he added, "When I was changing the s-spare the last time."

"So both your spare tire and your back tire are gone and your jack is also broken," Reed said.

"Yeah!" Bill said.

"Are you telling the truth?" Reed asked. "Because it does not seem like you are. But you do not have to tell me if you—"

"Take the jack from the other car," I said.

Reed said: "I only asked her if we could borrow her spare tire. I did not ask her if we could borrow her jack."

"I think it's OK, Reed."

"We should ask her," Reed said, then went back to the house.

REED

YOU SHOULD ALWAYS CHECK with the owner of something if you want to borrow that something, no matter what it is.

I knocked on the front door again.

"Yes?" Liz called out.

"Thank you, Miss Moyer, for letting us use your spare tire."

"Uh, you're welcome."

"May we use your jack too?"

"What?"

"We need to use your car jack to lift our car up so we can put your spare tire on our car. But when I say 'our car,' I mean, their car, because it is not mine."

I heard a man grunt.

"Sure," Liz said. "You can use the jack."

"Thank you," I said. She did not say anything and I wondered if she had heard me, so I said again, louder: "Thank you!"

"You're welcome, damn it!" she yelled from inside.

LIZ

I STEPPED OVER Kap to answer the door. But before opening it, I turned back around and gave him a sharp kick to the ribs for good measure.

I opened the front door. The guy standing there was barely more than a teenager. I'd seen him before, at the high school. Reed something. Nice kid. I looked over his shoulder. In the driveway in front of my house was another car, this one parked askew. Reed asked to use my spare tire. Heck, I didn't even know if there was a spare in my new used car. I'd bought it mere hours ago and hadn't looked. But then I heard Kap groan and just told Reed yes and shut the door fast. I didn't mean to be hasty, but a drug-dealing ex-con who'd broken into my house and attacked me was lying injured on the floor, so I gave myself a pass for minor rudeness.

Kap looked up. I said, "If you move a finger, I am going to split your skull wide open with this."

He brought his hand back and I raised the fireplace poker high.

"Wait, wait!" he said. "I was only checkin' to see if I still got brains in my head!"

"If you ever had 'em in the first place."

He moaned a little.

I said, "There's a bunch of people outside. If I scream, they'll call the cops, and you'll get busted for breaking and entering. So don't you even think about touching me."

I probably didn't need to issue that warning. He was dazed. I worked fast: From inside my big grandma handbag, I took out the roll of duct tape and a utility knife I had there. I wrapped the tape around his wrists ten times. Then around his legs the same.

"You can wiggle free of that in a few minutes, I bet. But it'll give me enough time to get out of here—or to brain you again. Or both."

Then there was another knock on the door and, from outside, Reed asked if he could also use the car jack.

Jesus Christ, will these people ever leave me alone?

CARLA

REED TOOK THE JACK from the other car and carried it over. Billy grabbed the tire iron and began loosening the lug nuts. I lit the area with a flashlight; I had to do something other than stand there and worry and sniff the air for any odor coming from the trunk.

After Reed jacked up the car and removed the rim, Billy crouched to his knees to fit the spare into place, then finger tightened the lug nuts. He finished the job with the tire iron. Reed grabbed the old rim and motioned toward our car.

"Just leave it here, Reed," I said. I was too tired to think up another excuse for why we couldn't open the trunk and getting cranky from the throbbing pain in my hand.

"Are we good?" I asked aloud.

Billy nodded.

Reed said: "We did an excellent job."

That was enough for me. Billy put the jack back into the other car, then started his. We were both in a hurry to get out of there, but something didn't feel right. Someone was in the house: Why didn't she come out to offer help or to see what our problem was? That didn't sit well with me, especially in a place like Locksburg, where neighbors knew everything from your maiden name to the

220

vegetables you planted in your garden last spring. Also, I wanted to be sure that she hadn't for some reason called the police.

"Let's thank her, Reed," I said. "You said it was a woman, right?"

"Yes. She used to work in my high school. In the office, answering phones."

I probably knew her, then.

Reed and I went up and knocked.

Following a very long moment, Liz Moyer opened the door a bit, then slipped outside. When I waitressed at Zinger's she played on the small stage some nights. We shared a laugh here and there and a "Hiya" in the supermarket when we saw each other.

"Liz!" I said. I stepped forward then stopped rather than hurt my hand anymore. I motioned to it as my excuse not to hug.

"Carla!" she said. "Oh my gosh, did you just hurt that?"

"No. I cut it earlier. I didn't know you lived here. I'm sorry that we bugged you, but my car broke down and the spare tire is flat."

"You said that the spare tire was being repaired," Reed said.

"Oh yeah, that," I said. "Anyway, Liz, we'll return your spare as soon as possible. Thank you so much."

Liz peeked back inside, then quickly closed the door behind her, the move of a woman who didn't want you to see who was in there with her. My guess: She was with someone's husband or boyfriend or—who knows?—maybe someone's girlfriend. If so, I'd soon hear that gossip around town.

"I'd, ah, invite you in but . . . I'm sorta busy right now."

"Oh, no problem at all. We're leaving. Thank you."

"Why are you out this way, Carla?" she asked before I could go. "There's nothing down here. And I know you weren't visiting me."

"Billy, my son, he, um, he's back from college and we decided to drive around and talk some."

"The three of you?"

"No. Reed here, he was . . . taking a walk, I guess. Is that right, Reed?"

"I was walking," he said.

A grunt sounded from inside. Liz said hurriedly: "OK, well, have a great night!" and scurried inside. She slammed the door behind her.

I wondered again what was going on in that house. She was definitely acting strange. But I don't examine the dental work of gift horses, especially those with spare tires that might save my son and me from getting stranded and arrested before the night was over.

No, on a dark summer night, with a body in my son's trunk, at the very last house on a vacant road not far from the river, I don't question anything like that.

REED

UP ON THE PORCH, I did not want either of the two women to ask me why I had been out walking on Tharp Road because I did not want to tell them about my plan or lie to them. So I stood there quietly like I do when I want people to talk to each other and not to me, and it mostly worked.

Once, I looked back at Billy, who was sitting in the front seat of his car with a very impatient expression. Then I turned to Carla and Liz and realized that they both had the same impatient expression. I was nervous: It was getting late and I had a long way to walk before I got to the cemetery. So I guess I was like the three of them too. And that was funny in a not really funny kind of way how people can all be feeling the same emotion at the same time but hiding it from the other persons.

That is what I love most about Little Jimmy. He is never afraid to tell you how he feels or what he thinks. Maybe, when you get older, what happens is that people get more scared or embarrassed or unsure of what they feel, so they tamp it down. I hoped that would not happen to Little Jimmy, but I guess it might.

I stared at my feet as Carla and Liz talked and I waited for them to finish. Then I gazed up at the sky. There are always so many stars out in Locksburg, but we were further away from town and there were more to see. I imagined someone high up there looking down at us. Not a god but only another person. And that person would see the three of us from above. The three of us, just these regular people, standing on a small porch in central Pennsylvania, each of us worrying about something but afraid to say anything to another person.

After a short while Carla and Liz finished and we all said good night to each other and smiled smiles that were more uneasy than happy though we all pretended that they were cheerful.

And then I set off down the road on my own.

LIZ

I WAS STANDING over Kap, thinking through what needed to be done, when he began pulling against the tape on his wrists.

"I'll let you go," I told him. "But not just yet."

He was lying on his side. I propped him up against a coffee table and wrapped duct tape around his chest to bind him to the table. Not a perfect job but one that would keep him immobile for a little while longer.

Someone knocked at the door. Yet again.

"Go ahead and yell if you want," I said to Kap. "If they call 911, I'll have to tell the police that you broke into my house. You'll be in a jail cell within the hour."

"Then let me go."

"I'll cut you loose after they leave."

I opened the front door a quarter way. I was about to scold Reed but saw that someone was with him. It was Carla, a waitress at one of the bars where I sometimes played.

We said hi and she told me about her car's flat and how she'd return my spare tire to me soon. I slipped out to the porch before anyone could see inside.

Getting back inside the house was my priority, but I couldn't help being curious as to why she was in the area. In the daylight there were times when no car would drive by my house for a half hour at least. At night, that could stretch on for several hours. Carla said that she and her son were out riding around and happened to come down this way.

My ass, I wanted to say. I was still trembling from my encounter with Kap, who was likely getting angrier by the minute, taped up inside the house. But I could recognize a load of bullshit when I smelled it. And I smelled a whole pasture full here, in the way Carla was acting, and in Reed's silence, and in both their twitchy moves.

Something was way off. And something reeked worse than their bullshit. The remains of the burnt tire, sure, but something altogether rancid underneath that. I sniffed the air and looked at Carla, then at Reed.

I didn't have time to quiz them, though. Something sounded like it had fallen off the coffee table where Kap was taped. I told Carla and Reed good night and went back inside.

There was work to do.

CARLA

WE PULLED AWAY from Liz's house on the new tire. The drive felt smooth as ice after the earlier rumbling. Two miles later we passed the cemetery. Another mile, and we came to the river.

Billy pulled into the empty parking lot by the towpath and moved as far south as we could go. Then he reversed so the trunk would be closer to the woods. We donned our hairnets, caps, and gloves.

"What if someone comes?" he asked.

"Once we get out of the car, don't stop moving: Take one end of the sheet. I'll try to hold the other. We're going to a spot about a hundred yards away. We'll hide her there. I don't want her to be found until we write the letter to tell them where she is."

Billy opened the trunk. Putrid smells wafted out. I'd left the VapoRub at home when my hand had been cut. Now, after the restaurant fire and the flat tire, neither of us was in any shape to complain. I bunched the sheet in my uninjured hand and we lifted her out. Then we walked.

From the first steps, nothing went right. We each tripped in the dark. Bugs stung us, and with every breath I seemed to inhale some fly or mosquito. Stray branches clawed and snagged the sheet, stopping us several times when we heard ripping.

Fifty yards later, the insects that we'd seen earlier on Doreen must have felt the movement and crawled out. They crept onto our hands and up our arms. Neither Billy nor I could let go, so we let them scuttle over our skin.

At one point I sunk into mud. I tried to jump away quickly and fell. I yanked my foot free, and the mud sucked the shoe off. I reached into the muck and pulled the shoe out. Billy had to help me put it back on. My injured fingers pulsed with agony. Then we picked Doreen up and began moving again.

When we arrived at the spot, we lay Doreen down and got to work, covering her with leaves and branches. Now and then we'd freeze, convinced that a sound from the nearby water or woods was a signal that someone was near. After a few moments of listening, we'd resume. Within twenty minutes we had her hidden.

"That's enough," I whispered. "Let's go."

"Wait," he whispered.

Billy knelt down in front of the pile of brush. He looked over his shoulder at me to do the same. I joined him there. We both folded our hands.

We'd long been atheists or agnostics or whatever you call people who don't believe or simply don't bother to care about such things. I didn't begrudge Billy, though. I don't know what he said in his head or who he said it to. But I asked Doreen to forgive us for this and explained to her that we had no other choice. I told her that, the times I'd seen her in town, she always seemed like a nice young woman. And I said I hoped that she had found some kind of peace.

Only when Billy and I got up and took the towpath back to the car did I realize I hadn't said anything at all to God.

* * *

When we returned home, Billy began filling the hole in the yard. I gave up within a minute, unable to maneuver a shovel with only one hand. He finished with the dirt, then fit the pieces of sod back on top like a jigsaw puzzle. Come daylight, you'd be able to see that someone had been digging there. That wouldn't be the case in a week or two, when the grass re-rooted and any rain helped tamp down the soil.

We went to the car trunk and carefully removed the shower curtain, folded it, and slipped it into a paper shopping bag. Then we wiped the inside of the trunk with bleach.

Billy undressed in the mudroom, I in the shed, and put on the fresh sets of clothing we'd left there earlier. All the old stuff, hats and hairnets included, were stuffed into another bag. The bags went into the fireplace. I sprayed them with lighter fluid, then lit them up. As it all burned I took a fifth of whiskey and drank straight from the bottle.

"You need to go to the h-hospital for your hand," Billy said.

"Relax for a minute."

"What's left to do?"

"The hole is filled in. Your trunk is clean. Did you wipe the shovels with bleach?"

"Yeah."

"So we're done for tonight. Unless you want to sit here and watch the fire."

"I'm taking a shower, to get the smells off me. Then I'll drive you to the hospital."

He went upstairs while I sat on the recliner, watching the fire. I threw another log on, though there was no need: Everything there was now ash. The evidence was gone.

I took another long pull from the whiskey bottle.

Then another.

Billy never made it to the shower. The next day he told me that he'd sat on the bed, only to lean back and fall asleep within a minute. Downstairs, a stomach filled with whiskey and a warm fire coaxed me into closing my eyes. They didn't open until the next morning, when sunlight crept across the room and onto my face. My hand immediately screamed with pain.

I went upstairs and peeked in on my sleeping son. Then I wrapped my bandaged hand in a plastic bag and showered before heading out.

Locksburg General Hospital is a squat building with ten beds that are usually unoccupied save for minor emergencies or cases in which patients didn't have the time to dither or to travel: kids who got cut on rusty barbed wire or dairy workers whose bones snapped when a cow stepped down hard on their feet. Most women choose to give birth in Harrisburg if they can help it, as do other patients who need any kind of scheduled surgery.

I didn't know Dr. Willis, the physician on duty, very well, though I'd seen him here and there in Locksburg. He was retired from some other small town, I'd heard, though he spoke so much, it wasn't easy to ask him anything.

"Well, let's see what we have here!" he said, seemingly pleased that, despite my injury, someone had come in to make his day interesting. He breathed through his teeth as he unwrapped my hand, going extra slow when he came to the gauze that had become glued to my wound.

The doctor said: "Last week, we had a farmer in here. Get this: He was from Bear Gap. He had his truck up on jack stands in the garage behind his house. So he's sitting on the ground and installing new brakes. One of the springs in the brakes gets stuck. He yanks at it with a pair of pliers. Then he really pulls. The spring . . . well, they spring, right? The pliers slip. The spring snaps back, goes into the white of his eye."

"Ouch."

"Yeah. A two-inch wire spring impales him in the eyeball. It's sticking halfway out. He starts screaming and flailing. Stands up. Falls against the truck. The trucks slips off the jack stands. Bam! Three thousand pounds of Ford F-150 land right on his foot. Crushes every bone there before he can pull it out. Toes broken too."

"You sure you want to be telling me this?" I asked. "I'm not feeling so—"

"The guy's half blind from a wire in his eye, and now he's got a crushed foot. So what's he do? He has to get to the hospital, and the phone is out. Remember those thunderstorms last week? The whole area still doesn't have service. I mean, Bear Gap isn't exactly on the phone company's list of high-priority areas."

The doctor kept rubbing my hand with alcohol, taking off the crust little by little while talking more and more. I guess he thought he was distracting me. Maybe he was.

"So the farmer can't call anyone for help, and he's got a piece of nine-gauge wire stuck in his eye that he doesn't want to pull at, in case his cornea comes out with it. And he can barely walk. What do you do?"

"Go to your neighbors?"

"He's *got* no neighbors! He's home alone in Bear Gap. Locksburg is the heart of Chicago compared to that henhouse of a town."

The doctor filled a syringe and injected it into my palm.

"Give this a minute. Let it numb. So what happened to your hand again?"

"I was in the garage. My son leaves everything around. Old skateboard. I slipped, put my hand out to stop myself, went with all my weight right onto the shovel blade."

"Why'd you wait so long? This was . . ." Dr. Willis gazed into my hand as if he could divine the crusted blood into a time. "This was last night."

"I was drunk. I didn't want to drive. So I bandaged it and—"

"You couldn't call a friend?"

"I passed out on the sofa. Half a bottle of whiskey will do that to you."

"So will a quarter bottle. Try that next time instead. Cut down on your drinking."

"So what happened?" I asked to keep him from inquiring any further about my injury.

"Huh?"

"To the Bear Gap guy."

"Oh yeah! No phone. No neighbors. So what's he do? He has to drive here to the hospital, right?"

"So he drove all the way?"

"How could he drive? He was repairing his truck!"

"Oh, I forgot."

"With two tires removed! And now half the truck is fallen off the stands!"

"So what did he do?"

232

"What do you think he did?"

I shrugged. My fingers were becoming numb.

"He repaired the truck!" the doctor crowed. "Jacked it back up. Put the brakes on, put the tires on, tightened them all."

"You're kidding."

"No! Fixed it all, while the wire was hanging from his eye and his foot was crushed like a bag of potato chips! Took him an hour. Did a damn fine repair job too! Then he drove fifteen miles here."

"How is he?"

"Luckiest son of a gun. We removed the spring from his eye, sent him down to Wills Eye Hospital in Philly, to make sure all was well, and it was. Got a cast on his foot for the next couple months. He's back home now. He better wear eye protection from now on."

"Right."

"And you better tell your son not to keep his skateboard lying around."

He pinched my hand. It seemed meaty and thick as a pillow. "How's that feel?"

"It's numb."

Dr. Willis cleaned the rest, a little less gently now, as I studied anything around the office—the charts, the white cabinets—to keep my eyes off the wound. I couldn't help looking at least once, though. The severed piece of pinky was purple-black and almost entirely off now, just below the top knuckle. Something yellow was seeping from the wound.

The doctor said: "We'll have to stitch that second finger up. It isn't so bad. The top half of that pinky, though, well, we're not going to bother with that, you understand?"

"I do."

"It'll have to come off. I mean, it's pretty much off anyway. Before I do it, you'll have to sign a form telling me it's OK to amputate it."

He opened a drawer and took out a form, then called for Paula the nurse. I knew her from town and smiled when she came in. She was the kind of person I could commiserate with, maybe share my worries, woman to woman—she had an ex-husband in prison and a run of bad luck that everyone in town liked to gossip about—but I didn't dare.

The doctor repeated what he'd told me, and I acknowledged that I understood what he had explained.

Paula signed her name to the form as a witness, as did the doctor. He put the form in front of me. I signed. Three minutes later he cut the upper part of my pinky away clean with a scalpel that shaved off the top of the bone. As he stitched the wound closed, he nodded to the piece of finger, which he'd dropped into a stainless steel pan.

"Do you want to keep that? Some people do. Put it in a jar with—"

"No."

"OK. It's here if you change your mind. Once you walk out, though, you'll never see that finger again."

Billy was in bed when I got home. He'd been there for close to fifteen hours and came down when he smelled the lunch I was cooking.

"You OK?"

He shrugged.

After another minute of quiet, he said: "We did a good thing, right?"

"We did the best thing we could."

"I know. It's still tough to believe."

"I'd love for you to stay and help with the restaurant, but Nestor and I have it under control. Did you call school?"

"I just got off the phone with Dr. Cooper at the computer lab. He said there's a job opening for the rest of the summer. So I took it."

"Good," I said. As much as I'd wanted Billy here, it seemed best for him to get away from this town and from what had happened. It would help us both to forget.

Following lunch, we sat in front of an old desktop computer that Billy had once trash picked, and fifteen minutes later we'd finished the letter.

> *Doreen Shippen's body is wrapped in a sheet and under a pile of branches, about 100 yards south from the parking lot at the dead end on Tharp Road. She is close to the towpath, maybe 50 yards away.*
>
> *On the night she disappeared, Doreen was using drugs. She mistakenly overdosed and died. I was asleep. When I woke I became scared and buried her body, then later moved it to where it now is.*
>
> *To her mother and her family: Doreen made a terrible mistake. I hope it is a comfort to you that before she died, she seemed happy, and was in no pain. I apologize for taking so long to let you know. I am very, very sorry.*

It wasn't good. How could anything be good about that kind of letter? It served its purpose, though. We debated ending with something like "God bless" or "Take care." Billy backed the cursor over all of them. The fewer words the better.

Billy hooked up a dot matrix printer, one that he had found years ago. It took a while to connect to the computer. The extra time was worth it, he said, because the old printer couldn't be traced.

The letter rolled and clicked its way out, and we both stared, as if it might grow teeth and snap at us. I put on gloves, folded the paper, and placed it in an envelope, then wet the glue with tap water. The envelope, addressed to the police station in block letters and with no return address, went into a plastic bag to keep it clean before it could be mailed.

"All back roads to Allentown," I said.

"All b-back roads to Allentown," Billy repeated.

"And when you get there—"

"Mom. I know."

"—and when you get there, find a deserted street with a mailbox. Check that there are no security cameras around. Then mail it. And—"

"Mom, I said I know."

We'd devised the plan earlier. And while Billy seemed to think I was repeating it out of nervousness, the repetition was for safety. We needed to get this final part right.

Billy had loaded up his car to return to M.I.T. But first he'd take back roads south, far off the path to Cambridge. When he reached Allentown, he'd mail the letter, then head north and drive to school.

"Pull the battery from your cell phone and don't put it back in until you are in Massachusetts."

He nodded. Soon I was talked out and we stood around the driveway, delaying his departure for no good reason.

"Oh, wait," Billy said. He'd taken his car to a mechanic the day before and had a new tire installed and had Liz's spare in his trunk. He put the tire by the side of the house. "Make sure she gets this."

"I will."

After all that had happened, what could be said? Billy and I had never been about spoken words anyway. We put our foreheads together a long time, hugged and moved apart.

Then my boy left our small town and went back to school.

They found Doreen five days later.

Whether the letter got delayed by the Post Office or sat around unopened at the police station, I don't know. But someone eventually received and read it, and Kriner himself went out and located the body.

Within an hour telephones rang all over town. Patty dialed my number after being called by a supermarket friend, who found out from a librarian, who heard it from a retiree whose son was one of the eight members of the Locksburg Police Department. The rest of the story I pieced together from Harrisburg's TV stations, which ran the report that night, and from the *Leader*, which covered it in detail for weeks. According to the reports, the area by the towpath was locked down and combed over. Except for Doreen's body, nothing out of the ordinary appeared to have been found, and the letter itself yielded no other clues.

Kriner told reporters that the body would be autopsied and tested, with results expected in several weeks. Two people were soon released from jail: The first was Doreen's drug-dealing former boyfriend, whose alibi was suddenly found valid. The other was her mother, who had served half of her short sentence for her own offenses and was freed by a sympathetic judge who warned her not to use narcotics again. The town grapevine said she'd already been seen high or drunk or both. I made no judgments. My heart hurt for her.

The day after the discovery, paranoia slithered into my brain, asking, *What if you left something behind?* and *Are you sure no one saw you?* and maybe this or that or the other thing.

My self-induced mania peaked after a week, then faded away each day that passed without a cop car showing up outside my front door. Besides, I had a restaurant to build.

Billy called and, in a kind of shorthand code, told me he'd seen the news online. We talked around it, then he set out on an act, as if someone were listening in.

"Mom, something happened," he said.

"What, honey?" I asked.

"I really messed up the car."

"Oh no. What did you do?"

"It was an accident. I scraped the entire passenger side against a guardrail. The door was crumpled in; the fenders too. I went to an auto body shop. They said the car wasn't worth fixing. So I junked it."

Neither of us wanted to take the chance that some small piece of evidence was hanging around in the trunk. So Billy bashed the car on purpose in Boston, then took it to a junkyard, where it was probably being dismantled for parts or melted down as scrap metal. It would never be found.

For Billy and me, everything seemed to be working out according to plan.

Maybe that's why I couldn't shake the feeling that something would come back to bite us.

REED

CARLA AND BILLY offered to give me a ride before leaving Liz's house. I told them no, and they did not seem unhappy. Some people, when they try to give you something and you do not want it, almost force it on you and make you feel bad for not taking it. Carla and Billy said only "OK," then drove off quickly.

I began to walk down to the cemetery and decided that if any headlights came along, in front or behind me, I would hide in the woods. I had had enough of cars.

I tried to convince myself that I had had enough of Locksburg too. Though I liked living in town, I knew that Greg was going to send me to Pittsburgh and I could not stop him. So I decided to focus on the not-so-nice things because maybe that would help me to feel better about leaving. That is called a coping strategy.

So I thought I would not miss the people who drive loud pickup trucks and turn up their stereos as if they think that everyone else wants to hear their music. I would not miss Dan Malloy. I would not miss the abandoned houses that always made me feel like someone was in there watching me.

Yet the more I thought about it, the more I realized that most of those things would be anywhere I went. Even if Dan Malloy

240

stayed here, there would be mean people elsewhere, and abandoned houses and loud trucks.

But all the good things that were in Locksburg would not be anywhere else. Creamy Bros. ice cream is not in Pittsburgh. And neither is Warren Creek or the old train bridge or St. Stanislaw Church, which, if you arrived at the right time, seemed to glow blue and purple and red inside from the sunbeams traveling through the stained glass. It did not seem fair that if I went away I would still find bad things, but these good things could not come with me.

Also I will have to leave behind Terri Spencer.

THE STORY OF MY HIGH SCHOOL CLASSMATE TERRI SPENCER

Terri and I were in the same grade in high school. She would some-times say hi to me and I would say hi back but I was a little scared of her. She was medium height and thin and some people called her a tomboy but not to her face. She had short red hair and once punched a linebacker on the football team who had pinched her butt and knocked out one of his front teeth. Later I heard Mr. Norman, our physical education teacher, say to another teacher, "I boxed in the Marines and even I wouldn't mess with Terri Spencer."

I did not want to go to the prom, but Mom made me go. It was not a formal event like the proms you see in movies, where everyone wears expensive clothes and sits at a table with candles. Ours was called the Senior Send-Off Dance and was held in the high school gym because we had a small graduating class that year, and even if a senior found a date, it would likely be another senior from our class anyway. Most people came without someone else. Some people wore suits. Some wore jeans. Some treated it as a joke. I only wanted to go home.

I had two slices of plain pizza and decided that when no one was watching I would leave and walk home slowly so that my mom would think that I had spent a lot of time there. I waited for ten songs to play, then prepared to go. Near the door, Terri Spencer was sitting on the bleachers with two friends. The other kids called them the cowgirls because all three of their dads had livestock farms. Terri saw me and said, loudly and not exactly nicely: "Where you goin', Reed?"

I did not say anything.

"You're leaving early, aren't ya?"

She was the only person who had spoken to me all night. I stood there and looked at the floor and she said: "Come over here."

I was afraid of her not like I was afraid of Dan Malloy, because all Dan could do was beat me up and that would heal. With Terri I was afraid that maybe I would embarrass myself in front of her and that would be far worse than being punched, though I knew she could hit hard too.

I walked over to Terri. She stared at me. If I had counted I would have gotten to ten or fifteen before she said something.

"Well?" she said. It was practically a bark.

"Well what?"

"Aren't you gonna ask me to dance?"

I did not say anything. I looked behind me in case she was speaking to someone else. But she was not.

"I'm waiting, Reed."

"I do not know how."

"It's simple. You just say, 'Hey, Terri, do you want to go out there and cut a rug?'"

"No. I meant, I do not know how to dance."

"See?" Terri said to her two friends, as if this proved some point. "This is exactly what I've been saying all along about these Locksburg guys. Their mommas do everything for 'em. Probably even hold their peckers for 'em when they pee. You have to teach them *everything*! Jesus H. Christmas!"

Then Terri pulled me out onto the dance floor.

She was the first girl my age who had ever taken hold of my hand.

"Now, don't step on my feet, you hear?" she said, not too quietly. I stood there with my hands at my sides. She rolled her eyes and said, "Puhhh!" and took my one hand and put it on her waist, then took my other hand and held it in hers. Then she put a hand on my shoulder and started to move a little and I tried to move a little too.

"There ya go," she said, and it sounded nice. "Now you're dancing." I kept watching our feet because I did not want to step on hers until she said: "Look me in the eyes, will ya, you oaf?"

And I did.

Then someone to my left said, "Oh my gawd!" and squealed and we both turned to see that it was Christie Hauk, who no one liked but a lot of people had to act like they liked unless they wanted her to be an enemy, which they did not want. Christie was dancing with Dan Malloy, who had already graduated from school but who went to the dance with Christie. Dan laughed out loud then whispered something in Christie's ear.

Christie looked at us and said: "Ewww!"

During my freshman year one of the boys said: "Terri don't take shit from nobody," and only at that moment did I understand what that boy had meant.

"You got something to say, ya twat?" Terri said right to Christie's face. It was almost as if she smacked her. Christie's mouth went wide, as if she could not believe that someone would talk to her in that way. Terri saw that and said, "If not, shut your piehole. You look as dopey as my dad's cows."

Dan said, "Hey!"

"Speaking of dopey," Terri said, "there's another world-class example."

Then Terri sized them both up and announced: "You two dip-shits were *made* for each other."

A couple of people nearby heard that and giggled. Christie and Dan both sneered but I could tell they did not want to say anything more to Terri, so they moved away.

Terri turned to me as if nothing had happened. Then she said: "Your hand's sweaty, Reed."

I quickly brushed it on my pants, then went back to holding her hand and hoped it did not sweat again. "Better," she said.

The music changed. Terri said: "Oh my god, I love this song!"

And the song that came on was "August" by a singer named Taylor Swift. It was another slow song.

Terri took my hand and put it on her waist like she did my other hand. She said: "I ain't gotta warn you not to get fresh, do I?"

I shook my head because I was scared to get fresh, which I think meant trying to touch her inappropriately. No matter what it meant, I was not going to do it.

Terri put her hands up to my shoulders, then moved them behind my neck where her fingers intertwined and we swayed slowly back and forth to the music with my hands on her waist and it felt as if what was happening lasted so very long and also went so very fast, at the exact same time. Her perfume smelled wonderful. She was warm. She hummed along to the song softly and I felt her breath.

And I was sad when the song finished and tried not to show it. "Not too shabby, Reed," she said.

We walked back to her two friends. Then three guys walked over to them and asked them to dance and they were going out onto the gym floor and Terri said, "Thanks for the dance, Reed. Yer cute," in a way that I think meant I was nice. There are some times when I will think about her words and try to figure out exactly what she meant. I will parse them. "Parse" is a good word.

But one thing I will not do is listen to "August" by the singer named Taylor Swift. Every so often it will come on the radio and I will change the station because I do not want that song to mean anything else to me except for the night that Terri Spencer took my hand and danced with me.

I sometimes see Terri when I walk by the feed store because she works there. She will not automatically act pleased to see me, like some people do, with a singsongy voice. And she will not automatically avoid me like some people do when I see them and they move to get out of my way. Instead she will say, "Hiya Reed," the same way she does to everyone, and that means something to me, that she treats me no different from anyone else. And I know that she is dating Mike Stevenson, whose dad owns the feed store, and there is a rumor around town that Mike was at the jewelry store pricing engagement rings because he is going to ask Terri to marry him, and I try not to think much more about Terri because . . . I do not know why. There may not be a good word for it.

But I can say that if Terri wants to marry Mike Stevenson, then I hope that he will ask her because I want her to be happy.

THAT IS THE END OF THE STORY OF MY HIGH SCHOOL CLASSMATE TERRI SPENCER

That night of the Senior Send-Off Dance was a lot like the night when I was walking on the road to the cemetery. There was the soft breeze that comes off the hills and no clouds in the sky and it makes you feel that Locksburg is hidden away from everything in the world as if it were a special place.

After a while I came to the side of the cemetery. About fifty yards further down the road was the main entrance but that was locked at night, so I climbed over the small wall and walked slowly so as to not trip in the dark. There seemed to be more gravestones at night than in the day. I looked at them and thought that underneath each one was a person who had lived an entire life, and everything that that person had ever felt or believed was now gone. Except for maybe the young children, all those in the ground had had enemies like Dan Malloy and all had had special times like the dance I had with Terri Spencer and all had had people they loved like I loved Mom and all had had people who they both sometimes loved and sometimes did not love, like I felt about Greg, and all had had people they wanted to protect like I wanted to protect Little Jimmy. That seemed to be one of the biggest thoughts I could ever have, and it was both very sad that the people under the gravestones were all like us at one point and very amazing too that they were all like us at one point.

LIZ

I STEPPED OVER Kap and opened the closet on the far side of the room, examined it up and down, decided there was nothing in there that I wanted, then did the same to each drawer in the kitchen. I never used the second bedroom but gave it a once-over anyway.

I returned to the living room.

"Will you let me go already?" Kap said.

"Shush it for a minute, will ya?"

Earlier I'd scoured every square inch of the house with the futile goal of finding something to sell. So I knew exactly what I owned, and it wasn't much. Still, I was never coming back here and wanted to make sure there was nothing left behind that I needed. I took the last few toiletries from the bathroom, shoved them in a bag, then carried both duffel bags into the living room and put them by the front door.

"Where you goin'?" Kap asked.

"Over these hills, then far away," I told him.

"You owe me money."

"Correct."

I picked up the fireplace poker.

"Let me go and we'll call it even," Kap said when he saw that in my hand.

"Nope. We're not calling it even."

He continued to give off a dangerous vibe. But he wasn't stupid. He knew that if I decided to clobber him, his head would be cracked open like a raw egg in seconds. I saw him work against the duct tape while trying not to show that he was struggling. I tapped him on the shoulder with the poker and shook my head. He stopped.

"If I called the cops and told them you broke in, what do you think would happen to you?"

"You know what would happen," he said.

"Tell me."

"I'm on parole."

"And . . . ?"

"They'd throw me back in the can."

"Righto." I waved the poker in front of his face, just for a little drama.

"If I killed you in my house, what do you think would happen to me?"

"Probably nothing."

"Righto once again. Hell, they'd probably give me a medal. But I haven't called the cops, have I?"

"No."

"And I haven't killed you."

"No."

"If I were a petty person, I'd say you owe me for that."

I put the poker back by the fireplace. Kap was visibly relieved.

Then I took my grandma bag, put it over my shoulder, and reached inside.

I brought out a thick wad of money. I was hoping his expression would be astounded. I wasn't disappointed.

"Correct me if I'm wrong, but I owe you five hundred and sixty dollars for the so-called repairs to my car. Is that accurate?"

"That's right."

I peeled off five one-hundred-dollar bills from the stack, tossed them into Kap's lap. Then three twenties and dropped them there too. "OK, that's paid for. And I don't think I'm being impolite when I say your subpar automobile repair skills leave much to be desired. You're lucky I won't file a grievance with Triple A or leave you a nasty online review."

"I put in a new fuel pump and tried to save you money on the fuel line!" he said. "And I—"

"Yeah, yeah, whatever. We'll call it a difference of opinion. So we're even on that, yes?"

He nodded his head but I wanted words.

"So we're even on the car repairs, yes?"

"Yes."

"Now, the meth that you fronted Luke. Remind me how much that cost."

"Three grand."

I counted off a thousand. Dropped it in his lap. Counted off another thousand. Dropped it in his lap. Then I counted the third and dropped that there too.

"There's three thousand for the meth. So we're even on the drugs, yes?"

"Yes," he said, and he was no longer sneering. Now he was gawking at all that cash in his lap. His lips parted slightly in a smile, and a few yellow teeth peeked out.

"Now. How much will it cost to have you forget me forever?"

"Huh?"

"I want you to forget that I ever existed. That means if I were to come back to Locksburg, you don't know or care. Or if I have relatives here, you don't know or care about them either."

"I'm not sure I follow you."

"What will it cost to get you to forget about me and to forget about all that happened tonight? Not that you didn't deserve it for breaking into my house."

He gazed at me, perplexed.

"Five hundred?" I said to help him along.

He gave it some thought. "A thousand."

I counted out the grand. Acted like it hurt to hand that over, though I would have paid him two thousand if he'd asked. Dropped the money in his lap. The remaining wad of bills went back into my bag.

"So I have your word?" I said.

"You have my word."

"There's close to five grand in your lap. But wait, there's more! I'm leaving now. I've taken everything I want from this house. Feel free to take whatever's left. Go get a truck if you want, to move the stuff. The sofa's still got some life in it. The TV's ancient, but it works. The bed is soft too, and the frame is solid. I've seen where you live, and I bet you need better furniture."

"I sure could use it. How about that easy chair over there?"

"Anything you want is yours. I'm leaving town."

"Cool," he said. "I'll take it all."

"How'd you get here?"

"My bike's up the road, hidden there."

"Gotcha. OK. Well, Kap, I'd like to say it was nice meeting you, but it wasn't nice meeting you. Stay out of trouble, though. Or at least try."

"You gonna cut me loose?"

"Nope. You're a strong guy. You can wiggle your hands out of that tape in ten or fifteen minutes."

"Fair 'nuf," he said.

I picked up my duffel bags. Gave the house another look, though I had no nostalgia for the place.

"By the way, what kind of name is Kap?"

"Kevin Albert Paulson. That's my Christian name."

"Ah."

"You're the first person to ask me that."

"I can't imagine why," I said.

As I was about to go outside and put the bags in my new used car and take off for good, Kap said, "Hey."

He nodded toward my handbag, where he's seen me put the wad of cash, then nodded to the bills that were in his lap.

"Where did you get all this money?" he asked. "You gotta tell me."

I smiled.

"Trust me on two things, Kevin Albert Paulson," I said. "First, I don't want to tell you. And second, you don't want to know."

CARLA

TWO MONTHS AFTER the fire at my restaurant, Nestor accompanied me to county small claims court. The electrician refused to provide a refund for his shoddy work and fought my request that he pay for the damages. Nestor testified to the guy's inept job and the fact that we'd gotten flat tires from the metal pieces that he'd spilled in the lot and failed to clean up. The fire chief was there too, and had his say. At the end, the judge squinted over his reading glasses at the electrician: "I've seen you in my court before, haven't I?"

We left with a judgment in our favor. As we walked out the judge said: "Does your restaurant have a name yet?"

"The Starting Gate," I told him.

The *Locksburg Leader* landed in my driveway.

I'd stopped checking the website every day, too busy with the restaurant and too eager to get that night off my mind. Over time, it drifted further from my thoughts.

The newspaper's story led with:

Doreen Shippen had heroin in her body, though there are signs that violence may have contributed to or caused her death, Chief

253

*Joe Kriner of the Locksburg Police Department said, citing the
autopsy report.*

*"Her neck may have been compressed, or at least badly bruised.
We're not sure yet," he said. "As of now, those tests are inconclusive.
She was buried for a year, so that complicates matters." Additional
tests will be done when the body is moved to the State Police lab in
Philadelphia.*

*Though Chief Kriner declined to discuss potential suspects, citing
the ongoing investigation, he did say that there was important new
evidence. A bloodstain found on Doreen's jeans was apparently left
there long after she was dead.*

*"It doesn't match her blood type," he told the Leader. "We suspect
that it is from whoever transported her body."*

The missing top of my finger seemed to tingle.

I dropped the newspaper, then picked it up and read the story
twice more, analyzing every sentence. Afterward I paced the house and
cursed at nothing. At times I gazed out in the yard, where the grass
had regrown lush and thick. When I composed myself, I called Billy.

"I'm in the computer lab," he said. "What's up?"

"Go home."

"What's this about? I—"

"Do it."

His apartment was a ten-minute walk from the lab, but it took
him thirty minutes to call back.

"I've been standing by this phone! Where were you?"

"I had to find someone to c-cover for me at the lab."

"Did you read the story? On Doreen?"

"No. What?"

"There were drugs in her body, like you said. But she—"

I couldn't bring myself to say it flat out, or even to ask. I had to turn the question around, to soften it, in an effort to keep me sane.

"Did you and Doreen . . . did you have a fight, or did anything else happen that night?"

"Why are you asking me that?"

"You can read it online. My god, we shouldn't be talking like this on the phone!"

"You're allowed to call me. You're my mother, and I'm at cuh-college."

"I should have called you from a pay phone or—"

"Mom, what happened?"

"The autopsy said she had drugs in her system. It also said there may be some signs of a fight."

"The story didn't say 'fight.'"

"I thought you didn't read it?"

A pause.

"I'm reading it now."

"It says that her neck . . . Please. Billy. Tell me what happened."

"Nothing happened!"

"Nothing at all?"

"Wait! I know what it is! I know what it is!"

"What?"

"I . . . when I carried her out to the yard. I dropped her. She was heavy. She landed, like, on her h-head or her n-neck."

"Are you . . . are you telling me the truth? Please tell me the truth, Billy."

"I dropped her," he said.

"Is that the truth?"

"Mom, don't you trust me?"

"You never told me this before."

"They found your blood on her," Billy said.

"I guess when, you know, the shovel cut my hand."

"Right."

"They'll have it on file now," I said.

"Don't use any of those genealogy sites or get your b-blood tested or anything like that," he said.

"I won't."

"I shouldn't either, huh?"

"No, I guess you shouldn't."

"Because that w-would . . . I mean, they can tell it's your DNA, even through me."

"Right."

"So I won't get my blood tested either. I'll do that for you. For us."

"OK."

Billy said, "You'd l-lose everything. If they found out."

I paused.

After a moment I could only say, "Yeah."

We tried to reassure ourselves by reading aloud sections of the story that said: "No arrests are imminent" and "There is speculation that those connected with the death may not be from Locksburg."

After we'd gone over the same words in a half dozen different ways, we began to tire. Before we hung up I asked Billy my standard question out of habit: "How's school?"

"Fine. I have . . . I guess you'd call her a g-girlfriend."

"Oh. Good."

"She, uh, wants me to come to her house for Christmas."

"Are you planning to go?"

"I am, if you're OK with that."

"Go," I said, and my heart hurt a little at the lie. Of course I wasn't OK with that. I'd never had a Christmas without him, since he was born.

"OK," Billy said. "I have to get back to the cuh-computer lab. Call me if . . . you know . . . you hear anything else."

A pause.

"Wait," I said.

He must have been pulling the phone away from his ear, because it took him a little longer before he said: "What?"

"When you came home, in June . . . why did you tell me about Doreen then? Why not at Christmas break last year? Or some other time? Why then?"

When he didn't answer, I started to speak my thoughts aloud.

I said: "Was it because that was the day I told you I'd remortgaged the house? So, if I lost the house, someone else might move in? And if they dug up the yard, they'd find her and—"

"Mom, you're rambling. What are you trying to say? I told you then because it was b-bugging me."

"Bugging you."

"Yeah. Driving me c-crazy."

"Billy. Are you telling me the truth?"

"I dropped her," he said. "Or maybe, you know, when she wouldn't wake up, I sh-shook her. You know?"

The line was silent for a long time.

"Mom, you've known me from the st-start," he said. "You need to believe me."

Neither of us spoke anymore.

The quiet sat there.

Then Billy hung up the phone.

I didn't sleep that evening and wondered how I would ever make it through an entire night again. I doubted everything Billy had said, then believed each word, then oscillated between the two for hours until the sky began to lighten.

A story is made up only of the facts you choose, and every time I chose a different fact to believe, I changed what I thought.

I know my own son, though. I knew him at the starting gate.

I went on hounding myself until exhaustion set in: *How do you know they didn't get in a fight, or she laughed at his stutter, and that was his breaking point after eighteen grueling years in Locksburg? And he's smart enough to think ten steps ahead. Maybe he intentionally injured you with the shovel, to connect you to the crime. Are you sure he's the person you first thought he was?*

Such ideas agonized me as I went to work on the restaurant, where I found myself obsessed with carefulness so as not to cut myself. I didn't want to draw any blood.

"What's the matter?" Nestor asked. I practically jumped, surprised, when he spoke and snapped me from my thoughts.

"Nothing . . . Tired is all."

"I don't believe you," he said. "What is it?"

"I'd rather not talk about it."

"Tell God."

"Doesn't he already know?" I said, angrier than I'd wanted it to sound.

"I told you before: You don't pray to change God's mind. You pray to change your own."

When I got home that night, I walked the rooms of the house, wondering what to do if the police showed up. If that happened, I could create some story, take the blame, and save my son.

But was he worth saving?

I knelt down by my bed and began to pray and begged God to give me an answer.

REED

I DID NOT WANT to use my flashlight as I made my way across the cemetery in case someone saw the light. The cemetery is huge for such a small town because Locksburg was not always such a small town. At one time it was thriving. For years and years there were a lot of people in Locksburg, but most of them left when the coal mines closed. You might ask what happened to all the living people and where did they go, but you never ask what about the bodies. That is because most times bodies stay where they are buried. The living do not take the dead with them.

I turned down the wrong path once, then went back the way I came and after a few minutes found our family mausoleum. There, I took the key that looks like a skeleton key and unlocked the front gate then stepped in and closed it behind me. The small room was cooler than it had been that morning. I sat on the stone bench inside and got the flashlight from my backpack. When it was lit, the shadows became large and moved across the ceiling and that made me anxious, which is a better word to use than "scared." I put the flashlight on the bench on top of the backpack and aimed it at the place on the wall that had my mother's name.

With one of the drill bits, I popped out the four little pieces of metal that hid the screw holes. I got the drill and switched it to reverse mode and removed the screws. Then I took off the plate and put it on the floor. Everything that moved sounded very loud.

The front of Mom's casket was visible. I grabbed the handle and pulled. The casket slid out on a roller tabletop with legs that unfolded, the same way I had seen the undertaker put it in there that morning, just opposite.

The casket did not have a lock but rather a clasp that sealed the rubber between the lid and the casket. I unhooked the clasp and the lid popped up some. The lid could now be opened when I was ready.

From my backpack I took Miss Molly the Dolly. Then I brought her to the casket and started to talk to Mom. I knew Mom was dead and she could not hear me but I could not help talking to her like people talk to animals who cannot talk back, and like Mom used to talk to Dad when she came to visit. And here I was, doing the same thing that she always did, but to her.

"Hello, Mom," I whispered. "Greg forgot to give Miss Molly the Dolly to the undertakers, so they did not put her in there. I came here to put her in with you like you said you wanted. It has been a very difficult day. I wanted to talk to you so many times, to ask you what I should do, but you were not there. But maybe that was not so bad, since you always said I needed to do things on my own. So I did this all on my own and I did not quit because you said we were not quitters. You told me I could do anything. That is what I kept thinking."

The more I talked, the better I felt and the less anxious I was of being in the dark with the big shadows.

"I will put Miss Molly the Dolly in with you and put your casket back but I wanted to tell you something first. I want to tell you about what happened last week."

I put my hand on the casket. The metal felt cool, so I put my other hand there too. The casket was about chest-high. I stepped closer and pressed my forehead against it.

Then I asked Mom to forgive me.

THE STORY OF MY LIE

Last week Greg stopped by the house early in the morning to drop off Little Jimmy so Mom and I would watch him while Greg was at work.

"Here's our cutie-patootie!" Mom said when Little Jimmy ran in the house. "Now our electric bill is going to go through the roof!" She did not mean that the bill would rise up and move through the ceiling. Mom meant that we would be paying more money because Little Jimmy turns on the lights. We had cereal for breakfast and Mom said she was going to lay down because she had a headache and maybe later we would bake a cake.

"Keep it to a dull roar out here," Mom said, because her bedroom was right next to the kitchen downstairs. A dull roar did not mean we should roar dully. It meant to keep quiet.

"Can we go to Warren Creek?" Little Jimmy asked.

Mom said: "If Reed wants to take you." Then she turned to me: "Remember: Never leave him alone down there," Mom said. Then to Little Jimmy she said, "Some girl drowned in the creek years ago. Scares me still." She said to me: "Promise me you won't let him out of your sight."

"I promise."

"That's my boy," she said.

Mom went to lay down.

I sat on the sofa and put on the television until ten or fifteen minutes later when Little Jimmy turned it off. Then he turned on the ceiling fan and the light switch and I knew he was getting antsy, so I said, "Do you want to go to the creek?" He said yes and I said, "I will go to the shed and get the net so we can use it to catch minnows."

The shed is behind the house.

Little Jimmy had followed me out. He reached inside and shut the light off and giggled and ran away into the house because he wanted me to chase him. But after I came out of the shed with the net, he had gone through the house. He ran out the front door, then down toward the creek. Instead of going inside the house, I ran alongside it so I would not let Little Jimmy out of my sight like I promised.

Warren Creek is about four football fields away. I ran after Little Jimmy and caught up with him before it turned downhill then we walked together to the water. We netted a few minnows, then let them go and walked down further to see if we could catch a sunfish but they were too wily. "Wily" is a fun word. So is "critter."

After maybe an hour, Little Jimmy and I sat on the bank of the creek and Little Jimmy said: "I like it here."

"So do I. What other things do you like?"

"I like it when you chase me!"

"That I know."

"I like how you get so angry when I turn stuff off and on."

"I am not really angry. That is acting."

"I like turning the switches and dials."

"I know that."

"I turned them all on so you would chase me even more."

I nodded and stared out at the water.

Then I said, "What did you turn on?"

"I turned all the dials in the kitchen! You were in the shed and I ran through the house. That's why you chased me, right?"

I stood up fast and said: "We need to go."

"Chase me!" he said, and ran in the other direction.

I wanted to run back to the house that very second. But I had promised Mom never to leave Little Jimmy alone at the creek. I chased him and he laughed, but this was not something to laugh at.

I was not anxious. I was scared.

"Get back here, Jimmy!" I yelled. But that is what I used to yell at him every other time I chased him. I ran and tripped and cut my forearm when I hit the ground. He got further ahead, and by the time I caught up with him, we were further away from the house. I grabbed him by the hand and hurried to go back.

I got there and opened the front door of the house.

But I could not go inside at first.

There was too much gas.

The ambulance took Mom away a while later.

Before that, I had kept the front door open, then ran around back and opened that door too. Then I burst into Mom's bedroom next to the kitchen. I could tell that she was not alive by the way her skin looked. Little Jimmy was coming inside but I rushed to keep him out and called 911. Little Jimmy asked what happened. I had to think up something fast and it is hard to lie but I told him that before I left the house and went to the creek, I turned on the oven to make a cake and put milk on the stove to boil for the frosting but the milk overflowed and put out the flame but the gas stayed on and I kept talking and using lots and lots of words to confuse him because he is only five and I said, "Do you understand? Uncle Reed made a big mistake." I had him repeat that and repeat that and repeat that, and then he believed it.

I spilled milk on the stove before the ambulance came and later, after the police had called Greg to come over, Chief Kriner said to me: "What happened here, Reed?"

And instead of thinking about what happened here, I thought of the future. About how Little Jimmy had turned on the gas dials and how he would be known all over Locksburg as the kid who killed his grandmother and how Greg, who never forgave anyone for anything, would hold it against him even though he would say he would not hold it against him. I know how it is to be pointed at and talked about. I could not let that happen to Little Jimmy.

"Reed?" Chief Kriner said.

"Yes?"

"I need you to tell me the truth here, all right?"

"I'll tell you the truth," I said.

"Did you turn on the gas?"

I nodded, because that seemed like less of a way to lie and Mom said never to lie.

"Reed. I need to hear it from you. Did you turn on the gas?"

It took a while, but then I said: "Yes. I turned on the gas."

"This town is going to hate you," Greg said to me the next day. "That's the way they are."

I did not say anything.

THAT IS THE END OF THE STORY OF MY LIE

* * *

"Little Jimmy did not mean it, Mom. You know that."

I took my hands off the casket and my forehead off the casket and I stood holding Miss Molly the Dolly and I said:

"You said never to lie. But you also said to stick by your family. So I had to follow the second. I do not want to go to Pittsburgh but more than that I do not want Little Jimmy to be in trouble. I know what it is like to be ostracized, and that is a word I do not like. It is better that only one of us is marked. So I did not always tell the truth, Mom. I am sorry. Please forgive me."

I opened the lid of the casket only a quarter way and saw a bit of the blue dress that Mom had on. I put Miss Molly the Dolly in the crook of Mom's arm. Miss Molly's brown yarn hair looked nice against the blue and I think Mom would have liked it.

"Take care of her, Molly," I whispered.

I closed the casket and did the reverse of what I had done minutes earlier. I latched the casket, rolled it back into place, and screwed the plate onto the wall. Then I locked the mausoleum and went out into the night.

I walked away from the cemetery and up Tharp Road and past Liz Moyer's house and through Locksburg and by the police station and got home long past midnight and Greg was there with the light on in the house, waiting for me in the living room. Little Jimmy was curled up asleep on the sofa.

Greg stood when I walked in. He seemed ready to shout something angry or to demand to know where I had been.

But before he could speak, I walked over and put my arms around him and hugged him. And Greg was surprised and he went quiet.

After a little while he hugged me back.

And the two of us stood there in Mom's house, hugging like good brothers.

We did not say anything.

LIZ

I PULLED OUT of my driveway in my Honda, gave a goodbye salute to the burned-out Chevy, then headed toward I-81. Pitstops aside, I would drive straight through to Tennessee. I patted the grandma handbag on the seat next to me. Sometime later I would find a bank and deposit the thousands of dollars that were in there. I didn't want to be carrying that much cash around. What a new and lovely problem to have.

There were other things I didn't want to be carrying around. I pulled into the parking lot of the Coal Miner Diner, the last business before the Locksburg town limits. There I took the utility knife and the roll of duct tape from the grandma bag and tossed them into the trash can.

Then I pulled out of the lot. Fifty yards later, I crossed the Locksburg line.

Next stop, Nashville.

On the morning of Luke's cremation, I didn't believe I'd be able to do what needed to be done. I examined my scheme from every angle and knew, theoretically, that it was possible. But could I go through with it?

"Act as if ye have faith, and faith shall be given to ye," I remembered reading somewhere.

So I prepared as if I were going to do it. Maybe then I would.

I searched my house. Found a utility knife, with its razor gleaming and sharp, in an old toolbox. A roll of duct tape too under the sink. Still sticky.

I put them all in the grandma bag along with a long pair of yellow rubber cleaning gloves that were in a bathroom drawer.

Even at nine in the morning, as Stacey opened the chapel, I didn't think I'd go through with the plan.

But then Stacey began to hum.

I said to her, "What's that tune?"

She said: "Oh. Sorry. That new country song: 'Baby, We Won!' I keep humming the darn thing."

I closed my eyes hard. Maybe she thought I was holding back tears. But I was pissed: At Luke for swallowing the coin. At the mess I was in. At the shitty songs and the no-talent twits who sang them. And at my own rotten luck. So perhaps it was spite that spurred me on.

I said to myself: *You want to get ahead? Then get ahead.*

"Can I have some time alone?" I asked Stacey.

"Of course. Of course," she said. "I'll be in the office if you need me."

I nodded and she left.

The door closed behind her.

I locked it.

Then I opened Luke's cardboard casket. His body was wrapped in a simple white shroud, much like a long nightshirt, as Stacey told me it would be. I took hold of the shroud, pulled, and flipped it up to cover his face. I didn't want to look at that or at the staples they used to seal his split-open skull. Someone had put him in a white pair of boxer shorts, perhaps the cleanest he'd ever worn.

I donned the yellow rubber gloves. Then took the utility knife and slid the razor out.

And god forgive me, but to keep my mind off all this, I started to whisper-sing a couple bars of a song that I'd been working on.

I placed the edge of the razor against Luke's belly. Cringed. Then I pressed my weight down and sliced across his gut. Blood didn't come squirting out. Instead, a brown and viscous fluid oozed from the incision. I stopped after six inches to see a yellow layer of fat, and beneath that, the wrinkle of intestines.

I'd cut too low.

There were three choices: make another incision, give up, or stick my hand inside. I didn't have enough time for the first, and the second was no longer an option—not after coming this far.

I dug my fingers in, pushed past the cold guts, and forced my hand higher. Soon I was up to my elbow in Luke. When I leaned down, my face was inches from his chest. I didn't know exactly what to search for—I graduated high school without even dissecting a frog—but a bulbus organ was there, above the rope of intestines. I squeezed and felt something solid inside: the coin.

No time to lose. I pulled my arm free of Luke, took the utility knife again, and slid my hand back inside with it. Then I reached up and sliced open his stomach.

I retched at the gaseous smells and at the squirmy texture of it all.

The way to a man's heart is through his stomach! I thought out of nowhere, and gagged.

I moved my hand inside the stomach and pinched the coin between my finger and thumb. I pulled my arm out. It made a moist, slurping sound.

In my hand I held the hard plastic container containing the Seated Liberty dime.

I quickly tossed everything into my bag—the coin, the knife, the gloves—then took the duct tape and sealed the incision so that nothing would slide out before the cremation.

I secured the cardboard lid and hurried back to unlock the door. Less than a minute later, Stacey returned, somber expression in place.

"Will there be any more guests?" she asked.

"No," I said, and wiped my eyes, which had watered from the odor that hung around the room. If Stacey smelled something, she was nice enough to ignore it. "I think it's time."

She pointed to the button. "Would you like to . . . ?"

"Yes," I said, and pushed it.

The cardboard casket traveled the fifteen feet to the crematory chamber doors, which slid open. Once the casket cleared that, the doors shut and we heard the whoosh of flames.

I took my bag and made for the exit.

"My condolences," Stacey said.

"For what?" I asked, genuinely puzzled. Then I realized what she meant.

"Oh yeah, him," I said. "Thanks."

* * *

271

Ed at Berwick Numismatic examined the coin and smiled with sad nostalgia.

"Where does the time go?" he said. "I'm telling you, it seems like yesterday when your dad came in to buy this. I was in my thirties then. Look at me now! Older than dirt! And nowhere near as pretty!"

As he strolled down memory lane, I discreetly examined my fingernails to check yet again that they were clean.

After leaving the chapel, I speed walked the two miles home. There I turned on the sink and scrubbed my arms raw with a bar of soap, then cleaned the gloves and put them in the trash. I rinsed the plastic container that held the dime. Through it, the coin sparkled.

Ed said: "You want to sell her, huh?"

"Yes. It's time. So can I get four thousand for it?"

"Can you get *four thousand* for it?" he said.

I didn't like the way he stressed the price—and wasn't fond of his tone of voice either. I liked it even less when he repeated the words. "Can you get four thousand dollars for it? That's a strange question."

"Well, can I?"

"Sure. You can get four thousand for this coin."

"OK, then."

"But it's worth fourteen," Ed said.

If I could transcribe what I said, it would be a string of stunted words and half starts interspersed with stammering and muddled with confusion. While I babbled, he typed something on the keyboard and examined his computer screen.

"Last sale of one of these was a month ago, according to the dealer database. That was for fourteen thousand seven hundred and fifty. And I know a collector in Philly who will pay fifteen at least."

"My dad said, the last time he checked, it was four thousand."

"Must have been a while back," Ed said. "Past couple years, Seated Liberty prices have skyrocketed. You still wanna sell?"

"You still wanna buy?"

"If the price is right."

"Give me thirteen thousand," I said. "Then call that collector in Philly. Make yourself a nice profit."

"Take a check?" Ed asked.

The bank teller thought I misspoke when I requested it all in cash. I repeated myself and added a wide smile.

Fast Eddie's Sunoco had a used Honda on the lot, waxed to a shine and with a FOR SALE sign in the front window. That six-thousand-dollar car was mine for five-five following a short haggle. I bought the biggest bunch of flowers that Luhr's flower shop had and walked into Hillview with those in one hand and a coin collecting kit that I'd bought from Ed in the other. It had a few hundred dollars' worth of coins that I knew Dad would have a blast inspecting and showing to the nurses. I also bought back the buffalo nickel to keep with me for luck.

"Pop, I sold the Seated Liberty dime," I told him.

"How much?"

"Thirteen thousand."

"That's more than four thousand."

"Correct. After I leave here, I'm packing my stuff, then driving to Nashville. If it works out, you and I can get a place there, together."

"*When* it works out," he corrected.

We sat for hours, and when it grew dark, we went to his room. I held his hand until he fell asleep, this dad who'd once carried me on his shoulders and hopped up and down like a horse until I was breathless with laughter. This man who had taken a wrench and removed the training wheels from my bike, stood behind me holding on to the seat, then let go, and I found myself pedaling on my own.

I've loved those memories. I've tried a dozen times to turn them into songs. It's never worked.

But even while pulling that dime out of Luke's chilled and slippery innards, I was making up rhymes and humming a half-made melody about how I found myself in a jam and broke into my old house, then fled the scene.

On the drive to Nashville I'll shape all of that into a tune.

I've always cherished the good times. But the bad times make for some great songs.

Acknowledgments

From the time I saw my first Clint Eastwood western, I longed to be the terse and silent loner, someone who relied on nobody, who had no baggage, who walked this world alone.

Then I grew up.

It took a while to learn that not only do I sort of like people, I was surrounded by so many exceptional ones. First and foremost: Michele, Hope, and Troy Jaworowski. Close behind: Everyone with the last name of Bier, DiPietro, Simons, and Wallace.

Annemarie Heideck says she's the president of my fan club, but secretly, I'm the leader of hers. I'm a member of other Heideck fan clubs too: I'm looking at you, Ginny and Bob, as well as Laraine Heideck Gallagher and Tom Gallagher.

Theater people who deserve the brightest spotlight: Thomas Coté, Jed Dickson, Tracy Newirth, Dee Dee Friedman, Ted Thompson, Tony Sportiello, Riley Jones-Cohen, Emily Zacharias, Alex Dmitriev, Elysa Marden, Seth Bauer, Ben Sumrall, and Eva Heinemann.

Book people who keep the pages turning: Joe Brosnan, Morgan Entrekin, and Doug Stewart.

Hey, Sandy Gonzalez and Dave Wilson—you always show up for me. I appreciate it. Hey, Andy Webster—stop making me laugh. Wait, don't.

I spent my life insulting New Jersey, only to move there and find wonderful friends: Dorothy and Patrick Holmes, Missy and Chris Pirrera, Robin and Tommy Zovich, Cathe and Bruce Moritz, Sue and Ari Kolker, Blanca and Parshu Shah, LeaEllen and Kevin Collins, May and Mark Rowland, Tracy and Shane Daly, Katie and Ray Gallagher, Eileen and Ravi Sattiraju, Donna and Neil Genzlinger, Connie and Peter Lusdyk, Margarita and Marcos Gomez, Pam and Nick Potenza, Kate Mellor and Mike Sherman, and Christine and John Santa Maria.

Superior writers: Alex Finlay, Dean Koontz, Meagan Lucas, Jahmal Mayfield, Hank Phillippi Ryan, Lisa Scottoline, Mark Stevens, and Anna Quindlen.

Ken Bruen inspired me. His words live on.

Who needs cowboys when you've got librarians and bookstore workers. They are real heroes.

And to you, kind reader: So much thanks.